D1570298

SOMETIMES IT'S
NEW YORK

Other Works by Claude Stanush

Fiction

The Balanced Rock and Other Stories

All Honest Men
(with Michele Stanush)

Nonfiction

The World in My Head (essays)

The Newton Boys: Portrait of an Outlaw Gang
(an oral history, with David Middleton)

Films

The Newton Boys
(with Richard Linklater and Clark Lee Walker)

The Newton Boys: Portrait of an Outlaw Gang
(a documentary, with David Middleton)

The Lusty Men
(inspired by a story by Claude Stanush)

SOMETIMES IT'S

NEW YORK

Stories

Claude Stanush

Edited by Michele Stanush

San Antonio, Texas
2007

Sometimes It's New York
© 2007 by Claude Stanush

Cover photograph, "111 Waverly Place," by Barbara Evans Stanush.
Manipulated by Bryce Milligan. Used by permission.

The publication of this work was made possible in part by a
generous grant from the City of San Antonio, Department of Cultural Affairs

First Wings Press Edition

ISBN-10: 0-916727-18-1
ISBN-13: 978-0-916727-18-5

Wings Press
627 E. Guenther
San Antonio, Texas 78210
Phone/fax: (210) 271-7805
On-line catalogue and ordering: www.wingspress.com
All Wings Press titles are distributed to the trade by
Independent Publishers Group
www.ipgbook.com

Library of Congress Cataloging-in-Publication Data

Stanush, Claude, 1918-
  Sometimes it's New York : stories / Claude Stanush ; edited by
Michele Stanush. -- 1st Wings Press ed.
      p. cm.
  ISBN-13: 978-0-916727-18-5 (alk. paper)
  I. Stanush, Michele. II. Title.
  PS3619.T367S66 2007
  813'.6--dc22
                                    2006033502

CONTENTS

SOMETIMES IT'S

NEW YORK

NEW YORK, NEW YORK

In the 1950s New York was one of those magical places, like Baghdad of the *Arabian Nights*, where everything seemed possible. I remember my first trip to New York, I stood at the foot of the Empire State Building and looked up in awe – small-town ogler that I was – wondering how something so tall could ever have been built so high into the clouds. Of course, there were dozens of other skyscrapers on the tiny island of Manhattan, some almost as tall, and if one took the tourist boat around it, as I did shortly after my arrival there, one could only marvel at the skyline and the technology that had made it possible as well as feel a great American pride that nothing that men had built anywhere else in the world could equal it.

I was drawn to New York for the same reason that my great-grandfather had been drawn to Texas from Tennessee a century before. Texas in the 1850s was on the edge of the frontier, and the frontier was where the action was; where the very air you breathed had the smell of opportunity. Everybody was "going West" – that is, everybody with ambition and courage. By 1900 the frontier had ended at the Pacific Ocean and the focus and locus of the American Dream had shifted eastward again, to New York especially, with its Big Money, High Culture and Empire State Buildings pointing up to infinity. If something had a New York label on it, you could count on it being first-class. And if you could make it in New York, you could make it anywhere. So to Gotham they came, by the tens of thousands, America's talented young men and women, fired with dreams and energy, seeking fame and fortune – from Idaho, California, Iowa, Mississippi, or even, like myself, from a state (Texas) that had scant regard for "all those Yankees crammed together up there on that filthy little spit of land."

They were right about one thing: There were a lot of people up there, and with the United Nations newly headquartered in New York, they'd come from everywhere. On the crowded sidewalks of Fifth Avenue people in stylish clothes bumped into Westerners wearing cowboy hats and boots or into people from other parts of the world in dress strange to Americans at that time: turbans, saris, fezzes, leopard-skin caps, togas and tunics. For me, new to that kind of experience, it was exhilarating – all those people, and the diversity. Scary too; there were not only too many people on the sidewalks, bumping into each other without an apology, but too many people after every job in New York, all pushing and shoving to grab the golden ring. Companies like the one where I was hired eventually even encouraged a certain amount of inner-office tension, of sparring and footwork, "to keep everybody on their toes."

In the five years I had worked for Perkins & Smith, Publishers, I felt I had learned most of the survival tactics. Yet there was always the danger, if you let down your guard, of a left hook. So when Louis Elliott, the senior editor, brought John Spears into my office one day to introduce him as my new assistant, at the same time that I was smiling affably, I was mentally measuring his reach.

Perkins & Smith prided itself on publishing good books: quality in the content, quality in the paper and binding. Naturally it expected its employees to be quality too. Though I hadn't gone to an Ivy League college in the East (the standard for quality held by most New Yorkers back then), I had graduated *summa cum laude* from one of the best liberal arts colleges in the Southwest. And my enthusiasm must have impressed Elliott, whose policy was to hire talent from wherever it came. Within three years I had become an editor of manuscripts, with one assistant. My previous assistant, a Dartmouth graduate, had been inept; no threat, but no help either. And so when Elliott informed me that he had hired a replacement, he assured me – or warned me, I'm not sure which – that the new man would be different. "He's going to give you a run for your money, Karl." Of course, Elliott had a somewhat perverse sense of humor. But the better part of prudence was to take him at his word; I visualized someone with a quick jab, fast on his feet.

Seeing Spears finally in the flesh, I was almost disappointed. He certainly didn't have the build of a Joe Louis: too pudgy. Also, he was too neatly done up: his round pink face scrubbed, every strand of his sandy hair in place, like someone going to school for the first time. And his clothes! The tan-and-white sports coat with the large plaid and the wide, padded shoulders!

"You can hang your coat up there," I said.

He took the tartan off and hung it up carefully on the rack.

"Where are you from?" I asked.

"Kansas."

I knew it! He had to have come from Kansas, or some place like Kansas. Yet the young man's hand, when I shook it, wasn't exactly the hand that gripped the plow that broke the plain.

"Elliott's recommended you highly," I said.

"I didn't know that," he replied, modestly. "I haven't had much experience."

"Meaning?"

"I was at *The Kansas City Evening Star* for three years. Before that, I wrote for the college paper: art, music, the theater. That's about it."

Art, music, the theater. I registered this, while Spears explained that his knowledge of the arts was strictly second-hand: books, records, magazine articles. Except for playing the banjo!

"I'm sure you'll do fine," I said. "I imagine Elliott's already explained to you what your duties'll be."

He nodded.

"Okay then," I said. "If you have any questions, please don't hesitate to ask."

He didn't hesitate. He nearly drove me crazy. Questions burst out of him like popcorn. He wanted to know absolutely everything about the office operation; everything about everything. And he was always hoofing it off to the public library, to bring back whole armfuls of books for research.

No question about it, the quality of his reports steadily improved and before long he had demonstrated to everyone's satisfaction, including his own (I could tell it from the subtle change in his manner), that he was "in."

Often I felt that with his constant, persistent questioning he was steadily draining me like a child emptying a soda bottle with a straw. On the other hand, I needed someone wise to the job. And Spears demonstrated that he could give as well as take. On nights when he knew that I wanted to leave, he'd offer to stay late himself to perform the mopping-up chores.

Sometimes I accepted, sometimes I didn't. Spears didn't push. His tact, his friendliness, his openness were disarming. Grudgingly I found myself liking him. We frequently lunched and often, when working late, we'd finish up the day by having a drink at a bar.

Spears had one area of reserve: He seldom talked about himself or his background, to the point where my curiosity was piqued. One evening, after we had had a couple of stiff bourbons together, I asked boldly, "John, what does your father do back in Kansas?"

His face reddened. "He's a stockman."

When I didn't react, he went on to explain: "He fattens livestock, grows his own feed – corn, sorghum."

"Sounds like a good business arrangement."

"It is if you're a big operator." He paused for a second, pushing an ice cube down into his drink with the tip of his finger. "My father's not. He works harder than anyone I know, but at the end of the year there's not much to show for it."

"What's the magnet then?"

"Cattle. He loves working with cattle and he loves talking about cattle. He even loves talking *to* cattle." Spears took a long drink. "Besides, it's the only business he knows. It's the only business most of them back there know. The older folks, that is. The young ones, like me – we're all leaving. God, how I hated Sundays. Always the same thing: church; fried chicken or baked ham; baked ham or fried chicken; apple pie or lemon pie; lemon pie or apple pie. Afternoons: it was coffee, cards, and talk, talk, interminable talk about corn and cattle and weather and the prices at the market. The only person I think I ever really enjoyed talking to was my Uncle Wade, the one who taught me the banjo. He had a little orchestra; he traveled around, played at church picnics, county fairs. You know."

It was a little embarrassing, his being so frank about his family and where he came from. I wanted to tell him that my father talked not only to cows but to horses and goats and turkeys and chickens and his pickup truck, and that the talk around our dining table was usually about grass, grass, grass, the tallness or shortness of it, the desperate need for rain, or, conversely, the devastation caused by too much rain, and (of course) the prices at the market. But Spears' skin had returned from red to pink, and I decided it was time to change the subject.

"I gather you like it here," I said, "living in the Big Ant Hill."

"Oh, God, I love it! New York's a great city!" His eyes were glowing. "You know, I've always been fascinated by ants. They're tough little things, biologically." And with a swish of his hand, he was back on the Great Plains again. "Back home, they're all over the corn fields. Big, red ones. My poor father; he's forever pouring some kind of poison down their holes. He's even tried burning them out. Nothing! The ants just pack up their bags, wave 'so long,' scoop out another hole, and nod 'hello'. ''

I had to laugh, in spite of myself, the way he picked up on my metaphor. But was he pulling my leg? Was he smarter than I gave him credit for? I couldn't tell from the look on his face.

"Of course, there're some things I like about Kansas, don't get me wrong," he went on. "Things most New Yorkers probably wouldn't like. The flatness, the distances, even the emptiness. It gets under your skin, when you're a part of it."

Did this explain why Spears, when he looked at you, never really seemed to be looking at you but always through you and beyond you into space? Maybe, maybe not. Cowboys and sailors develop squints from trying to look farther than their eyes can see. Spears never squinted. His eyes always remained round and wide open.

"When you're used to living under the Big Sky, when you can see in every direction, as far as the eye'll take you," he was saying, "you don't like your eye running into mountains. I guess that's why I'm not too crazy about mountains. They surround you."

"I can understand that, coming from where I came from," I said. "Only these tall New York buildings can close in on you too."

"Nothing like mountains," he replied. "You know, last Sunday, I decided to take a walk across the Brooklyn Bridge right about dusk. And when I got to the middle, I turned around and stood there and just looked at the City. It was dark in most of the business district, but in the apartment buildings, my God! Nearly every window in nearly every one was lit up – like cells in some huge golden honeycomb. Except every cell had people in it. And I thought about how, if you could talk to them and listen to their stories, there'd probably be a novel behind every one of those windows."

"I doubt it, John," I said, swilling the last of my bourbon and letting the glass hit the table with a clink. "I know a few New Yorkers who've lived here all their lives – and, yeah, maybe they'd make a novel. Born-and-bred New Yorkers are tougher than those ants in your father's cornfields; I don't think you could exterminate them with an atom bomb. But most people move in and out of here like it's a train station."

We were both bachelors, we both loved New York, but whereas I was satisfied to flirt with the city, to know and enjoy it as I encountered it, willing perhaps to move out someday and transfer my love back to the state where my roots were, Spears courted the city as if he meant marriage. He read *The New Yorker* and the just-launched *Village Voice* as if they were the Old and New Testaments. He bought a guidebook and visited all the celebrated landmarks, never seeming to tire of Times Square, Rockefeller Center, Greenwich Village or the Museum of Modern Art. "It's an addiction," he said. "I don't know whether I could ever live anywhere else again." He even changed overnight from bourbon and beer to Scotch and martinis.

Yet I wasn't prepared for a sudden caterpillar-like metamorphosis that took place one week. I had come to the office early and was sorting out papers when I looked up to see a strange figure standing in front of me. It wore a narrow-brimmed gray felt hat and a narrow-shouldered, narrow-cuffed Brooks Brothers suit that was so pointed at the extremities that the person in it looked like the diamond on a playing card. On his arm dangled a sharp-angled black umbrella that New Yorkers were accustomed to bring to work with them when the skies looked like rain later in the day.

"Top of the morning to you," Spears called out, hanging his umbrella and then his coat on a rack in the office. "How do you like it?"

"Terrific," I replied, lying.

I myself still wore clothes I had brought with me from Texas or bought when I was home on vacation: some padding in the shoulders, but only lightly so. On occasion, I'd wear my black cowboy boots and my one-gallon Stetson to work. I just couldn't bring myself to buy or wear a Brooks Brothers suit – and though Brooks Brothers prided itself on its clothes having "the natural look," Spears' hat and suit somehow just didn't look natural on him.

Nobody else in the office seemed to notice or care. It was not unusual, in fact it was expected, that newcomers to New York would sooner or later adapt their clothes to the city, like some animals change fur with a change in the weather or environment. I was more or less an exception, and Elliott more or less accepted that too, sighing, "Once a Texan, always a Texan."

Anyway, that evening, while Spears was putting his coat and hat back on, he revealed yet another mutation in his life. He had rented an apartment down in the Village. "Not right in the Village, the rents are too high. More on the edge of the Village," he said. "And it's really not an apartment. More of a cold-water flat, the kind writers *used* to rent in the Village. But it's only $55 a month, and I'm going to put in hot water and have the walls replastered with the money I save. The only real inconvenience will be that I have to share the toilet with an old lady who lives next door and keeps six cats. She's a bit peculiar."

"Six cats!" I whistled. "Let me tell you something, John. Anybody who keeps more than one cat in a New York apartment has got to be crazy."

He laughed. "Don't worry. I'm only going to share the toilet with her."

Spears painted his flat himself, working evenings and weekends, and when he was through with it he invited me down for an inspection tour. There was no categorizing the place; like Spears it was made up of a lot of incongruous elements. But it did have a certain charm. The walls were oyster white, the woodwork red. The combination would have looked ludicrous in most settings, though here it gave the whole place a bold, bright, cheery tone, like the stripes on a circus tent. Spears explained that the walls were copied from the Museum of Modern Art, a reference that needed no elaboration because there were van Gogh, Gauguin and de Kooning prints hanging in every room. What's more, once Spears was firmly settled in his new home he enrolled in night classes in painting and sculpture and set about producing his own art. Out of wire clothes hangers and paper mache he fashioned tall, spare Giacometti-like figures which he set up on little platforms around the rooms or hung from the ceilings; and in bright colors – red, orange, purple, vermilion – he painted huge canvases of swirling, vortex-like abstractions with big, glassy fish-eyes at the center. One by one he hung his own paintings on the walls to replace the processed prints.

When I asked Spears why he had gotten so interested in art when our profession was literary, he replied, "I guess I've always been interested in art, even though I never had much contact with it back home. Good art, that is. Besides, I read somewhere that the art of one art translates into the art of others, and one thing I've learned in working on manuscripts is that the best writers think visually as well as verbally."

It was a seemingly offhand remark: "The best writers think visually as well as verbally." Natural, too, for someone whose job was to work with manuscripts, to judge the effectiveness and quality of the writing. Yet all of a sudden, way down deep inside of me, something exploded. Was that seemingly offhand remark a clue to that strange, faraway look in John's eyes, particularly when coupled with that previous remark of his looking back at Manhattan from the middle of the Brooklyn Bridge and seeing a novel behind every lighted window of New York's tall, multi-storied apartment buildings? Was the ambitious young man from Kansas possibly thinking of a leap upward in the established literary hierarchy, from a reader and editor of manuscripts to an author of them? The very possibility of that happening, no matter how remote – or how remote the possibility of it being successful, even if it happened – was the spark that had set off the explosion inside of me. I recognized it immediately, for subconsciously I had felt a powder keg of anger, resentment, and jealousy building up within me for a long time, only waiting for the right spark to set it off.

Once I had had the thought myself – nay, call it a dream – of becoming a "writer." I say call it a dream because the idea had been pretty remote for me when I was a kid, even though I grew up in a family of story-tellers – my grandparents and my parents were always telling tales about the hardships and dangers of settling on the frontier; of outlaws who robbed banks and trains; of quarrels between neighbors over fence-lines and broken fences that sometimes led to shootings; of droughts and dust storms and catastrophic cyclones, one of which picked up a 2,000-pound Brahma bull and dropped it on the other side of the fence in a neighbor's pasture. But my "writer" dream really only began when I was in college and one of my teachers, a Professor Ronald Harris, complimented me on my theme papers and encouraged me to try my hand at fiction. When I wrote a couple of short stories and had been accepted by a couple of so-called "little" magazines, I could hardly believe it. A writer? Maybe not one like Chekhov, Balzac or Melville, but the thought of being any kind of an "author" was enticing. I couldn't help fantasizing about seeing more of my stories in print – many more; of creating men and women, indeed whole worlds, out of nothing more substantial than the imagination; of making these men and women love and hate and live out their destinies under my omniscient eye; of being, in other words, like a God to whom there is no power and no joy like the power and joy of begetting and of providence and predestination. It was that dream that eventually prompted me to head for New York, for if New York was the place to be for an aspiring actor, artist, a singer, wasn't New York, the publishing capital of the United States, also the place to be for an aspiring writer? And when Elliott hired me after looking over some of my writing, the impossible dream suddenly seemed possible. During my early days in New York, I spent my weekends, and even nights after work, writing, writing, writing, devoting hours and days of drudging labor, trying desperately to create stories in which real people moved, and moved others. I endured the tortures of hell, draining myself of life in order to give life to the people in my stories. And yet somehow, for whatever reason, I could never quite do it; my people always remained gray clumps of words. Finally, deciding that I had not really been given the gift of the Muses, I had given up, feeling that it would be folly and presumption to try further. The day I decided that was perhaps the blackest day of my life.

But if Spears was hiding inside of him the dream that I once had, he gave no further evidence of it. At least not in the days immediately ahead.

Apart from his work, in which he was becoming increasingly competent, he seemed most interested in absorbing what New York had to offer, on developing his persona in his new environment. In fact, it wasn't long before he was entertaining in his flat, and invariably, as his closest associate, I'd be invited.

At his parties Spears would drift around the room wearing his best smile and he'd be the host *par excellence*, replenishing drinks and making sure that his guests had plenty of canapés and nuts to munch on. There was always pleasant music playing on his record player, classical and pop, and, at least once in the evening, at the urging of his guests, he would get out his banjo and sing folk songs, with everybody joining it on the choruses:

> *Bird in a cage, love, bird in a cage . . .*
> *Dying for freedom, ever a slave;*
> *Eeeeever a slave, deeeear . . .*

I always had a good time at these parties; except once.

This party, to which about ten people had been invited, started out well enough, with everyone drinking martinis and growing more expansive with each one. But trouble was fated, if only because of the nature of Spears' date, a long-faced young woman named Susan Wicker. A recent graduate of Sarah Lawrence, Susan Wicker was one of those aggressive, intellectual types who can't be happy unless they are skewering something or somebody. It was Spears' first date with Susan and her first visit to the flat. By her third martini, she was finding all sorts of hidden and pejorative meanings in his paintings. "Do you always paint in spirals?" she asked

Spears, her mouth itself ironically twisting to one side in a kind of half-spiral.

"Not always."

"Then why is every single one of your paintings in the form of a spiral?"

"Is that bad?"

Susan swirled the olive in her glass. She smiled smugly. "Depends on who's making the judgment. I'm sure you know that spirals are a universal archetype and that they are found in the art forms of all cultures with deep sexual repressions."

Turning away from his date, Spears whispered, "Bullshit," in my ear. To her he said, "What about Frank Lloyd Wright's design for the new Guggenheim Museum? It's a spiral and the *Times* says everybody who's seen the blueprints loves it."

"You've just proven my point," Susan came back. "We're a Puritan culture to the core." And for the rest of the evening she went on and on about circles, triangles, and trapezoids in the art forms of different cultures and what they meant psychologically, meanwhile downing one drink after another like a winded plug-horse at the trough. At one o'clock, when everybody had left but Susan and me, she refused to budge, demanding another drink and telling Spears that he probably needed to see a psychoanalyst. Spears, acting as if he hadn't heard, got out the coats. Whereupon Susan grabbed hers with a snort and headed for the door.

We were no sooner out on the street, where you never knew what or whom you were going to encounter that time of night, than we were confronted by a disheveled, rheumy-eyed wino who moved up close to Spears and coughed in his face. "I'm sick, Jack, can you help me get some medicine?" Spears drew back the couple of steps. But the man moved with him. "C'mon now, I know you can spare me something." When Spears retreated still farther, the man went right along, like a tango dancer hewing to his partner.

Susan eyed them both contemptuously. "Oh, for God's sake, John, why don't you give him a buck? It's not going to break you!"

"Because I'm not as gullible as you are," Spears snapped back, his face reddening. To the panhandler, he said, "Get out of my way!"

The man didn't budge.

With that, Spears gave the man a shove on the shoulder. In the man's unsteady condition, it was enough to send him reeling. He fell to the sidewalk. And there he lay as if paralyzed, his bloody eyes fixed angrily on

Spears. Finally, with all the strength he could muster, he screamed at my friend and colleague:

"You cheap little fink! *Fink!*"

Spears' face turned from red to white. He stood trembling. It was embarrassing for all of us.

I walked over to the wino and grabbed his arm to lift him to his feet. He pulled back and started to flail at me, like a comic mimicking a boxer. "I c'n get up myself, when I get good and ready," he shouted at me. "Your pal's a cheap little fink! Whole bunch o' ya are!"

The next morning Spears apologized to me profusely for the incident.

"I probably should have given the guy a buck and let it go at that," he said. "But I never know whether you're helping or hurting those men. And when Susan put her oar in, that did it. I was fed up to here with her," and he moved a finger across his nose.

I frankly didn't know what I would've done myself under the circumstances. I don't think Spears should have shoved the man (maybe he'd had too many martinis), but I myself had become increasingly resistant to the panhandlers who confronted you everywhere in New York, particularly when you had a woman with you.

For a couple of days, Spears remained uncharacteristically aloof, trying, I suppose, to get his bearings again in the light of the unpleasant incident. I understood, because in New York back then one was always under pressure to shift gears, and sometimes it took a little time and introspection to know what gear to shift.

Then it happened.

I say "it" because some things in life just happen impersonally, no matter what you do or don't do. They're in the stars, as the astrologers in the third-floor hovels on Times Square would tell you for four or five dollars.

"It" began when Elliott called in the department heads one day to announce a new company policy: more rapid growth, more aggressiveness, possible entry into the foreign field which until now had been left to other firms. "We've got to quit sitting around on our status quos," Elliott growled. "I want a longer and stronger list; I want some fresh and original new writers; and I want to know how to find them. And I want suggestions from everybody, even the office boys."

I passed the word on to Spears and other members of my department. My plan was for them to submit their suggestions to me, and after eliminating repetitions and far-out notions, I would combine them into a single memo from the department as a whole.

But when Spears submitted his suggestions (he worked on them for two weeks, mostly on his own time) they were so comprehensive, they showed so much thought and effort, my whole plan was thrown into a cocked hat. If I merged Spears' ideas with the others, wouldn't he feel, perhaps with some justification, that he'd been short-changed? On the other hand, if I submitted them apart from the department's . . . well, wouldn't it show us all up to his own advantage; especially me?

To be truthful, Spears hadn't asked for any special consideration; but the more I thought about the dilemma he had put me in, the angrier I got. Especially since way down deep inside of me I had the smoldering suspicion that this supposedly rough-cut kid from Kansas was moving ahead methodically, step by step, according to a carefully conceived plan in which ultimately he would be the winner, and I, inevitably, the loser.

For two days I kept his report on my desk and did nothing. In the end, I decided that I was being childish and petty: I submitted his memo to Elliott intact.

The Grand Sachem was delighted, so much so that he took Spears out of my department and assigned him to the new foreign division under an editor named Harvey Alcock; and to launch the budding project with a big bang – Elliott's way of doing things – Alcock and Spears were to make a trip around the world (yes, around the world) to meet and ingratiate themselves with foreign publishers and authors, hopefully to bring home provocative books and manuscripts that could be translated into English and republished in the United States. It was a plum of an assignment, a rare one in the business. When I heard about it, I almost headed for the Hudson River. As I congratulated Spears, I tried desperately not to show my feelings, though I knew that both my ears were flopping.

Spears, for his part, reacted modestly. "I'm sorry to be leaving your department," he told me, saying it as if he meant it. "I owe you a lot." But as he walked around the office, treating secretaries, office boys, and the like with an overflowing courtesy approaching courtliness, I could see him growing taller by the minute, and there was a completely new air about him. If before he seemed to be looking through you and beyond to some distant landscape, his eyes seemed now to be looking beyond the earth itself to some extraterrestrial destination.

It was the same when he and Alcock returned from their world tour; triumphantly, with a whole truckload of manuscripts and contracts. Into the office Spears walked wearing an English fedora, a suit and coat that had been made for him in London, and a smile that reached all the way from the Atlantic to the Pacific.

"How was it?" I knew the question was redundant.

"Wonderful! It was wonderful!" he replied, and handed me a large, heavy cardboard box.

I took the box rather sheepishly.

"Go ahead; open it," he said, and while I tore the cover off, he stood balancing himself first on one foot and then the other, his ear-to-ear grin still there.

A bronze Dancing Shiva! Not one of those shiny factory-made ones they sell to tourists but an old one with a patina. He had bought it for me in New Delhi from an art dealer, for the mantelpiece in my apartment.

"I'm flabbergasted." The truth was, I felt very guilty.

"I thought you might like it."

He had brought back presents for other people in the office – perfumes from France, blown glass from Italy, nielloware from Bangkok, wood-cuts from Japan – but nothing like the Dancing Shiva. How could I hate him?

In Spears' new position with the foreign department, he had many opportunities to mingle with the so-called international set – mostly people in the foreign publishing business but also in the arts and United Nations – and every chance he had to include me in he'd do so. In spite of myself, it brought a new spice to my life. I tried to reciprocate.

One way, ironically, was to lend an ear to Spears' "lover's lament." For at one of the international cocktail parties Spears met and fell head over heels in love with a young Hungarian woman named Anita Kadar. And when I say "head over heels" I mean just that.

Anita was the daughter of Marie Kadar, a shrewd, enterprising widow who had parlayed a small jewelry shop into big business by the following formula: she would hire cash-hungry artisans in upstate New York to copy the design of necklaces and bracelets and such from a wide range of eras and countries – ancient Greece, pre-Columbian Mexico, Africa, China, et cetera – and then sell the reproductions to wealthy *matronas* in South America. Anita had her mother's good looks – luxurious jet-black hair that shimmered like a bird's wing; deep black eyes; and soft, smooth olive skin; but whereas her mother was a targeted extrovert, surrounded always by a coterie of satellites, the daughter was a quiet and retiring person who preferred books and classical music to the world of fashion and commerce. Mornings she spent at Columbia University where she was taking graduate courses in English literature, the other half of the day she worked for her mother. Once Spears got to know her, the Holy Grail itself was not pursued with more fervor.

Anita kept him guessing. And when she would decline one of his invitations, without giving an explanation, he would be devastated. He dragged around the office day after day looking like a sick cat. And when we'd have lunch he'd pour out his woe and frustration upon my shoulders, over and over again to the point of complete boredom.

"Do you think she likes me?" he asked me one day for the umpteenth time.

"She must," I answered as I always did, "or she wouldn't go out with you at all."

"But how much does she like me?" He bit his lip. "Maybe she just tolerates me. . . . Maybe it's my looks."

We were on our third martini, the barricades were down. "Look, Spears, you're no Cary Grant. But not all women fall in love with looks, certainly not in the strictest sense of the word. Who did Venus marry? Vulcan. Meantime, Napoleon was short. Clark Gable had problematic ears."

Spears sat up. But only for a moment. "If she likes me, why does she turn me down so often?"

I punched a toothpick into the olive in my glass. "Maybe it's because you ask her *too often*."

His eyes looked past me. "I don't think she'd like me at all if I were some timid little . . . mouse."

"Right. But John, not every woman wants to be stormed like a fort."

Now he was the one who punched at the olive. It slipped off his toothpick, and with a look of exasperation, he crooked a finger into the glass, grabbed the olive and plopped it into his mouth. "It's not just her beauty," he said. "She's incredibly intelligent. She's the most intelligent young woman I've ever known. You think I'm ridiculous, don't you, Karl?"

"No."

His face brightened. "Why not? I need to know." He seemed to be holding his breath.

"It seems to me," I felt I had to say something quickly, "that there's absolutely nothing wrong with being in love with the most beautiful, most intelligent girl in the world, *if.* . . ."

"If . . . what?"

"If she's in love with you."

His mouth dropped open.

Spears and Anita were married!

Time, moreover, seemed to justify his ebullience. As a married couple, they seemed to have many interests in common, and in other areas to complement one another.

Anita became more outgoing and gracious, even more feminine. She took a greater interest in clothes than before; her natural beauty she enhanced with jewelry from her mother's shop. Spears, for his part, acquired a poise and a self-assurance that went beyond cockiness; he seemed inwardly relaxed for the first time since I'd known him.

I wondered whether they would move out of Spears' flat but Anita settled that quickly. "I love the place."

As an old friend of the family (I had even been best man), I was often invited over for dinner or drinks. Mostly we talked about books, authors, publishing. Anita, who read two or three books a week, always seemed interested and frequently stayed up with us until the wee hours. I envied Spears that he had not only married beauty and brains but someone so completely in tune with his professional interests. With her help and his own drive I could easily visualize him someday as one of the top officers of the company – assuming that was what he wanted, and at that point I had begun to think that that was really what he was after.

So certain was I that his immediate goal was moving upward in the company that I was totally unprepared for the "announcement" that Spears made one evening at his flat. It had been a most pleasant evening: dinner of beef bourguignon, Beethoven's Fifth Symphony on the stereo, several rounds of brandy while we all sat in front of the fireplace. Anita had gotten up to brew coffee. Spears and I continued to stare meditatively and contentedly into the flames, the red glow of the fire upon our faces.

Finally, Spears broke the silence. "Karl," he said, "I've got some news I want you to be the first to hear."

I looked up. "News? What kind of news?" Anita . . . pregnant? Another promotion – for Spears?

"I'm resigning from the company."

This time I was the one who almost quit breathing.

"What? *Why?*"

"I want to write."

"Write?"

"You know, that thing that happens before a book gets published." He smiled, a Cheshire-cat kind of smile. "Publishing's a great business, you and I both know that, Karl. But I've decided that what I really want to do, more than anything else in the world, is write."

I tried not to betray how I was feeling inside. I smiled back. "Well. Writing, huh? As in 'The Great American. . . . ?"

He looked at me almost with contempt. "Someday I'd like to write a novel. Perhaps. But right now, I want to write short stories. I've already written a few, in my spare time. They're not very good, but. . . ."

"Don't believe him," Anita broke in as she returned with the coffee. "They're *good* stories."

"My claque, my loyal wife." Spears smiled appreciatively.

"But, but, why do you have to quit your job? Couldn't you. . . . "

"No." Spears' jaw went out. "I don't want to play at writing. I want to write. Full time."

"*Oui!*" Anita echoed.

I looked over at her. Her own jaw was set, she had the same faraway stare in her eyes that Spears did.

"Good," I said. "I only have one other question. . . . "

"You don't even have to finish." Spears laughed. "Fortunately, the rent on this flat isn't much" – the pieces were beginning to fall into place – "and if we get into a bind I have some savings. . . ."

"And after that, if I have to," Anita interjected, "I'll go to work full time for my mother."

"Wow. What a woman."

"She offered," Spears said, as he sipped his coffee.

What more could I say? I felt left out, and not only empty but about as angry as I had ever been in my life. Angry that somehow I had been deceived all along about Spears' real intentions. Angry that Fate had dealt him a better hand than it had dealt me. And angry perhaps most of all at myself, that I had let opportunities slip through my fingers.

Surprised, angry, jealous, all at the same time. Yet I somehow maintained enough equilibrium to offer some gratuitous advice.

"Now, John, don't go at it as if you're trying to build the Great

Wall. And don't be disappointed if . . ."

"Don't worry," they both replied, almost in unison.

My God, I thought, it's uncanny. Frighteningly uncanny.

For some time after this evening, I suffered from a deep and strange depression. Moodily I ate my meals, hardly tasting what I put into my mouth, and I slept badly: Neither work nor play provided much zest. I say strange depression, and yet was it really so strange? Wasn't *he* behind it all? Not personally: he hadn't done me any overt wrong. But ever since he'd won the foreign department post and made his triumphant world tour, his simple presence in the office had been a constant, irrepressible canker in my side. Now, ironically, it was his absence that was the canker – an even more painful and depressing one than before. For wasn't he possibly about to realize what I had dreamed about myself – and failed at? He had already shown me what could be done by stretching one's powers, thinking the extra thought, walking the additional mile. Of course, it was still too early to say whether he would succeed or fail. To wish him to fail would make me not more of a man but less. But to wish him to succeed was almost more than I was capable of. The very thought soured my stomach and spirit, as they had never been soured before in my life, not even during that awful period when I had decided to give up trying to write.

More than a year went by before I learned anything. Even then, it wasn't from Spears, who would talk about almost anything these days except his writing. Opening *The Hudson Review* one day, I saw a story there by "John Spears." It was patently autobiographical – about a sensitive farm boy breaking through the hard crust of New York life – but it was well-written, and what's more, it was a published story. I immediately telephoned Spears to congratulate him.

Six months later he had a second story published. It seemed to confirm that he not only had talent but some future as a writer. I was happy for Spears, while burning with envy. Particularly so since I had spent a gloomy, frustrating two years in my own job since he had left the office and was agonizing over whether I should leave the office myself.

With the publication of the second story I would have expected Spears to loosen up and talk more about his writing. The very opposite happened. He became increasingly diffident, even antisocial, and there followed a period in which I saw him and Anita only rarely. They quit giving parties at their flat, quit going out to them. Anita explained that it was partly to save money, Spears' earnings on his two published stories had hardly been enough to pay for his stationary; but mainly because he was hard at work on a novel now. "By the end of the day," she said, "he's so tired he doesn't want to do anything, not even talk. He just lies down on the couch and before you know it, he's sound asleep. I wish there was something I could do to help him. When I ask him he just waves me off, says it's something he has to do himself, that there's nothing anybody can do to help him."

"He's right, in a way. It's hard work, writing. The hardest," I said. "But I still think you can help him by getting him to come up occasionally for air – or at least a good cocktail."

"I'll try," she said, smiling, a faint smile like the glimmer of a distant light, but fetching.

Months and months went by before I talked to Anita again. During that time I had fallen head over heels myself for a young woman named Anne Friedrich and was so preoccupied that I almost forgot about John Spears, the aspiring young writer. Then one sunny spring afternoon I went into John David's to buy shirts and there at the counter, making a similar purchase for her husband, stood Anita. Though she smiled and was friendly, she seemed to be in a hurry to get her package and leave. I couldn't resist asking about Spears.

Her brow furrowed. "He's still at it."

"The end in sight yet?

Her frown deepened. "I wish I knew. But he doesn't tell me." She set down her parcels; having said that much, she seemed to want to talk more. "I've been trying to get him to take a vacation and he keeps promising he will, *soon*, but the farthest I've been able to get him is Van Cortlandt Park. Last Sunday, I packed a picnic lunch and we drove out there. He didn't say a word, the whole way out, or while we ate. After lunch he said he wanted to go for a walk in the woods, by himself. He was gone for nearly two hours and by the time he got back, I'll tell you, Karl, I was absolutely frantic. I asked him to please promise me he'd never do that again, and he promised. But I'm worried, Karl, I'm really worried. Goodness knows what'll happen if he doesn't finish the book soon or let up a little. I want him to succeed at what he's doing; as much as he does – but my God. . . . And we can easily afford a nice vacation now. I don't suppose I told you that I've gone back to work for my mother full-time?"

"No."

"Since December. It gives us a steady income again, it also keeps me from moping around the apartment and getting in John's hair."

"That's wonderful. With a wife like you, I don't see how John can fail." Anita's face lit up like a window at dusk.

I went on. "I'd like to help too, if only by helping John get out of himself. Look, I've got someone I want you both to meet. So why don't we drive by early Sunday afternoon – don't tell John we're coming – and we'll try to talk him into a ride out to the beach. This girl's great and between the two of us I guarantee you we'll break through whatever this wall is he's built around himself."

Anita gave me look of appreciation that turned my heart to jelly.

Spears wasn't overjoyed to see us. Dressed in a rumpled old red T-shirt and white dungarees, he looked hung over. He'd put on a lot of weight.

He wasn't exactly unfriendly, but when I suggested a drive out to the beach he balked. "There'll be traffic jams all the way out and back, I just can't take 'em."

I said I'd do the driving; then Anne joined in, saying Spears just had to see the peek-a-boo swimsuits the girls were wearing this year and she wanted to show him some "magic" food she had to attract seagulls; and all of us, including Anita, coaxed and pulled until finally he agreed to go. But only on condition that we take their car and that he do the driving. (Anita had been given an old '39 Ford by one of her mother's clients.) "I'll tell you why I wanta drive," he confided. "I've been pretty keyed up lately, I've got to do something with my hands."

He did: he took us on the wildest ride of my life. In and out of traffic lanes he wove as if he were trying to take over the lead at Indianapolis. Down the straightaway he drove in fits and starts, bobbing his foot up and down on the accelerator until we were all getting white under the gills. The conversation went in fits and starts too, with little continuity or coherence. All of us visibly shared a great feeling of relief when we arrived at the beach and headed over into one of those over-size parking lots that with their white stripes look like gargantuan grills.

Hundreds of cars already crammed the lot, and we had to look hard to find a vacant space. Finally Spears saw one and headed for it. But another driver had also seen the space and with a burst of speed nosed in ahead of him. Its big red stoplights flashed in Spears' face.

Spears was furious. His hands clutched the steering wheel as if he were about to tear it off.

"No use fretting about it," Anita said. "It's a big lot. We'll find another space."

Spears didn't say anything but I could tell by the tightness of his jaw and the perspiration that appeared suddenly on his forehead that he was boiling inside. Round and round the lot he drove several times without finding another space. Everybody in New York, and their brothers and sisters, and uncles and aunts, must have been at the beach that weekend. Finally, unable to control his anger any longer, Spears went back to where the other car had nosed in ahead of him and brought his front bumper up against the rear bumper of the other car. "John, what in heaven's name are you doing?" Anita asked. Anne Friedrich, anticipating that something unpleasant was about to happen, grabbed my arm.

Then Spears put on the gas and his car pushed up hard against the other car. It didn't budge.

"John, for God's sake, stop!" Anita screamed. "There's another lot down the beach."

But Spears didn't stop. Backing up a few feet, he revved the motor and drove his car headlong at the other's rear. Whambo! The impact was so great that the bumper on the other car snapped, and so did Spears' own front bumper; and both his headlights were smashed.

Anita, too mortified to say anything, covered her face with her hands.

The damage to Spears' car only infuriated him the more. He backed up and was about to leave the lot when all of us at the same time saw a space that another car was just vacating. Spears literally plunged his car into it. But the whole rest of the afternoon he spent grinding his teeth and growling to himself. Not least because Anita, who had taken the license number of the car Spears had struck, insisted on turning the matter over to their insurance company.

At one point in the afternoon, while we were all lying on the sand sunbathing, Anita asked me if I would go with her to the concession stand. And when we were out of earshot of the others, she exclaimed: "I think he's gone mad, absolutely mad! Crazy mad!"

I suppose I should have commiserated with her. Instead I laughed. Because for some reason – call it a perverted sense of humor if you will – the incident had struck me as more comic than tragic, reminding me of the Terrible-Tempered Mr. Bang of the comic strips, who was always kicking at things, only to stub his toe. "He'll come to his senses when he hears from the insurance company," I said.

Anita didn't appreciate my comment. "Karl," she said, "the John who hit that other car is not the John I married. Something is radically wrong. Anybody who did what he just did ought to see a doctor."

Nothing more was said until we had gotten our sodas and peanuts and were strolling slowly back down the beach: Then Anita told me she was worried about something else. "His writing. I know that some rewriting is necessary, but why should John rewrite the same material over and over again, seemingly endlessly? He doesn't let on that he does, but I can tell, from the way he works."

"Because it's hard, extremely hard, to put down on paper – in black, bloodless words – what you think and feel."

"I know it's hard, but not *that* hard," Anita answered, " – if it's right for you. And that's what's starting to worry me. For the first time, I'm beginning to wonder if . . . I don't know . . . if maybe his train isn't on the wrong track. For lack of a better way to put it. What do you think, Karl?" Her question, and the way she put it, reminded me so very much of the querying that Spears used to do when he was courting Anita.

"It's hard to say." I was digging a long furrow in the sand with my heel. "I've only read two of his stories."

"And what did you think of them? Be honest."

"They were well-written."

"Then he *is* a writer." She seemed greatly relieved.

"Not necessarily." I halted because I wanted to think about it for a moment. It was a big question. Not only for Spears but for myself and all other wannabe writers as well. "Not necessarily," I repeated. "It depends on what one means by the words 'writer' and 'well-written.' Some people are wizards with words, others are like jugglers and acrobats, but the real magic of literature isn't that of musicians, jugglers and acrobats. Dickens, Dostoevsky, many other great writers, even wrote clumsily at times. The people who wrote the Bible weren't primarily what we call 'writers.' Nor was Thomas Jefferson. But the words of the Declaration of Independence are like a call to arms to all the peoples of the world forever. I know that doesn't answer your question about John. But I don't think I can."

The season was late autumn and I was feeling like the weather, cloudy and morose. My courtship of Anne Friedrich had ended, sunk by the submerged reef of temperamental differences. At the office, I was nearing an absolute dead-end – my work no longer seemed challenging enough, I desperately felt the need to test and expand my powers, such as they were, in new directions. But where? Moving up the administrative ladder of the company didn't interest me; the only other editorial job that might have – the foreign department – was completely filled. Going to work for another publishing company would only be playing musical chairs. This fall evening, having finished dinner, I was sitting in an easy chair, sipping a cup of coffee, feeling very lonely and sorry for myself, listening to a classical record with rolling, tumbling rhythms that somewhat soothed my troubled soul, when the buzzer rang.

It was Anita, though I hardly recognized her. So pale and thin, skin waxen, cheeks hollow, eyes big and agitated.

"I'm so sorry, Karl," she stammered, "but I had to talk to somebody." She broke into tears.

Good God, I thought, what's happened now? Putting my arm around her, I led her inside to a couch. She continued to sob, so I took her hand and tried to calm her.

"Karl," she exclaimed, "something's happened. It's horrible. . ."

"John again?"

She nodded. "I don't even know how to tell it. It's a long story. You know part of it already; you've *seen* part of it. And I can't help but think that some part of it is my fault."

"Take it slow and easy, Anita." I got up and mixed her a toddy, and as she sipped it she became calmer.

She began with the time the past spring when we had all driven out to the beach together; when she had been angered, embarrassed and frightened, all at the same time, by Spears' "irrational" behavior. That outing, even with the tragic-comic bumping of cars, hadn't been a total waste, she explained, for the next day Spears seemed abashed at what he had done and anxious to make up for it. He began taking her out to dinner and to the movies and, for a period of several weeks, seemed more relaxed and in better spirits. But then came a return to the old habits: unrelieved, desperate work, writing and rewriting, writing and rewriting, the only letups on Sunday when he would flop on a couch and fall asleep from sheer exhaustion.

"It was like quicksand; he'd pull out one leg and the other one would just sink down deeper. But what could I do? He hadn't let me read anything of what he'd written, I had absolutely no way of knowing. Finally, the strain on me was too much. I couldn't stand it. One Sunday, while he was sleeping, I picked up one of his chapters and read it. I know I shouldn't have done it, but I just had to do something, find out *something.* . . ."

Anita looked up, her eyes searching mine for approval. I said merely, "Go on."

"I, I only read one chapter. Maybe if I could have read more. But the next day John noticed the papers on his desk had been shifted. Slightly. I don't know how he'd notice something like that. But he asked me if I'd been reading his work. I had to tell him the truth. He went through the ceiling! He was shouting at me, Karl. Shouting! 'Don't ever, ever touch my papers again!' From then on, he locked his papers in his desk at the end of every day. And he kept the key in his pocket."

"I know that you only read one chapter," I said, "but what'd you think of it?"

"I don't know. It seemed disorganized. Like there was no focus. Maybe if I could have read more. . . . I know it's not fair to judge a whole novel on one chapter."

I told Anita I sympathized with her, but that I also sympathized with her husband, knowing how he felt, since I had gone through a similar experience myself.

"How *he* felt?" Her eyes suddenly glowed with anger, her voice rose. "Can you imagine how *I've* felt, living with this man month after month this way? He hardly knows I'm alive. He speaks to me in monosyllables, when he speaks to me at all. And every day I see him sinking deeper and deeper into, I don't know what, some . . . abyss."

She was trembling: I began to wonder whether it was she, and not Spears, who had been working herself each day deeper and deeper into an abyss.

"This morning, everything came to a head at the breakfast table," she said. "I told John he had to make a choice, one way or the other. I don't think he understood what I was saying. He stormed out of the kitchen, stormed into his workroom, slammed the door. For the next hour, I could hear him banging the typewriter. Then he came back into the kitchen, walked right by me, didn't say a word, and poured himself a drink. And when he finished that one, he came back and poured himself another one. And then another one. He did that the whole morning –

drinking and banging on that typewriter. On one of his trips to the kitchen he kicked a chair out of his way so hard it broke. That's when I got really, really frightened. I was actually afraid of being in the same house with him."

Here Anita broke into tears again and I couldn't help feeling very sorry for her. I wanted to put my arm around her, to console her, to love her.

"I had to get out of that apartment," she sobbed. "For about an hour I just walked around and around the block, like I was in a daze. I was wondering whether I should go to my mother's and never come back; whether I should call a doctor; whether – I hate to admit this one – whether I should call the police. At one point, I actually went into a pharmacy to call the police. Then I thought that'd be completely silly. That John was just exhausted: mentally, emotionally, physically; that what he really needs is rest and some kind of change of scenery; he needs to go somewhere where there aren't any pencils or paper or typewriters – or maybe even me! I decided I'd leave him alone for awhile, go to a movie, and when I got home I'd try to talk him into going down to Nassau or some place like that. . . ."

I put my arm around her. She rested her head on my shoulder.

"I got back," she went on, her voice increasingly weak, "about five o'clock. I opened the door and I peeked in. I was trying to hear his typewriter. But I didn't hear anything. The place felt so empty, like nobody even lived there. And I couldn't hear anything. Nothing. Not even the slightest sound. It gave me the shivers. I knew he was there, somewhere. And I knew – although I can't tell you how I knew this – that he was okay, physically. And I did want to go in; I felt like I *should* go in. But I couldn't. I just couldn't, Karl. I closed the door and went back out to the street and I caught a cab. And here I am. I honestly don't know what to do. I think I'm at the end of my rope. . . "

"It's all understandable, Anita. You've been through a lot," I said, laying a hand over hers. "But I'm sure, I'm absolutely sure, that you don't need to be afraid of John. He might bump a car, or bang a typewriter, or kick a chair, maybe even kick a cat in this state, but to hurt somebody – you – I'm sure he wouldn't do that."

Anita took her head off my shoulder. She turned toward me, and put her other hand in mine. "I hope not, Karl," she said. "But you didn't see the look he had in his eye today. It was different – it was different than anything I've ever seen before. That's what scared me the most. You remember the day at the beach, when John bumped the car, I told you I thought he'd gone mad. I didn't really mean it then. But today he looked like he had. Like he was crazy mad. I can't even explain it. It was this look in his eye – wild, frenzied. Like he was a wild animal. . . ."

"John's mad, all right," I said. "He's mad at the whole world and everything and everybody in it, including himself. I felt that way myself once. Mad enough to blow up the whole world, me included."

"You did?" She looked at me with a queer kind of expression.

"I sure did."

"Well, maybe you felt that way. But I'll bet you didn't go around tearing things up."

"Only because I didn't have the strength. I just shoved my manuscripts into the bottom of a closet and fell asleep, and slept for three whole days."

I squeezed her hands gently and got up from the couch. "Anita," I said, "I think we need to go back and see him."

"No, no!" she cried. "I can't go back there. I don't think you could drag me back there."

"You don't have to go in," I said. "I'll go in, alone. I'll talk to him."

"No, no," she retorted. "I couldn't let you do that. He might, might. . . ."

"Don't worry," I said, putting on my coat. "Come on, let's go."

On the way down in the cab neither Anita nor I spoke very much. Spent emotionally, she sank back in her seat and pulled her coat tight around her, as if she were having a chill. Her skin sagged and she didn't look very attractive to me now.

And the more I looked at Anita, the more I wondered whether I was doing something quixotic, assuming that Spears was in some kind of hopped-up emotional state. What business was it of mine? Why should I intrude? I began to have second thoughts, wished that I could tell the driver to turn around and take me back to my apartment.

Too late for that. We were there.

Leaving the cab, we started the hundred or so feet toward their building. I still hadn't made up my mind what I was going to do, or even what I'd say if I confronted John.

"Anita," I said when we were right at the apartment, "maybe you'd better go over to that coffee shop down the street. Why don't you wait for me there?"

"What are you going to say to him?"

"I'm not sure. I'll think of something."

She grabbed me by the sleeve. "I'd feel better if someone went in with you."

"Who?" It came out involuntarily. Embarrassing, after all my bravado. What was I getting so queasy about? Spears just wasn't the type. . . . Then I recalled the anger and violence he had unleashed on the car at the beach. Who knows what a person backed up against the wall and struggling to survive will do?

"Who?" I repeated.

"I don't know. I don't want any of the people in the building to know what's going on. Some of them would probably love to call the police if they thought we were having trouble."

"Then I'll have to go in alone."

"All right, but before you go I want you to do something; for my sake. You know there's a walk on the side of the building, over by his study. Look in the window there and see if he's still in his room: and if everything looks okay, you can knock on the door and make out like you've just stopped by for a visit."

I said I would if only she'd get over to the coffee shop. She turned to go.

I went around a corner of the building and moved toward the window of Spears' study. I felt very silly. Like I was playing cops and robbers.

The walk separated two buildings and it was very dark along it except for a couple of spots where light poured out of windows in beams. No one would be likely to see me if I didn't step into those beams.

One of the windows out of which light streamed was Spears'. By that I presumed that he was in his study, working, reading – or perhaps, by now, if he had gone on hitting the bottle, dead drunk.

I edged up against the window. The light was shining against the glass, making it look opaque. The light shifted and the glass glittered as my head moved slowly up toward it. I peered inside.

There was Spears, slumped in a chair under an overhead light, his hands dangling to the floor. He looked grossly overweight, his face as round as a beach ball, heavy jowls under the chin. His hair was disheveled, his shirt open almost to the waist. He bore only a vague resemblance to the Spears I had known.

He looked dead. Not dead like murdered, or suicide, or from a heart attack. Rather, it was as if somebody had opened a valve in his head and let out all the juices.

Directly in front of him, only a few feet away, stood one of his own paintings, a sweeping, swirling red abstraction with a big blue-white fish eye in the center. The way he was sitting, it was as if he had been staring into the eye when whatever had happened had happened. Or, in another way, as if he were looking into a mirror and the huge blue-white eye of the painting were a magnified reflection of his own eye.

However, the more I looked at him the more I saw his eyes weren't focused on the painting at all, or on the wall behind the painting, or on anything. They were glassy and opaque, *they* were the mirrors reflecting the big blue-white fish eye in front of him.

Then I noticed what was on the floor all around Spears. Scraps of paper. Scraps and tatters of paper strewn all around in such quantity that in some spots they were almost ankle deep. Like a mammoth rat's nest.

For some time I stood at the window, my eyes fixed on Spears, as if I were dead too.

Finally, I withdrew. Anita was waiting anxiously.

"He's there," I said.

"What's he doing?"

"What's he doing?" I repeated. "Nothing."

"Then he's all right." She breathed a sigh of relief.

"I hope so. I sure hope so." I told her what I'd seen.

"He's sick, Karl. He's very, very sick." Now she began crying silently. "He worked so hard. He gave it everything he had. It was just too much for him."

"No, Anita. It wasn't that. Not entirely anyway. You know it was more than that."

"Maybe it was my fault, Karl. He loved me – I know that, even when he didn't act like it. Maybe I put too much pressure on him."

"I think it was more than that, too."

"He was such a perfectionist. He wouldn't . . . he couldn't . . . compromise."

"Maybe it would have been better to compromise, a little. In his case."

Now Anita's eyes flashed angrily. "Are you saying there's something wrong in wanting the best? Whatever it was in John that made him want the best was good. No, it was great!"

"Even if it was beyond him?"

"Yes, even if it was beyond him!" Her eyes were blazing. "Can't you understand that? I'm sorry for you, Karl, if you can't. . . . John wanted the best but he didn't want it for nothing. He was willing to pay for it. With whatever it cost. Do you understand that?"

I didn't answer. What could I say?

* * *

What eventually happened to John and Anita I'm not sure. John obviously needed medical treatment and I helped Anita get him into a clinic in upstate New York in a rural area where she thought that the beauties of nature – the hills, the trees, the lakes – would be healing. After that, I lost track of them; they moved somewhere (forwarding address not given) and even Anita's mother moved elsewhere, to Buenos Aires I heard.

I moved too, back to Texas where my roots were and where, because of my experience in the East Coast publishing business, I was hired to teach English at my alma mater. Surprisingly, I took to the job like a duck to water. I say "surprisingly" because I had never before thought of teaching as something I wanted to do. But over the years, and particularly during my time in New York, I had not only learned something of human nature but something of the qualities that distinguish what we call "literature" – that which will live longer than the men and women who created it – from that which will die before the author does. In time I'd also come to see that these qualities of literature – integrity, a searching for the truths of life, a feeling for the struggles and follies of humanity – were the same that made a human life worthwhile. How could one read Tolstoy, Dostoevsky or Melville without one's own life being affected?

Sometimes, when I brought students over to my home (later shared by a wife and a daughter) to continue discussions we had started in the classroom, we'd talk on and on until late in the night. And there was nothing more exciting to me, during those discussions, than those moments when I would see a spark come into the eye of a student, signaling that a connection had been made. In those moments I felt as Thomas Alva Edison must have felt when he brought two wires together and created light.

Every so often, I'd think about Spears and I'd wonder whether he might eventually have moved back to Kansas, as I had to Texas, and perhaps become a teacher, as I had. In spite of his ambivalence about Kansas, that's where his roots were and where his tenacity, like those ants in his father's cornfield, had come from. I doubt that he could have moved back to New York: It would not only have been too painful but, with developments in technology, the eye of the world had quit focusing so directly and so adoringly on the little island of Manhattan. As astronauts walked on the rocky surface of the moon and as television cameras on spacecraft showed us our Blue Planet whirling through a vast emptiness, the eye of the world was not only on itself (the whole world), but on the mysteries of outer space: where had all that stuff out in space – the asteroids, the comets, the planets, the galaxies of billions of stars – come from? If it had all started with an incredible explosion, a "big bang," as many astronomers believed, who or what had lit the fuse?

Now, ironically, in what I suppose are the twilight years of my life, I am trying my hand at writing again. As with this story of my experience in New York in the 1950s. But the difference between my writing now and what I had done before is that I am no longer trying to be a "writer." Whether I am doing it well or not, I am doing it because something deep within me is telling me that this story needs to be told. Not everybody can be a Tolstoy or a Chekhov. But if a story is demanding to be told, I've decided it needs to be told, no matter who tells it or how clumsily. Of course, as regards this particular story, the New York of today is a very different place from the New York of the 1950s. And although the Empire State Building that I once ogled still stands, the Twin Towers of the World Trade Center (built a few years after my departure back to Texas) have indeed fallen. In a monstrous and apocalyptic way. Does that make this tale about the quiet rise and the private fall of a young writer from Kansas, who courted the city of New York with such a passion so many decades ago, too insignificant to tell? I hope not. Indeed, I hope not. Because don't they both – the private falls and the blazing apocalypses – essentially emerge from the same mysterious source?

Nowadays, as a New World emerges in a new century, the action is everywhere – and where people live, or where we come from, or what school we have gone to seem much less important to me than what is going on inside the human head and the human heart. I have even begun to write some stories set in Texas, stories that have grown out of my experiences in my home state, that are demanding to be told. And as I write, the stories I am telling seem suddenly to come to life, in a way that I have never experienced before. Of course, I could be imagining that; we humans have an almost infinite capacity for deceiving ourselves. But it's something I've stopped worrying about. If something has the power of life in it, it lives. If it doesn't, it dies.

BISHOP O'HARA

Third Avenue, New York City, 1965

Gertie Gallagher panted over to the big, plate-glass window of Paddy McClairty's Irish Pub and pressed her nose against it. A look, that's all. My God, she just had to stop a minute and give her boiling body some relief. Her dress was already wringing wet, and not even halfway home. Against her nose the glass felt cool; cool and comforting.

Cupping her hands around her eyes she watched as huge mugs of beer – flowing over with froth – went sliding down the front-bar to eager fingers. It had been a blazer of a day. When Gertie'd stepped out on the sidewalk from work, it was like stepping out on a giant hotplate; even right here, under Paddy's tent of an awning, she could feel the heat from the cement coming up through the soles of her shoes.

Inside the bar the light was dim (that's the way Paddy liked it, cozy), but by squinting, Gertie could see almost everything: the sawdust-covered floor, the people at the tables, even the black-bordered photograph of President Kennedy which hung high up on the back-bar. The counter at the long, mahogany front-bar was strung solid with shirts – white, blue denim, loud sporty ones – with Paddy's head bobbing up every now and then among them.

Although Paddy's beer was certainly the same brew that was served at all the other bars, there was something special about it, and every frosted, foaming mug that went sliding down the counter made the dry wad in Gertie's parched throat seem bigger, and bigger, and bigger – until she didn't know how much longer she could stand it. She thirsted, oh, how she thirsted; every ounce of her one hundred and seventy-six pounds thirsted.

But she wasn't going in, she wasn't giving in. This time she was sticking by her guns!

Hey, there was Goof Lavelle and Jack Tyner, at the end of the line, facing her. And Rosey Franciosa. The other men standing at the bar, with their backs to her, she wasn't sure of, though the fellow at the extreme right, with the wide shoulders, looked for all the world like Tommy Ryan. Tommy Ryan? It couldn't be. Tommy was supposed to be somewhere on the high seas, on an oil tanker. Yet who else had shoulders like that? It had to be him. *I'll bet half this week's paycheck it is. He'll turn around in a minute, I'll prove it is.* If it was Tommy Ryan, it wouldn't be long either before he would be plunking down a couple of twenties, setting up the whole house.

Hail Mary, full of grace, don't let me go in.

A yell came from the far side of the bar and Paddy flipped on the TV. It was mounted high up in a corner, so everybody could see it. Gertie could see it too, though the sound coming through the glass was a little scraggly. Two boxers were slugging it out; one in green trunks, one in orange. Gertie's eyes remained fixed on them: she liked a good prizefight. Whenever one of the fighters landed a solid blow, a chorus of cheers arose, loud and lusty, from supporters in the pub. Judging from the loudness of the yells, each fighter had about the same number of fans. That was the way it always was at Paddy's whenever there was some contest, because the people who drank there liked things even, and that was another thing (besides the beer) Gertie liked about the place.

It was a furious, lashing fight, with lots of cheers and boos back and forth, and for a few moments Tommy and her thirst were forgotten.

Then something connected.

The Bishop! He's on tonight, right after the fight.

Gertie looked at her wristwatch. The Bishop would be on in exactly ten minutes. She couldn't possibly get home by then, not even if she ran all the way.

There was no choice. Paddy wouldn't mind. And better to see the Bishop here than not at all.

She stepped inside.

Nobody even noticed her, they were so preoccupied with the fight. She took a seat at the only vacant table in the place, to the far left, away from the TV. From here she could see, in profile, the man with the wide shoulders. He wasn't Tommy, though he sure did have shoulders like him. None of the men in the bar was Tommy. In a way she was relieved. There were six or seven other women in the place, all sitting at tables with men and all cheering and booing with them. Let 'em. She was here to watch Bishop O'Hara, nothing else. She took off her hat, set it to one side on the table, leaned back in her chair, and mopped her forehead with her handkerchief. Though it was cooler here in the bar (the breeze blowing from the ceiling fan was making the feather on her hat dance), it wasn't as cool as it had seemed from the outside; this was just one of those days.

Paddy spotted her and waved; she waved back. It was amazing the way he could keep his eyes on the whole place, all at once, yet give everybody special attention. It was amazing too, considering his size, the way he could work behind the bar, drawing beer with one hand and clanging the cash register with the other, grabbing a bottle of bourbon off the back-bar while reaching under the front-bar for the ice, sliding from one end of the counter to the other as if he were on grease, rattling the cocktail shaker on the way. In just about a minute he'd be at her table, asking her what she'd have. . . . And sure enough in just about a minute he was there, looking like one of his kegs of beer with an apron tied around it.

"Nothing today, Paddy. I just came in to watch the Bishop. I hope you don't mind."

"But nothing to drink, on a day like today?" He was squinting at her incredulously. "You must be outa yer mind, dearie! Just look at 'cha. Yer boiling over."

"I know. But I . . . can't."

He roared. "Oh, c'mon now! If ya don't put some liquid in ya pretty quick, yer gonna burn out a bearing."

"No, really, Paddy. I'll settle for a glass of water."

"It'll be on the house. Just for you!"

"Just water. Please."

"Okay, okay, okay, okay. But I think it's against some kinda criminal law to drink water on a day like today."

When he brought it, she took a couple swallows of the water. It was awful. But that's the way it had to be. For what was the use of it, walking to and from work, skipping the movies and the hair dresser's on Saturdays, scrimping every penny to go to Miami next month, if she was going to appear on the beach looking like a big, god-awful lumpy potato? Looking like she did last Sunday when she put on her bathing suit and stood in front of the mirror? Any man taking one look at her would turn and run the other way, and she wouldn't blame him! For a brief moment she hated Paddy and his beer, because wasn't it coming into Paddy's that was the cause of it all?

The prizefight ended – in a draw. Catcalls and Bronx cheers filled the bar, as if everybody there had paid good money to see somebody busted. "You know it! You know that was a fix!" yelled one.

"Ah, hell! They was playing patty cake."

"How do they get off, matching punks like that?"

"They couldn't punch their ways outa Rosey's lunch sack! Neither one of 'em."

"C'mon, c'mon, c'mon now," Paddy yelled above the hubbub, "cut out the yak! Anybody wants another one, better order it up now 'cause Bishop O'Hara's about to be on, right after the commercial."

Gertie wryly took a sip of her water.

On the screen the Yankee second baseman was plowing paths across his lathered face with a new, improved "Super-Edge" blade. Then the screen went blank and there was a moment of expectant silence. Goof Lavelle noticed Gertie and waved to her. She waved back. Nice guy, Goof, if only he'd bathe more often.

A bust of the Blessed Virgin appeared on the screen; in the background a choir intoned a hymn, softly, fervently. From the Virgin the camera panned to the full-length figure of Bishop Dennis O'Hara. Skullcap on his head, a dark scarlet cape draped over his shoulders, his arms outstretched like Jesus beckoning to the little children, the Bishop stood straight and steady, statuesque, smiling. There was loud applause from the studio audience, with Paddy's patrons joining in. The Bishop raised both his arms even higher, stretching them up and out toward the TV studio ceiling, and nodded his head solemnly. A hush came over both audiences. The men in Paddy's who had caps on took them off and set them reverently beside their glasses.

As the camera moved in for a closeup, the smile faded from the Bishop's face. "My friends," he began solemnly. His face was so close now that Gertie could see a small mole on his cheek. "My friends . . . the past few weeks we have been considering the Seven Capital Sins, sometimes called the Seven Deadly Sins. They are called Capital, you will recall, because they are not only sins or flaws in themselves but are the sources of so many other sins. . . ."

"Could you turn it up a little, Paddy?" Gertie called.

"Got it," said Paddy, reaching up and turning one of the knobs. "Wanta sit up closer?"

Gertie shook her head. "I'm fine. Thanks."

"Shhh." From the back of the tavern.

"We have already discussed Pride, Covetousness, Lust, and Anger; and tonight we shall take up Gluttony – the very word is foul-sounding, is it not? And it is a foul word, a foul sin. Repulsive! . . .

"I can hear you saying, 'Me a glutton! No! Oh, I may overeat now and then. My waistline may be expanding more than it should. But a glutton, no! Gluttony was the sin of the Romans, those gross, voluptuous, corrupt Romans who gorged themselves until they were ready to burst, then retched so that they could gorge themselves some more.' Yes, I can hear you saying that, because few Americans today really think they are guilty of the sin of Gluttony. But if you say 'Oh no!' I say 'Oh yes!' . . . ."

"Yes-s-s-s." The last sounds rolled out of his mouth and across the room like the sibilant whirling of surf.

There was a pause. The Bishop was staring right at Gertie.

"Re-e-ead all about it! Hat-t-tchet murder in Gren-itch Village!"

A pimply-faced teenager, wearing a red hat with a high crown and carrying a bundle of newspapers under his arm, had appeared out of nowhere and was standing by the bar, screaming at the top of his lungs.

"Shhh!"

"Shut up, kid!"

"Re-e-e-ad all about the poet killed in his bed!" The boy held up one of his papers broadside. Large, black headlines echoed his shrill cry.

"No, dammit, no!"

"Paddy, can ya sweep this babbling idiot outa the way!"

"C'mon, Nick, scram," said Paddy. "Can't ya see the Bishop's on TV?"

"How th' hell should I know! I sell papers."

The boy silently threaded his way between and around tables, shoving papers into faces. A man standing at the bar called to him. "Hey, kid, over here! . . . Gimme three o' them papers. . . ."

"Isn't it shameful how we will diet for our health's sake, or to be attractive to someone of the opposite sex – and yet how many of us are willing to control our appetites for God's sake? . . ."

It's the truth; the revolting, nauseating, god-awful truth, Gertie thought. She ate too much; sometimes downright hoggishly when it was something she liked, like mashed potatoes, with gravy, or lemon meringue pie; she knew it. And when did she start dieting? Only after she had looked into the mirror and saw not the body that God had given her but a big fat dumpling.

"In most instances those who eat too much commit only a venial sin. . . ." (Well, that was *some* consolation.)

"Furthermore, eating to excess is not the only form of Gluttony, or even the worst. There is another kind of Gluttony which is far more serious. Which may not only be a mortal sin in itself but may also, as one of the Capital Sins, lead to other mortal sins. Yes, I think you know what kind of Gluttony I am talking about. Intoxication; drunkenness-s-s. . . ."

Again the Bishop paused.

Gertie lowered her eyes, wondering if by some gift of the Holy Ghost the Bishop could read her thoughts; she hoped not, because even while he was looking right at her, she was being consumed by desire for a frosty schooner. And if she had one, wouldn't she eventually be wanting another? And then another? And wasn't that it, wasn't that her sin, that she didn't know when to stop?

The man who had bought the three newspapers lurched over from the bar to Gertie's table. She'd never seen him here before. He was middle-aged and beefy, with a paunchy stomach jutting over his belt like a cliff. He wore a red-and-yellow sports shirt and carried a paper sack which he sat on the table on top of his newspapers. "Wanta read about the hatchet murder?" he asked.

Gertie shook her head, though she hardly heard the man.

"Ain't trying to sell you a paper," he went on. "It's free. Here." Unfolding one of the papers he pushed it toward her.

Her eyes went back to Bishop O'Hara.

"Okay," the man said. "You don't hav-ta read it. Mind if I set down at your table here?"

Gertie wagged her head: she did mind, but she didn't want to start an argument now; she wanted to hear what else the Bishop had to say.

"It's a terrible sin, drunkenness. It robs a man of his reason – the most precious gift that God has given to man." The Bishop's eyes were flashing, his whole body trembling. "It cuts the reins by which a man controls himself, lets loose the wild beast that is within every man. It stimulates the passions and arouses illicit desires. Oh, how many sins against the Sixth and Ninth Commandments are due to intoxication! . . . ."

"Bull!" The man at Gertie's table roared it across the room.

Gertie's arm jumped, almost knocking over her water glass.

"Bull! Bull! Bull!" The man roared it again. "Nothing but bull!"

"U-h-h-h." There was a loud collective gasp from around the bar.

"Bull's what I said – and I'll say it again. Bull! Bull! Bull!"

Sacrilege, sacrilege, Gertie thought; but she was too afraid to say it out loud.

"Hey, shut up, man!" Someone was hammering on the table with a mug. "Shut him up, Paddy!"

Paddy scuttered over, his face flushed, his arms swinging like a prizefighter coming out of his corner. "Okay, that's enough, mister. Now button up yer lip or out ya go!"

"Oh, hell, this is a free country, ain't it?" the man with the newspapers growled. "Ain't no law against a body saying 'bull' if he wants to."

"For God's sake, Paddy, let him have it!"

"Not in my bar ya can't! And not to Bishop O'Hara."

"Says who?"

"Says me! Now just one more word outa ya – and out ya go!"

"God created the first human out of mud, but into that mud He breathed an immortal soul; so while man belongs in one way to the earth his ultimate destiny is Heaven. This is man's predicament, his despair and his glory – that he is half brute and half angel. And the Big Question is whether the brute shall dominate him, or the angel!"

"Bull! Bull! Bull!"

"Okay, ya asked for it," said Paddy, grabbing the man by the arm. And in a flash, the two bodies were twisting and thudding against each other like mastodons. Paddy was trying to lock the man's arms behind him. He might have succeeded if he hadn't slipped on a swath of sawdust. The other man jerked free.

A chubby hand reached into the paper sack on the table. Gertie saw the glint of shiny metal. "Oh my God!" she screamed.

"And *you* asked for it," the man said, aiming the pistol at Paddy. The bartender stood with his mouth open, his knobby hands drooped to his sides.

Not a muscle moved anywhere in the bar. Every eye was on the gun.

"Don't shoot, please don't shoot." Gertie's throat was so tight the words stuck there like balls in a pipe.

"Put . . . put that away, mister," said Paddy. "I don't want no trouble in here."

"Yeah, well, I don't want no trouble either; I'm just warning you," the man said. "Now" – motioning with the pistol toward the bar – "you get back o' there and mind your own business – and nobody'll get hurt."

Paddy hesitated but moved back of the bar where he stood, his hands outstretched upon the counter, like a statue.

Returning to his seat, the man shifted his chair so that he could watch the whole bar; he still held his pistol. "What you looking at me for?" – to the frozen faces staring at him. "Look at him" – pointing to the Bishop; "Keep your eyes on him 'n keep your seats 'n nobody'll get hurt."

To Paddy he said, "If you please, I'll have another double beer."

Paddy brought him a king-sized mug. The man picked it up and drank a quarter of it without stopping.

"When a man drinks to excess, he is letting the brute in him rule him. Nay, he is worse than a brute! For the brute does follow the law of nature, eating and drinking only what he needs. Whereas the intemperate man flaunts the natural law, gorging himself until he is bloated. He wades and wallows in the muck. . . ."

"Muck, schmuck!"

Eyes moved furtively, nervously.

"Muck, schmuck!"

But not an arm or leg so much as twitched.

What a bunch of sheep, Gertie thought. He's committing blasphemy and nobody has guts enough to say or do anything. Why doesn't somebody defend the Bishop! She looked over at Paddy. He was looking intently at the TV screen, as if he hadn't heard. A good Catholic he was!

If I were a man, Gertie thought, I'd stand up and defend the Bishop. Lifting her water glass to her lips with a gesture of defiance, she tilted it all the way until she was sucking in empty air. Oh, if only she were a man!

"Bartender," called the man with the pistol; "lady here needs a beer. Would you bring her one please; a double one; on me."

"No, no," Gertie started to protest, for as much as she wanted one right now she didn't want it from him, this brute, this blasphemer; but the words only gurgled in her throat and when Paddy brought her the brew, looking at her quizzically, all she could do was nod. The man shoved a bill toward Paddy, "Take the lady's out of this – and bring me another double, with a whisky chaser."

"Modern psychiatrists – and oh, how smug they are because they think they are so modern! – tell you not to repress your impulses, that you'll injure your psyche if you do. But I tell you – and God tells you;" shouting the words the Bishop hurled his right arm forward like a baseball pitcher delivering a fast ball, "I tell you and God tells you! . . ."

The beefy man had finished his second mug and was smacking his lips.

"You gotta lotta nerve you have," he shouted back at the Bishop, "talking like you was God Almighty Himself!" Raising his pistol, he took careful aim at the screen.

Uh-h-h!" The whole bar gasped.

"I got a mind to just let you have it. . . ."

Good God, Gertie thought, he's really going to shoot the Bishop. Somebody do something, quick.

The man lowered his gun. "Maybe not. Maybe not yet. Maybe I should let my friends here to get their fill o' that glop."

"So you want another drink! Well, go ahead and take it. Gratify your desires! Indulge yourself! Then take another, and still another – if you feel like it. . . ."

If he raised that pistol again and pointed it at the Bishop, *she* was going to do something. What, she didn't know, but something. Oh, why did the Bishop have to talk on and on? The big clock above the back-bar showed that his time was up. He ought to be through.

But the Bishop showed no sign of letting up. He was pitching his words faster and faster, hotter and hotter: Intemperance does not wait until the next world to exact its price; it takes its toll in this world here and now; in heart trouble, in high blood pressure, in diabetes, cirrhosis of the liver, and schizophrenia; all of these medical science can trace directly to excess of some kind. . . . Gertie's heart sank. It was now five after seven; the program must have been extended to an hour. No telling what would happen before it ended.

And sure enough, in a few moments he was doing it again; sighting his gun at the Bishop. "I've had just about all of this hogwash I'm going to take, I'm gonna blast 'im."

No, he wasn't! She'd stand up to him. For the Bishop. She would! – But suppose he blasted her instead? Oh God! Oh God! Oh God! She'd better get in the state of grace, quick. Bless me, Father, for I have sinned. The Deadly Sins. Pride, Covetousness, Envy. Lies. Impure Thoughts. Gluttony. Gluttony. One, two, three, four, five beers; walking home tipsy; falling asleep on the couch without supper; waking up in the morning with a big head. . . . Would the Bishop be able to give her absolution over TV? It would be awful dying without the Last Sacraments! . . . But if she died defending the Bishop, wouldn't she be dying for her faith? Wouldn't that make her a martyr? Of course! And the souls of martyrs fly right over Purgatory into Heaven!

Gertie grabbed the mug in front of her and in a few quick gulps emptied it.

She stood up. And as she did, the man with the gun got up too. Oh-h-h. The bar was whirling around – and around – and around.

She was falling. The wages of sin are death. DEATH.

She grabbed the man's arm. It was hairy, fleshy, worldly.

"Oh, excuse me," she said, coming to her senses and realizing what she had done. Around the edges of her sight, she felt pairs and pairs of eyes – from every part of the bar – sliding to the edges of their sockets. Watching her.

"Where you going?" The man with the gun was looking up at her suspiciously.

"To . . . to . . . to . . ." Her head was still spinning. "To . . . to . . . the ladies' room. I'll be right back."

"The ladies' room?"

"Door's right there. In plain sight. I'll be right back."

His chin gave a twitch. His eyes gave a quick scan around the bar. "Okay, but make it snappy."

All the way to the ladies' room she held her breath, as if by holding it, with her back to the brute, she was miraculously impregnable. (All those eyes – on frozen necks – followed her.) Once through the door she closed it quickly and threw the latch; breathing again, deeply. "Thank God!"

Then she realized that she did, after all, have a pressing need.

Afterwards, she stood up, turned around, and pondered a small window, painted black, above the toilet. Could she squeeze through? Putting down the toilet seat and stepping up on it (as carefully and as gingerly as a large woman can stand on a toilet seat), she tried the window. It was stuck. She hammered on it. It wouldn't budge. Again she hammered on it, this time a lot harder, trembling for fear that that brute outside would hear. Lucky for her that the Bishop's voice had steadily grown in volume until it was now like thunder, reverberating through the tavern with such force that it was rattling the restroom door. With an "ugh-h," she threw her whole weight against the frame.

It gave.

For a moment she stood panting, measuring the window with her eyes, watching it grow smaller and smaller. Wouldn't it be something if she got stuck in there, like a pig in a butchering chute, the victim of her own gluttony? God-awful thought! Still she couldn't stand there on the seat forever. Any second that devil might come bursting through the door. And there she would be on the front page of the morning paper, lying crumpled on the floor in a pool of blood, the big, black headlines shouting her embarrassment to the world.

By standing on her tiptoes she could just get her shoulders through the window. "Well, here goes," pushing out as far as she could.

The window overlooked a narrow alley. Peering up it, Gertie saw clumps of squatty garbage cans, nothing else. In the shadow of the buildings they looked dismal and ghostly, but there was no question what they were, the stench went up Gertie's nose like a shot of sulfur. She looked the other way. There was someone, a man in a floppy hat and baggy pants taking things out of a can and loading them onto a pushcart. "Psst," she hissed.

The man went on about his business.

Blowing herself up like a balloon, though she could hardly stand the foul air she was inhaling, she let go with all she had, "P-s-s-s-t!" The man looked up and around. Throwing caution to the wind, Gertie cupped her hands and yelled. "Hey, mister! Over here!"

The man saw her, "Yeah?"

"Over here."

"What'daya want?"

"Emergency!" she screamed. "I need your help!"

The man shuffled over to the window. "What th' hell?" In the dark shadows his face was only a blur.

"Quick, call a cop," Gertie panted out. "Madman's inside. Paddy's Pub. He's about . . . to shoot . . . the Bishop."

"The who?"

"The Bishop. Bishop O'Hara."

"What're you saying, woman?"

"I'll explain later. Please, please go and call a cop before it's too late!"

"I dunno. It sounds nutty to me." The man turned and headed down the alley, at a walk.

"Hurry, please hurry!" Gertie yelled after him.

A cold chill came over her: that fellow wasn't very bright; no telling where he was heading or when he would get there. And while Bishop O'Hara's voice was still rattling the door, there was little comfort in that. She'd better get back – right away. Steeling herself, she unlocked the door and plodded back to her table.

Things were about as she had left them: Paddy behind the long, mahogany counter; all eyes either on the Bishop or stealing glances at her table; the man with the gun with a double beer and a chaser in front of him, his eyes skipping around the bar.

". . . The inebriate falling in the street, in the gutter, is the symbol, is he not, of fallen man? Of man who was given everything, Paradise itself, and yet wasn't satisfied. Who ate of the Forbidden Fruit because he wanted more and more and more than what God, in His generosity, had already given him. Who, by his very greed, brought about his own fall and his own corruption. . . ."

"Bull! Bull! Bull!" cried the man with the gun.

"I came back as quick as I could," Gertie said, taking her seat.

"Good girl." He shook his head and took a swig of his beer. "You didn't miss a goddamn thing. You don't know how that Bishop bugs the hell outa me. I oughta blast 'im right now and get it over with."

Too late. The Bishop had ended his talk, bowed his head humbly to the vigorous applause of the studio audience and the camera was panning back to the bust of the Blessed Virgin while the choir sang,

"Mother Dear, O Pray for me!
Whilst far from Heaven and
Thee-e-e-e,
I wander in a fragile bark,
O'er life's tempestuous sea-a-a-a. . . ."

"Oh Mother Dear, get me out of this fix and I'll never take another drink in my whole life," Gertie prayed.

"Hey bartender, I'm setting 'em up again for the lady," the man yelled to Paddy. "A double one for her and a boilermaker for me."

The man smacked his lips as he gulped his beer. But his hand was shaking and his left eye was twitching. And when he had downed his chaser, he rose and addressed the whole bar. "Okay, I'm leaving now, but nobody better move a finger till I'm outa here." He waved his pistol. "I'm warning you."

He backed toward the door.

Gertie held her breath.

"Oh, no, you don't!" Two long midnight-blue arms circled around the man's chest like giant tongs and held him tight; other blue arms moved to jerk the pistol out of his hand.

The bar exploded.

Cheers, curses, handclapping, the banging of bottles and glasses on tables, the scraping of chairs on the floor, shouts of "Stomp him!" "Murder him!" "The dirty son-of-a-bitch!" rocked the room. The noise drowned out a circus band blaring from the TV; only now and then the strident whine of slide trombones rose above the din.

Handcuffs went on the man. And one of the cops barked, "All right, what's the fuss all about? . . . No, no, one at a time. . . . Where's Paddy?"

"Here." Paddy pushed his way through the flesh that had massed around the officers and their prisoner. "This slob – I bring him a beer and he pulls a cannon on me! And any minute he was gonna blow the whole place here to Kingdom Come!"

"He was insulting the Bishop; he was gonna shoot him," added Gertie. Her voice was weak. When the cops had grabbed the man, every muscle in her body had gone completely limp.

"The Bishop?"

"You know." Her voice a bit stronger now. "The Bishop. Bishop O'Hara."

"Bishop O'Hara's here? At Paddy's?"

"He was on TV."

"On TV?"

"You know. It's Thursday night."

The cop wrinkled his brow, and then gave a sudden, knowing nod. "Oh, yeah, yeah, yeah! Thursday night. But how the devil could he shoot Bishop O'Hara when the Bishop's on TV?"

"Every time the Bishop opened his mouth to say anything, he'd blaspheme against him," Gertie declared. "And he kept saying he was going to blast him right off the screen."

The man looked down. "No."

"Is that right, you were gonna blast Bishop O'Hara off the screen?"

An angry murmur went through the crowd.

"Come on, don't lie to me. The lady here says you were, and she's got a lotta witnesses to back her up. . . . D'ya know what that means, threatening a man's life?"

"The man was on TV, for God's sake!"

"Well, he's alive somewheres. And a threat's a threat!"

"Oh, hell. It was all bull, don't you know. This thing ain't even loaded."

The cop opened the chamber; it was empty.

Sputtering noises came from the crowd, like a motor shorting.

"Yeah, well it's still against the law, displaying a deadly weapon," the cop said. "We're gonna have to take you in; and tomorrow you can tell it to the judge. . . . Bob, go call a car."

The prisoner shifted his feet and looked at the cop. "You can do what you want with me, but I tell you I wasn't trying to insult the Bishop. I'm a good Catholic myself; so help me, I am."

"Yeah, we're all good Catholics," sneered a man with tousled hair and a dirty white shirt.

"Dominush vobish-cum," intoned a short, round woman who looked like the Fat Lady in the circus.

"*Et cum spiritu tuo*," her woman companion responded.

"No good Catholic would do what you did," Gertie blurted out. "Threatening to blast the Bishop, scaring everybody half out of their wits."

The man's chin jutted forward. "Alright, alright, yeah, yeah, yeah. I had one too many. I admit it. But it's my old lady, what it is! My old lady's the one that drove me to it! Always bugging me, bugging me, *bugging me*, till she drives me right off my rocker. Hell, if I didn't take a drink now and then, and let off a little steam, I'd end up right in the booby hatch. . . . D'ya know what I mean, Officer?"

"All I know is that it's against the law to display a firearm. . . . Where'd you get that cannon?"

"Downtown. Mary's Pawn. But all's I was gonna do with the thing was take it home 'n scare my old lady, to cure her once 'n for all. I just come in here for a couple. Then the bartender started bugging me, and I jus' went bats."

"But why the Bishop?" Gertie said. "What did he do to you? You had no right to take it out on him."

The man looked across at her. "Tell you the truth, lady, he got under my skin too. Blasting off about a guy taking a drink 'r two, making out like you was going right to hell for it. . . . Better to take a drink 'r two, if you need 'em, than to go plumb off your rocker. Right, Officer?"

"I told you all I know is that you can't go around displaying a firearm."

"Well, to prove to you that I didn't mean anybody any harm, I'd like to set 'em up for the whole house; the bartender too. . . . Hey, bartender, set 'em up for the whole house; on me. . . . Officer, if you reach down in my right pocket, you'll find two ten-spots there."

"Man, you can't buy anybody any drinks. You're under arrest."

"Come on; make out like you found it on the floor."

The policeman groaned.

"And if the Bishop was here," the man went on, "I'd count him in too – God bless 'im. . . . He ain't living in no bed o' roses either; you can tell that jus' by looking at him. If it ain't the Cardinal or somebody bugging him all the time, it's probably the Pope; and if he builds up a head o' steam, he can't come into any bar and let it off, like you and me. All he can do is blast off over TV, like he was doing. But if he was here right now, I'd bet he'd say, 'Officer, go ahead, let Frank Malone set 'em up for the whole house'. . . . Right, folks?" – addressing the throng around him.

"Right you are," said the man in the dirty white shirt; and a cheer went up from the others that almost shook the roof off of Paddy's.

"Dominush vobish-cum," shouted the Fat Lady.

Gertie's eyes started to blur.

The cop thrust his arms into the air. "Here, here, things are getting out of hand. This guy can't buy anybody any drinks. He's under arrest. . . ."

Loud boos drowned him out.

"Come on," said the officer, grabbing his prisoner by the arm and pushing him through the throng toward a police car that had just come to a stop at the curb, siren wailing, red blinker spinning wildly. When they got into the car, the door was slammed and it sped away again with a screeching of tires.

Inside the bar everything was confusion, as curious ones from the street entered and milled about, asking questions right and left. "Was there a murder?" "A holdup?" "A fight?"

Paddy parried all questions directed at him; shouting above the clamor, "This here bar's for my customers, please. Anybody who ain't a customer get the hell out!" Few paid him any attention, and it took a long time for the crowd to settle down.

The TV by now was popping with a giveaway show for which there was a whole stageful of prizes – mink coats, washing machines, stereos, hair dryers, a motor boat, all surrounding a long, shiny Cadillac. "A guy can't even hear himself think with all this damn noise," Paddy muttered, snapping the set off. He trudged over to Gertie's table, where she was sitting blankly, a mug of beer in front of her untouched. "Go on, drink it," Paddy said. "He paid for it – and it ain't contaminated." He stood by the table, a kind of dumbfounded look on his face. "Some crazy things have happened in this place," he said, "but this was the craziest."

Gertie took a long draught of the beer. The Blessed Virgin would understand; even Bishop O'Hara might. And what did she care, right now, how she looked in a bathing suit! She took several more long swallows, almost emptying the glass. Then she pressed her lips together and shook her head. "That poor man! Driven half out of his head! Doing something like this! And no bullets in his gun. The cops might've killed him. . . . And he woulda bought the Bishop a drink, if he could. . . . He must have a real bitch of a wife!"

She motioned to Paddy to bring her another one.

THE OAK AND THE ORCHID

New York City, 1954

"Miss Owens, Doctor."

Dr. George Olsen nodded, and the nurse opened the door to admit Miss Nancy M. Owens, who had an appointment for 10 o'clock. Olsen glanced at his watch. Two minutes to eleven. He'd say something to her. . . .

As she walked – slowly, languorously – to the chair on front of his desk, his eyes followed. Going to be late to the lab again. Yet there was something fascinating about the way she moved; with premeditation, yet intuitively.

Taking a seat, she crossed her legs at just the right angle, and brushed down the folds of her skirt. Her hands, the calf of her leg curved like a bow; strange, he had never noticed that before. Beautiful legs!

"You're looking well, Miss Owens."

"Thank you; I feel awful." She breathed deeply. "That last medicine didn't seem to help."

"I'm sorry to hear that."

A sigh, unmistakable. "It's gotten to the point I can hardly drag myself to work."

"Hmm." He rubbed his hand over a shock of slightly graying, unruly hair, then down his craggy chin. How many times; how many times? "You know, if there's anything medically wrong with you, I certainly haven't been able to find it. I've run just about every test I can think of."

She was attractive, in an extraordinary way: her soft, dark hair cut short, like a pixie; her large, brown eyes strikingly set in a soft, milk-white face – a little too white, she could stand some iron; her frame lithe, though a little too thinly fleshed out.

She was staring back at him. Yet for some reason he had the feeling she wasn't really listening. He wondered if she had ever listened to what he said.

". . . It's what we sometimes call 'nervous fatigue'. Nothing serious.

But nothing that medicine by itself is going to cure. Quite frankly, Miss Owens – and I say this as your friend, as well as your doctor – you might want to think seriously about moving back to Arizona. Where you'd get some sunshine. Get back into the open air. And where – you have a lot more friends."

Her eyes dropped. "But what about my career, Dr. Olsen? It'd feel like such a defeat to even think about moving back home." Unhappy with him, that he hadn't shown her more sympathy; too bad; he disliked self-pity.

"We can't always have what we'd like, I'm afraid. Don't you think your health is more important at this point than living in New York City?"

If only she were a little plumper. If only he were a little . . .

"But then what about Elaine?" she asked.

"Elaine?"

"Elaine Vincent?"

"Oh, yes. Miss Vincent." He had lost track of the conversation. "What about Miss Vincent?"

"She's from Arizona and she doesn't get any more sunshine and fresh air than I do. And look how she's thriving here."

"Well!" His eyes suddenly twinkling. "I don't like to make comparisons between you and Miss Vincent," he said. "But some people are like weeds – they can grow anywhere, out on the sunbaked prairie, in rocky soil, even in sooty, crowded, ugly cities. You can stomp on them, even throw hot ashes on them. They keep growing, impudently. But other people – well, Miss Owens, some other people are like orchids; beautiful, delicate, sensitive. They require a special environment. Tender, loving care."

She appeared flustered. "Dr. Olsen!"

"Let's try something different. Here." He scrawled across his prescription pad. "What, what's the matter?"

Her lips were pouting. "What you just said; about orchids. Aren't orchids parasites?"

He laughed. A hearty laugh. "That wasn't my point. Beauty is its own justification. Particularly the beauty of a lovely woman. I can guarantee you there's not a man in the world who would dispute me." He pushed the prescription across the desk toward her. "Take one every morning, right after breakfast. And if you don't feel better in a two or three weeks, let me know. . . . Now, there's one last thing we haven't yet talked about. Your social life. Is it any better?"

The pout deepened. "No, not really. But I don't think it's my fault. It's this city. You just have no idea how hard it is to meet people in this city."

"Oh, nonsense," he retorted. "You've got to make more of an effort. I think you'd find it would do you a lot of good. Besides," he said, smiling, "beauty isn't meant for itself. Nature wouldn't have created beautiful things like orchids if it didn't mean them to be admired and appreciated."

She smiled (was that a blush?) and stood up smartly, with more animation than he had ever seen in her before. She smoothed her skirt. Her hands, her fingers, the curve of her leg even more pronounced now that she was standing up. . . .

"You know what you remind me of, Dr. Olsen?" she exclaimed, rather suddenly. "An oak! A big, stout oak! Like my grandfather used to have down in South Texas, on his ranch. I don't know what I'd do without you. Really."

Hmmmm. He hadn't expected anything like that; from her. He laughed, a little forced, and pushed his chair back. Escort her to the door. But she was still staring at him, in a kind of quizzical way (it did seem to be pink in her cheek!). Before he could do or say anything, however, she turned and almost skipped out of the office.

What was the matter with him anyway? Hadn't said anything to her about the time, and now he was going to be late to the lab. What did it matter? Something charming about her white languor, the blithe indifference. Beauty was its own justification, wasn't it? She had just proved it: He was sorry to see her leave. In fact, as the door closed behind her, his office seemed suddenly empty and lifeless. For several minutes he stared blankly at the closed door. Finally, he pressed the button to notify Miss Albright, his office manager, that if no more patients were waiting to see him, he'd like to go to lunch.

Tony was tapping his foot. "How's the chop, Doc?"

Lamb chop? Electron microscope, chromatograph, Harold Pagenkopf. No doubt about it, Pagenkopf needed an adrenal sufficiency test. But a new chromatograph? So expensive! Too bad about Mrs. Robbins. Been thinking about her all morning. Maybe should have tried something more radical. Incredible, when you stop to think about it, mice having the same glands as humans! Except Mrs. Robbins wasn't a mouse. Remind McGarity to keep his eyes on Cage 17. Seventeen; his lucky number! If only she were a little . . .

"Tony," he said, ". . . can you bring me a glass of port, please?"

"No lab today, Doc?"

"Not today."

Of course he was going to the lab. Why couldn't Tony mind his own business? The lamb chop was in his stomach, doing its job.

But wine at noon? He looked at his watch. So what? He wasn't a white mouse either, six grams of Purina mixed-chow at 12; six at 3. . . . Still, McGarity was waiting for him; impatiently, no doubt.

He held the port up to the light. A rich, saturated purple. Long white hands, fingers, tapering legs.

Pleasant.

Very pleasant.

He reached into the cage and picked up a mouse by the tail. It lay in the palm of his hand, the tail grasped tightly between the second and third fingers. Completely helpless, held that way, though its body was jerking convulsively, the heart beating wildly. Through the fur he made a rough count.

"What do you think of them now, McGarity?"

"No question about it. It's twitching all over the place."

He turned. "And you, Miss Owens?" (It was only incidental that she wasn't actually there.) "What do you think?"

Looking at him in that strange, quizzical way again. "Is it good for them to twitch like that?"

"Very good."

"And why would that be?"

"It means they're . . . reacting."

Her lips pursed. "Oh."

"Now, tell me Miss Owens, has that new medicine helped any?"

"Not really."

Not telling the truth. Her face was fuller; she'd put on weight, there was pink in her cheeks, definitely . . .

"I'm not surprised," he said. "It was a placebo."

"A placebo?"

"A harmless little sugar pill. I give them sometimes when I want to know whether a patient's reacting physically or psychologically."

"Oh." Now she seemed startled. Her cheeks flushed. It wasn't becoming, this time. He liked the delicate white of her skin. "And what have you decided, Dr. Olsen?"

"I'm not quite sure yet. Although I know what I'd give you if you were a white mouse. Adrenaline. Nothing like adrenaline to set a heart to pounding. . . . Pounding? My God, it's pounding so hard I can feel it in the flat of my hand. To be completely frank, Miss Owens – and I say this as your friend, as well as your doctor – I think your trouble is that you've never really experienced the pounding of a heart!"

"Off to the lab, Doc?"

"You asked me that yesterday, Tony."

"Sorry. You're usually in such a race to the finish."

"Not today. In fact, you can bring me another."

He didn't really want a second glass of wine, but he wasn't going to let Tony bully him. Besides, he wanted to do some thinking. Wasn't it time to do some thinking when you can't even remember what it is you've just eaten – chops or flank or stew? What was the matter with him? If only he were a little. . . . But maybe at his age it's too late for thinking: only makes you unhappy. Better to go see a movie! Or take a walk through a park! What would he tell McGarity? Tell him the truth, he was taking the afternoon off for no good reason. Didn't a man have a right to do that once every fifteen years? . . . Fifteen years! At hard labor, sometimes so intense he'd keep at it on and on, deep into the night, forgetting even to eat; often, usually, disappointed, discouraged, yet constantly probing – and refining. Always pushing farther, and farther; deeper, and deeper . . . deeper and deeper. . . .

He left the wine untouched.

The children were eating popcorn, and waving red and blue and green balloons on long sticks. He bought some popcorn himself, a tall puffy bag with lots of salt and butter; and some peanuts for the squirrels. . . .

It had been a long, long time, too long, since he had wandered through the park this way; walking aimlessly; stopping here and there to throw a handful of peanuts to the squirrels; letting the spirit move him as it would; thinking of nothing in particular; his fingers all greasy. He licked them. Not bad. Marvelous combination, really; butter and salt. Whoever brought the two together? Then he looked up, embarrassed. Old lady with a raptor nose was staring at him. Mind your own business, biddy. Other people lick their fingers. Is a doctor any different? . . .

This Friday afternoon, as he wandered. . . . Had he fallen in love? Ridiculous! Until yesterday he hadn't thought twice about her except as a patient. Besides, she was only twenty-eight, almost young enough to be his daughter. . . .

Then why couldn't he get her off his mind? Why? Why? When there were Pagenkopf, Mrs. Hendry . . . good old Mrs. Hendry, not giving up the fight. . . . The reactions of his white mice that he had waited four years for? . . .

If you hold the mouse in the palm of the hand, like that, the tail gripped tightly between the second and third fingers, it will be immobilized . . . except for the convulsion of the inner muscles, the wild beating of the heart. . . . God, what was happening to him?

Unable to keep his mind on "The Effects of Radiation on the Pituitary to Produce Thyrotropic Hormone," he shoved aside the journal and rested his head on his arms.

Miss Albright, entering, gasped. "Dr. Olsen!"

"Yes?" he asked, raising his head and looking at her through blurred eyes.

"My God! I thought you'd passed out."

"Just tired," he said, annoyed at her presumption. "We were up with the mice 'til three last night. After that, I couldn't sleep. . . ."

Miss Albright was searching his face. "You're not tired. What you are is exhausted. Completely and totally exhausted. I've seen it coming for a long time."

He rubbed his forehead. Arteries throbbing. Everything seemed dense. "I've been pushing it a little hard, lately. A few good night's sleep should take care of it."

"No, they won't. What you need is some real rest – and a change of scenery. Why don't you let me book you on that cruise to St. Thomas?"

"Now?" He shook his head.

She shook her head, too. "I know you, Dr. Olsen. Six weeks from now, three months from now, twenty years from now, you're still gonna be watching those mice. Ronald can watch your mice for you as well as you can."

He managed a smile. "Cruises bore me to death. Same kind of people. Same kind of conversations. Et cetera. Et cetera."

"Then what about a trip out West? Or to Europe? I can't think of anything more exciting than a couple of weeks in Paris. Or maybe a Greek island?"

"Very thought of it tires me out; when you've traveled as much as I have. . . ." The throbbing was driving him crazy. "But you are right about needing a break. I do need to get my mind off medicine now and then." He was groping through the fog. "That's it! A party. Why don't we give a party? We haven't had a party for a couple of years."

"A party?" She grimaced. "You remember what you said after your last party?"

"Refresh my memory."

"That it was time to stop when you got bored at your own parties. Same people. Same conversation. Et cetera. Et cetera."

"I did say that, didn't I? Well, our trouble was we tried to mix business with pleasure. That doesn't work, does it? No, this one'll be different. I'll have it at my apartment. People can spill out onto the terrace. And we'll invite some new faces. Fresh blood. No cadavers," trying to avoid the angry gaze of Mrs. Adolph Spencer III, who was wagging a finger. "Cadavers! You better think twice before you turn up your nose at cadavers, Dr. Olsen! Modern medicine couldn't exist without cadavers, and you know it. Furthermore, I am no cadaver. I intend to live forever – and I expect you to make sure that I do," letting drop on his desk a generous check toward the new chromatograph.

Everything was ready. Olsen hardly recognized his apartment, thanks to Miss Albright (who'd insisted on "helping"). New throw pillows. Fresh flowers. Trays and trays of hors d'oeuvres: smoked oysters, Panamanian shrimp, tiny Greek spinach pies. A well-stocked, lavish bar. It had been a good idea, the party. And if there was anything he hated, it was scrimping. He picked a tiny pink sweetheart rose from one of the vases. Pinned it on Miss Albright. "Everything's perfect," he said. "I don't know what I'd do without you." But why did she have to look at him that way? With those searching, yearning eyes?

Rowena McLain, a widow, arrived first. She was always very punctual. As he saw her through the porthole, he braced his shoulders. A bulldog, with her dewlap and diamond-encrusted collar. Before the evening was out, he'd probably be jumping fences to get away from her.

Next the five young interns from the hospital; the men in jaunty suits; the two women in bright colors. "So glad you could come," he said, taking the women's capes. No matter how he looked at them – and maybe it wasn't fair, seeing them every day at the hospital – they still reminded him of zinnias; hardy, but ordinary.

Then Mr. and Mrs. Phillip Tyson; Dr. and Mrs. Ernest Putnam; Dr. "Twig" Morrison and her husband; and so on. The apartment filled. The air thickened; scrambled talk; laughter; the clinking of glasses. Olsen, feeling better by the minute, moved from guest to guest.

He even promised to name his next hormone after Mrs. Spencer.

"You'll be immortalized in a somewhat odd – but integral – way," he said.

She giggled with delight.

Each time the buzzer rang, Olsen looked eagerly toward the door. He had hoped Miss Owens would arrive early, so each strident ring of the buzzer was like a pacemaker, setting the beat faster and faster. Each time the new arrival turned out to be somebody else.

Maybe she wasn't coming, after all. But why not? She had seemed thrilled. . . . He calmed himself, remembering always late, never on time, never, never, not even once. . . .

He was so lost in his ruminations that he didn't even hear the buzzer. Nor did he see her come in the room. All of a sudden, there she was, standing alone, looking around the room in that quizzical way as if to find a familiar face.

"Ay, my lovely orchid! Welcome! Welcome!" he exclaimed, rushing over to her. "Now the party can begin."

And there was no question about it, as he led her into the center of the swirl, stunning in a white silk dress that accented her dark hair and eyes, radiating a delicate French perfume, looking delightfully demure: The loveliest flower there.

Around her, the young male interns clustered like bees. And one by one the older men freed themselves from their wives.

Having given her a warm welcome, Olsen deliberately left her to the others. Let them exhaust themselves first. . . .

Still, as he circled the room, he couldn't keep his eyes off of her. Such a long, long time since he had had one so lovely in his apartment! Such a long time since he, his apartment, had been so alive! . . .

She was all smiles, eagerness, graciousness. Was it just possible that she was feeling this way, too?

His hopes grew as Miss Owens tired of the young interns. He could tell, the way her eyes moved restlessly. The more attention they paid to her, the less she paid to them. Eventually, they drifted away, leaving her alone with Dr. Clark. She and Reuben seemed to be enjoying one another. They were talking spiritedly and laughing. Clark had a brilliant mind. He was a good sport. He was 73. . . .

Olsen joined them. "I hope you don't mind my stealing into . . ." No doubt Clark would have taken the hint if Dr. McAllister hadn't edged his way over.

"You've got a real admirer here, George," McAllister said. "I told her we all admired you – though there's one thing I've never understood; why you've never gotten married. What a shame. A brilliant scientist like you – and no children!"

What an ass! He'd tell him so.

Clark did it better. "Some of the greatest minds in history never married," he said, laughing. "You know what Plato said, that anybody can have sons or daughters, but only the best men – people – can spawn ideas."

"Plato?" McAllister smirked. "The woman-hater?"

"Do you really think so?" Miss Owens entered the conversation. "Wasn't it Plato who said that man and woman were originally one?" Her eyes were sparkling. "I've always loved that story, how the first person was cut in half, half becoming the man and the other half the woman; so that ever since the two incomplete parts have been searching for each other; each man, each woman, trying to find his or her ideal partner. . . . Don't you love that story, Dr. Olsen?"

"That's a nice poetic notion but I think Plato's story was a little more complicated than that."

"But you do concede that the sexes are here to stay?" McAllister asked.

"You forget I'm an endocrinologist," he replied curtly. He turned his back on McAllister.

This time it was Miss Owens. And how cleverly. "Dr. Olsen," she said, "do you mind telling us a little bit about your laboratory experiments? Dr. Clark was saying that they're incredibly interesting."

He was touched. Foolish to get so worked up about McAllister. "You know, Miss Owens, in several of our experiments we've been able to bring about some pretty amazing transformations of nature. . . . Rabbits as fierce as wolves, wolves gentle as rabbits. And would you believe it?" he laughed. "Cats that are terrified of mice."

"Cats afraid of mice?" She laughed charmingly.

Dr. Clark laughed. Even McAllister.

"It's a frightening thought, really – so much of what we are due to chemistry . . . one man a hero, another a coward; one a poet; another a madman. . . . I mean, I'm an endocrinologist, but I can't exactly say I like the idea. I still like to think that I'm master of my own fate. . . ."

"But we are masters of our fate, don't you think?" said Miss Owens.

"Doesn't the Bible say that God made us out of the dust, but then breathed an immortal soul into each of us. That we have, within us, the power to choose good or evil. Do you believe that, Dr. Olsen?"

What could he say? Yes, yes, of course . . . her soul or her body? And what about his mice, with glands like humans; the mice in Cage 17?

She seemed to be holding on to his every word. Her lips were parted. How little he had really known of her, when she was only a patient? As sensitive and intellectually curious as she was beautiful! . . . He wanted to tell her more about what he had dedicated his life to. "Those mice in Cage 17, you know it's taken me four years. . . ."

But then she yawned.

Only a slight yawn. And her hand went swiftly to her mouth to stifle it. He made out as if he hadn't seen.

But his words trailed off. His chest was being crushed by a great heavy weight, more than he could bear. He couldn't catch his breath. The arteries in his forehead were throbbing again.

At last she broke in. "Well, I just think you're doing the most wonderful work, Dr. Olsen! And what a wonderful person you are for doing it! I could go on listening to you for hours . . . but I really have to say good night. You know how fatigued I get. And I've got to be at the office early tomorrow. . . ."

He found her wrap and escorted her to the door. It was only 11 o'clock. Only 11 o'clock, and the party was already over!

Why couldn't the other guests see that it was over? The silly giggles, the tinkling glasses; why didn't they stop all this nonsense and go home?

He couldn't be rude, yet he breathed a deep sigh of relief whenever anybody looked at his or her watch and said, "Time to be going, I guess." When the Coopers, who lived next to Miss Albright, offered a ride to her apartment, he encouraged her, over her protests, to accept. She wanted to stay and help him clean up. But what was the use of it? Why tidy up a dead apartment? Let the dead bury the dead. He wanted to be left alone.

"George, I want to talk to you. "

"Of course," he said, offering Clark a chair and slumping into one himself. He was not unhappy that his friend had remained.

"I'm going to be blunt. I don't like the way you've looked the past few months."

"I feel fine." But he knew he wasn't fooling his friend. "I suppose I have felt somewhat out of sorts of late. Not really ill, but strange. . . ." And suddenly he was talking, letting it all come out. "Like I've run out of fuel. What bothers me most of all, and this just isn't like me, I've lost interest. . . . I have to drag myself. . . ."

"And that's reason enough for you to come by sometime soon for a checkup. You're too young to be feeling this way."

"Well, I'm not exactly a kid," Olsen said. "Odd. Because right now, I do feel like an old man – who's behaving like a kid."

Clark smiled. "Not to get too personal, George, but there was only one time this evening when I saw a real light in your eye – and that was when you were talking to Miss Owens. Maybe all you need is a woman."

Olsen looked at him sharply. "How do you mean that?"

Clark laughed. "I don't know. But you're certainly reacting."

"Reacting? . . . Yes, of course. . . . Reacting all over the place." There was a bite in his voice. "Is that abnormal? For somebody my age?"

Clark tilted his head as if he hadn't heard.

"Is that abnormal?"

"Not at all." Clark's eyes sparkled. "I'm a lot older than you, and I have to say, I was reacting too. She's a real corker."

He was angry. At her. At himself, for being such a fool. He was even annoyed at Clark for suggesting that he might be ill. Though he felt completely enervated, that, he told himself, was only because he had stayed up until 3:30, long after Clark left. Miss Albright seemed as upset as he was, going around with a long face and dragging her feet on the floor. That depressed him all the more.

At noon Miss Albright rang the buzzer to say that Miss Owens was on the phone. . . . My God; how could she?

She couldn't thank him enough for the lovely, lovely party. It had been a long, long time since she had enjoyed herself so much. The young interns? Oh, they were nice, awfully nice. "But I have to say, Dr. Olsen, I think you may have spoiled me. Alongside you they seemed such little boys –." A pause. "Alongside you and that delightful Dr. Clark."

He wished she hadn't called at all.

He had to force himself to see Clark, he felt so drained of energy and will. Also, he knew he was going for nothing. Blood tests, X-rays, E.K.G., the whole thing. When he returned to hear the results, Clark gave him a long look and said, "I don't suppose you're feeling any better?"

He shook his head.

"Well, George," Clark continued, "none of your tests show anything. If you were one of my regular patients, I suppose I'd give you some harmless tonic, just to see what would happen. Then I might have to pull out the old chestnut; you know, 'Get more rest; put more fun into your life; take up a hobby; a vacation, if you can.' But I don't want to insult you."

"I understand."

Clark rose, shook his colleague's hand warmly. "If there's anyway I can possibly help, please call me. Remember, I'm your friend."

"Yes, I know." That was one thing he did know.

That night, he ate alone in a small delicatessen near his apartment. A thick piece of roast beef and some dark German beer. He wanted something with body and taste to it. It all tasted like nothing.

She kept coming back. Yes Miss Owens, No Miss Owens, Yes Miss Owens until his head ached. (Why couldn't he just call her Nancy?) He had a strong impulse to call her again and invite her out to dinner some evening. He had to do something! . . . Of course, he would only touch her arm, take her hand. Still, that would be enough. But what was the point, now, in taking her out to dinner? Would her arm and hand, if he touched them, feel warm; throbbing with blood? Or would they be cold and limp? Chuck everything, that's what he really felt like doing. His practice, the lab, his library of rare medical books, even his apartment which was more than he needed. Burdens all, they were the weight upon his chest. The walls of his prison. The leeches that drained him of blood and will. One by one, he disposed of them, mentally, feeling freer and richer by the moment. Yes, he would join some university or government laboratory where free at last of all catering and backslapping he could devote himself completely and wholeheartedly to research.

No; it was all an illusion. From a small prison he would only be escaping into a larger one; as the solution of one medical problem only opened up into a larger, more complex, more perplexing one. The very thought numbed. And angered him. "So we solve the problem we're working on and which seems so important to us at the moment," he said to himself, "so what? If we can't solve it, somebody else will. And if it isn't solved today, it will be tomorrow. Or if it isn't solved tomorrow, what difference does it make? Why this mad determination always to keep going; like children, always wanting one more, one more, one more; one more day, one more month, one more year; as if it were going to change anything, basically?"

That night, Olsen tossed and turned in bed. He twisted the sheets and blankets so crazily that in the morning he wondered if he could ever unravel them and put the bed in order again.

Fortunately, all his patients the next morning were old repeaters whose inner workings, physical and emotional, he knew so well that he could talk to them and prescribe for them in his sleep. It almost came to that – he was so tired! When he had seen the last patient on the list he slumped back in his chair like a sack of sand.

There was a light rap on the door.

"Yes?"

"It's Miss Owens, Doctor."

Oh, no!

She literally fluttered into the room as Miss Albright closed the door behind her softly. As always she was careful, as she sat down, to cross her legs at just the right angle and to brush down the folds of her skirt. But this time she was fairly beaming. "I'm sorry, Dr. Olsen . . . I know I don't have an appointment but I just had to see you. I'm feeling so much better. Those last pills are working wonders! . . . And I have a job offer in Arizona. The climate's so much better, and I have so many friends there. . . . I did want a career here. But my health, as you yourself said, needs to come first! . . . But I'll miss you . . . I don't know what I'll do without you. . . ."

Olsen didn't answer for a long moment. When he spoke, his voice was low and measured. "No one's indispensable, Miss Owens. There are some excellent internists in your home town. I'll give you a couple of names out of my medical directory. . . ."

He wrote the names on a prescription pad in a large scrawling hand, tore off the top sheet and handed it to her, standing up as he did so. She took the paper and rose also. There was a puzzled look on her face. In spite of himself, he walked around the desk to escort her to the door. Her arm; he was almost afraid to touch it; it looked so white. . . . But his hand went out. . . . Cold! Cold as a cadaver! He was sorry he had touched it.

Slowly he walked back to his desk. His body dragged. He sank into his chair. An effort for him even to sit. Resting his arms on the desk, he laid his head on them. . . . An effort to breathe. He breathed heavily. . . . Then, a sob.

His whole frame shook.

Miss Albright, entering the room, rushed to his side.

"My God, Dr. Olsen!," she exclaimed. "What's happened?"

No! No! Can't I have privacy in my own office?, he wanted to shout at her. Instead he said, limply, "Nothing's wrong."

Miss Albright was embarrassed. "I'm sorry I disturbed you. Would you like to see the patient list for tomorrow?"

"Yes, please."

She left quickly, returning with the list. And left again. He stared at the closed door, at its dark, blank paneling. Finally, he glanced at the list, more out of habit than because he really wanted to see who was on it.

At the head of the list, Mrs. Connie Wilson. Mrs. Wilson? Oh yes, nothing serious; hyperthyroid; need to slow down her carburetor. Then Mrs. Stella Minksy; nothing serious either; hypothyroid; speed up her carburetor. Next, Mrs. Carin Krumm; same old thing; she just eats too much and complains of her husband's losing interest in her. My God, how many times! How many times had he wanted to tweak Mrs. Krumm on her plump rump – not too low to be offensive, just low enough to make her giggle – telling her that he'd have to give up treating her if she didn't keep to her diet and lose some weight? How many and how fruitless her visits! Yet at least she was warm and jolly when he touched her. And how she'd probably love to be tweaked! Who knows why her husband had given up tweaking her? Because she'd gotten too fat? Or had she gotten too fat because her husband had stopped tweaking her?

"Who knows?" Dr. Olsen put down the list, not wishing or needing to read further.

He sighed, a long deep sigh.

CLAIRE

The incense was sweet, but cloying. It came from the convent chapel across the hall. Claire could see the backs of the nuns – some straight; some stooped; all in stark, black habits – from where she was sitting. *Tantum ergo sacramentum*, they were chanting.

The service was ending, but now the odor of the incense was getting stronger and headier, making her dizzy. And the room – stuffy hot, New York the middle of August. Couldn't the nuns afford air-conditioning?

Standing up, Claire walked over to a window. It was closed, the parlor behind reflected in the glass – shining, shimmering. The dark oak floor, the mahogany table in the center, the lithograph of Saint Joseph on the wall; all mirrors.

Claire lifted the window to let in some air. Not much help. Inside, outside, New York was one mass of hot, muggy, stagnant air.

Oh shit, where was Mother Carolina?

"I'm so sorry to have kept you waiting, dear." The mother superior suddenly appeared in the doorway, smiling. She could have walked out of a medieval painting: her round white face a pale midnight moon set against the black of her coif and veil; the cincture around her waist dividing her body into a scrunched figure 8.

Claire stood up, bowed her head. "I know it's a Holy Day, Mother. I wouldn't have come, except I was . . ."

The nun waved her words away. Swishing over to a chair, she motioned Claire to one across from her. Claire sat down limply, folding her arms in her lap. Mother Carolina rested her arms in her lap, too; her feet barely touched the floor.

"Yes, Claire?"

Claire strained forward like a long-distance runner toward the tape. Her voice was brittle. "I'd like to ask you to reconsider. Actually, I'm begging you to reconsider."

Mother Carolina seemed abstracted. She brushed away her veil.

"There's nothing I would like better, Claire. Particularly now, the way the world is. And the Good Lord knows we'd love to have more aspirants." She shook her head. "But I'm afraid it's final."

"Final?"

"Yes."

The way the nun said it, it was obvious that pleading would do no good, not even if she got down on her knees and pleaded until the night turned to day, the day to night; a lifetime. Suddenly Claire felt hollow inside: emptied of everything except pain; so empty and weak her head seemed to dangle in the air. Burying her face in her hands, she wept. Convulsively and unashamedly.

Wriggling out of her chair, the nun came over and put an arm around Claire. "Take heart, dear. Perhaps God has another plan for you," she soothed, reaching down and extracting a packet of tissues from a pocket hidden in the folds of her habit. "Can I get you some water?"

Claire didn't answer. She wiped her eyes. They burned like fire. "I still don't understand, Mother. I'm not asking you for anything. I'm offering you something. My life."

The tissues disappeared back into the folds. Mother Carolina patted Claire's shoulder, returned to her chair.

"How can one explain the ways of God, Claire?" she said, smiling faintly. "You're not only offering something to the order, you're also asking for something. A gift that can be given only by God. Why He gives it to some and not to others is a mystery. Certainly not for their beauty or worthiness. In God's eyes, I may be a much less worthy person than you. But the fact is that one cannot, should not, become a nun unless she has first received a calling. . . . Do you understand that?"

No, didn't understand. The nun was quibbling, not looking her in the eye. Plainly, they didn't want her. Not even on a platter. The very thought made her nauseous again; that, and the incense so heavy in the air that it seemed almost visible.

"Mother," Claire said bluntly, "how can you speak for God?"

"I don't claim to speak for God, Claire. I only serve God. But there are signs, indications we must interpret."

"And what did you 'interpret' about me that's a problem?"

"I tried to indicate it in my letter." Mother Carolina hadn't blinked.

"I'm sorry, Mother. Your letter wasn't clear."

"I'm afraid . . . ," the nun paused, "it's your motive."

"My motive?"

"Over and over you said you wanted to do something useful with your life, something for others. But I'm afraid that's not enough."

Not enough! Not enough! Her stomach churned wildly.

"No, Claire, there's one test above all others that we use to decide whether someone is to be accepted. The religious life isn't simply doing something useful. It's dedicating one's life to God *for the love of God*. And if that isn't your motive, your overriding motive, then you wouldn't really be happy as a nun."

"But, Mother, it wasn't my intent to be happy."

"Why not? What's wrong with being happy, dear? God created us to be happy. Even in trying times like these. And there are so many other ways to be happy and help others . . . " Clouds were passing in front of the nun's face; it was getting paler and paler. "Social work. Teaching. Even legal work, if it's for social justice. And what you do for a living sounds very interesting. Perhaps if you . . ."

"My job isn't . . .," Claire caught herself. How to say it now? She pressed her teeth together. "I don't think it's what . . . I was meant to do."

"Well, as I suggested when we spoke the last time, perhaps if you found a good spiritual director – the Jesuits make wonderful spiritual directors, by the way! – he might help you to come to a deeper realization of what God wants you to do."

"And as I said last time, Mother . . ." Claire's jaw tightened, her voice brittle again, ". . . I have a spiritual director and he supported my desire to become a nun."

"What I still don't understand about you," Mother Carolina went on, as if she hadn't heard, "is why you haven't married. You're a very attractive woman. You must have had many suitors. . . ."

"Suitors"? Quaint. But what was Mother Carolina driving at? Not pure and spotless enough to be a bride of Christ? To wear the sacred black wedding dress? No, she wasn't a virgin. But how many were these days? And Claire certainly wasn't the only one who was desperate for something. So was the Church! So desperate for nuns that some orders were recruiting on the Internet. Why wouldn't a desperate church welcome a desperate woman?

The mother superior was still talking, now as if to herself.

"I shouldn't confess this, I suppose, but what I wouldn't have given, when I was young, to be as good-looking as you, Claire!" The old nun laughed heartily. Folds of flesh under her chin bunched up like the gatherings of a ruff. "Look at me now! I'm fat as a goose. Well, I was born fat as a goose! No, don't ask" – and she was still chuckling – "I can see what you're thinking. It wouldn't have made any difference. Even when I was a young girl I knew I would be a nun someday. It was purely vanity on my part that I wanted the boys to think I was good-looking. But then most young people are very vain, aren't they?"

Not only young people. Middle-aged and old ones, too. Kings and peasants. Nuns, prostitutes, and editors of university alumni magazines. *Vanitas vanitatum.* All is vanity. Even a dog, or a cat wants to be desirable, wants somebody to want them – don't they?

"So odd, you know," Mother Carolina went on, still talking as if to herself. "We're such an old-fashioned order. And yet so many of the new ones seem to be drawn to orders like ours. They're not so young as in the old days, the new ones. Many are their 30s, like you. But they're so very devout. They like the holy hours, the rosaries, the novenas. After Vatican II, all that was considered so overly ritualistic."

Claire gasped for air. Why would the mother superior be talking to her now about "the new ones"? About the ones who made it in the eyes of God – or, at least, the eyes of a bunch of old, smug, sanitized nuns? Get out; quickly. Thank you, Mother Carolina. Take heart, dear. Find a good spiritual director. Try a Jesuit! The door! Out, out into the street. The door closed behind her.

Up the street she trudged, aimlessly, perspiring, past children playing on the sidewalk so intent on a game of hopscotch that they looked right through her. Past a Korean grocer with a white apron wrapped around his middle, stacking red and green apples on an outdoor stall past a maintenance crew covering a bare spot in the street with hot tar whose pungent smell stung her nose. Lucky, those men: faces gleaming with good sweat, able to swing their arms so purposefully!

Tired; tired of carrying that heart around. With each passing year it seemed to grow heavier and heavier. How heavy a heart can one carry?

She sat down on a brownstone stoop and stretched out her legs.

Voices she heard . . . dozens of them, each one as insistent as if it were the voice of God. Her widowed mother in Virginia. ("Your problem is that city, Claire. New York is a lonely, dangerous place. Why don't you come back home?") Her sister in Florida. ("You just need to find the right one, and you will; he's out there.") Her colleague, Charlie Dugan, one office down. ("I just can't understand how anybody as intelligent as you could be a Catholic. Why don't you join Rose and me at the Unitarian

Church some Sunday?") Father Joe, from whom she'd been seeking spiritual counsel at St. Catherine's for the past few months. ("What you need is a community of God.") Her last boy friend, Danny, whom she had hoped was Mr. Right, for five goddamn wasted years. ("You're too sensitive and emotional," he had accused her. "I think you need therapy.") They all, every one of them, had prescriptions for her life (every one different) which now lay in stacks deep down in her memory bank and which, when she tried to put them together, sounded like the gabbling of geese.

Not that there was anything wrong with geese; even Mother Carolina, who had given herself to God for the love of God, had called herself a goose. She didn't really mean it, but what's wrong with being a goose if, in the grand scheme of things, one is born a goose? If she, Claire, were a goose – a wild one she'd want to be – she'd know exactly what to do with her life. When the cold winds blew from the north, she would be on the wind, flying, flying, flying, by unerring instinct south, south to the cool, lush-green meadows; then, when the southern zephyrs blew she would wing back to the cool, lush-green north. Year after year, always escaping the snow and slush, never tiring because wild geese by nature have the strength to do what they're supposed to do.

But how silly to even imagine herself a goose! . . . To be honest, it made her tired just to think about it, flying back and forth, north to south, south to north, year after year, until she was shot by some hunter or eaten by a fox, a bear or some other predator that depends for its life upon eating geese.

Better get moving. Slog on, soldier, slog on, through dust and glaring heat to meet the enemy. The enemy. How horrible and wonderful! To face an enemy – eyeball to eyeball. To lock with him in battle. To have a sword thrust through that monstrous heart and release all the disappointed hopes stored in it. To be hailed as a hero, someone who had made the supreme sacrifice for the sake of something noble.

Charge! Block after block, she thought about the enemy and how she'd face him down. Charge! Once it was a cabbage-faced cop standing at a street corner. "Hey there! Blue skirt! You flippin' blind? You read English? '*Don't* walk.' That taxi'd a-hit you, you'd be wanting to sue him. Wouldn't you?"

Sue him? Of course not. Taxi drivers aren't the enemy, unless you're another cab driver competing for riders.

Past a newsstand where a *New York Times* headline blared: *President Unveils New War Tactics against 'Evil'!* But did the President have it right? Where's evil? Certainly evil had been in the 9-11 attacks on the World Trade Center that had killed so many innocents and shaken the city to its core. (Although, ironically, after the initial wave of shock, Claire herself had felt a strange surge of elation – a sense of solidarity with her fellow New Yorkers that she'd prayed, in vain, would last.)

Yes, certainly evil had been in those attacks! Still, evil wasn't only in the terrorists. Not only in *them*. Where else? Wasn't there evil in us, too?

Evil! Evil! Over here and over there! Over there and over here!

Easier not to think about it at all.

Past 74th and 75th Streets. At 76th street – o-h-h-h-h! – she leaned up against a storefront. Damn these heels! Maybe they were the enemy. Whoever designed them had to be a traitor to humanity, ought to be shot. . . . Incorrect. Wasn't the designers' fault that women's legs look better mounted on high heels. *Vanitas vanitatum*. But why had she worn high heels to a convent, for God's sake?

Look at those hats in the window. Designer hats, the sign says. And hats are back, aren't they? But what she needed more than a designer hat was a big, plain straw one. Her face was beginning to feel the burn of the blazing August sun, and perspiration was rolling down her face and body as if she were in a sweat room.

Nothing in the window that looked like a plain straw hat. In fact, nothing that really looked like a hat. But isn't it true that nowadays when women put something on top it's less to cover their heads than to attract attention? And isn't that what the sign in the window says. "For women who want to look distinctive"? *Vanitas vanitatum*. All over again!

But even if the shop didn't have simple straw hats inside they certainly had air-conditioning. And probably a chair so she could rest her aching feet. Entering, she stood for a moment by the door, breathing in the enveloping air. But only for a moment, the time it took for a clerk in the rear of the store to dash up to the front, a hawk-nosed woman with arching eyebrows.

"What kind of hat are you looking for? We have some very dramatic ones. Designed in Italy and France. You look like somebody who dares to be different."

"Well, really . . ." Claire stammered, "what I really need is something very utilitarian. I'm walking a long way. Do you happen to have just a plain old wide-brimmed straw hat?"

The woman looked insulted. "Nothing like that. Though we do have some very *stylish* straw hats. With bows. Or plumes. Or veils. Wherever you go, they'll know you're there. . . . Here, let's try one on."

The woman plucked a flaring hat off a polished brass hook and set it on Claire's head. "O-h-h-h! Lovely. This bow is bias-cut silk taffeta. Go look in the mirror. That will keep the sun off you – *and the men after you.* You know, you're a very lovely woman. . . . What's your name? . . . Oh, Claire. . . . That's a French name. . . . So this hat from Paris looks right at home on you."

In the mirror, the hat made her look like a circus clown. But beneath the hat, her face? Attractive? Mother Carolina had said so. But did she really mean it? Eyes into eyes, scared, seething, searching. Beauty, skin-deep. Beauty, in the soul. Fat goose. Nonsense! Damn that Mother Superior, damn her lily-white, smug soul. Whose fault? Hers? Luck? Hazel eyes, fair complexion, ash-blonde hair – why? Hers? Why not a vocation to be a nun? God's decision, not hers.

Secretly, deep down, was she relieved that God had chosen other-wise? Was this whole thing just hysteria? In recent weeks, hadn't she had three panic attacks, her heart beating so furiously against the chest walls that she could hear the thuds? Once, out of sheer fright, she'd managed to walk to a nearby fire station where they had the equipment to handle heart attacks. (Though she'd only stood outside the station, and never did go in.) But who had been the most outstanding and interesting influence in her life? Not her mother. Not her late father. No, it was Sister Mary Helena, her favorite teacher back in parochial school, a soft-spoken woman with a whimsical lilt to her head who had a soothing way of mak-ing everything in the world, everything in the Universe, even everything in the seventh grade, sound reasonable. When Claire had asked Sister Mary Helena if God was so wise why had He created human beings with the power to do all kinds of bad things and even to reject Him, the nun had had an immediate answer: "It was because He wanted beings with minds and hearts and souls whom He could love in a personal way, like parents love their children, and who would love Him in return. You see, even God, with all His power and greatness, didn't want to be alone."

Well, if God didn't want to be alone, neither did she!

Still, if not a convent, what? If not a nun, was she just a senseless cipher spilled out of a fax machine, meaning nothing, worth nothing?

"*Très joli*, don't you think?" The hat-store clerk was shifting her thighs impatiently.

"I don't know." *Did* know. How could they get away with selling monstrosities like that? $165. Ridiculous. "How about that one there?"

pointing to one with a wide brim but less *"joli."*

Too big, dropped down to her ears. But before she could take it off the clerk had two others to put on. Then two more. And two more. She couldn't leave the store without buying one. And finally she did choose. A black straw bonnet with cranberry trim and a brim that was at least moderately sized, if not wide. Only $76. The woman put the bonnet in a white cardboard box and Claire walked out of the store carrying it.

She did feel somewhat lighter, livelier, for after surveying herself in the mirror, with or without a hat, she'd decided that Mother Carolina wasn't just handing her blarney. She was attractive! That, if nothing else!

The feeling lasted one block. Even though the sun was blazing, Claire didn't even have the gumption to take the hat out of the box and put it on her head. *Vanitas vanitatum,* now that hat was the enemy! Pretending to be your best friend, so beguiling, enhancing your beauty. Liar! Traitor! Felt like flinging the box into a wire trash basket standing nearby. Only the $76 she'd just spent on the hat kept her from doing it.

Had to talk to somebody. Anybody. Anybody who could tell her that she was still alive and her name was Claire.

In the telephone booth at the corner of 79th and Third, Claire dropped two coins into the slot and called information for a number: a fellow member of the prayer group she'd joined at St. Catherine's. When the group prayed, the ten of them all together, Lorraine Hartmann prayed twice as loud as the others, in a nasal voice – and no matter how much the others pleaded, she wouldn't, or couldn't, lower the volume. Claire didn't really want to see her. But had to talk to someone. And who else would be home in the middle of the morning? Dropping more coins in the slot, she listened dismally to the ring on the other end.

Lorraine was there, and overjoyed. "Come right over. I'll put on a pot of coffee. Hurry!"

The cab tore up Third Avenue. Claire grasped the seat strap. She hadn't asked the driver to hurry, but there was something exhilarating about it, the cab cutting through space like that, the wind whistling by her ear. If she had the money she'd have told the driver to keep going. Past 96th Street. Across the river. Anywhere. Forever. Faster. FASTER.

At 96th the cab came to a jolting halt. Reluctantly Claire got out. Lorraine lived on the top floor. Claire had been there once before, when Lorraine had given a Sunday morning brunch for the group. She pressed the buzzer and got a resounding burr-r-r in return.

As she climbed, her toes scuffed the frayed red runner in the center of the stairs. A dank odor oozed from the yellow walls. On the second landing she had to stop to catch her breath.

From the top of the stairwell, like a tenuous ghostly voice echoing down a deep cistern, came a call. "Claire, Claire, that you?"

Looking up, she could only see darkness. Darkness, and, as her eyes adjusted to it, the bottom of the top landing.

"Hurry up, I've got the coffee on." Nail on glass! God in heaven, why had she come?

"Claire! Why don't you answer?" The voice sounded more irritated, and irritating, all the time. "Answer me, please."

"I'm out of breath," Claire shouted through cupped hands. And the echo was somehow pleasant. She tried again. "I'm on my way up . . . but I may not get there 'til noon. This is like . . . climbing . . . Mount Marcy."

Finally made it. Lorraine grabbed her by the hands and pulled her inside the apartment. "It's so great to see you, Claire. I've been s-o-o-o-o down today. What's in the box? Over there, over there, throw it on the bed. Here's your coffee."

The frayed Eames chair Claire sank into was so off-balance she had to tip her coffee cup in the opposite direction. Lorraine sprawled across from her in a similar chair, a spider on a pod with her long legs spread wide apart, her red skirt pulled up over her knees and her frizzy blonde hair on end.

"What a nice surprise!" Lorraine took swift sips of her coffee as she talked. "How come you're not at work today?"

"I had some . . . things. I'm not going to stay long."

"You can stay all day if you want. I'm taking the day off, too." She snorted. "Without pay. You won't believe what happened with Dr. Craven. . . ." And she launched into a story, which Claire found hard to follow, about how the woman before her had mixed up the records and when she'd handed the file to Dr. Craven it was the right one, only it had somebody else's medical history inside.

"Fired me. Right there. On the spot. Didn't even have the common courtesy to let me explain what'd happened. And that's what they call justice? Ha! Well, I was glad to get out of there. Nothing satisfied that man. And I wasn't the only one. He'd had four women in four months."

"I'm . . . sorry." Seemed to Claire as if Lorraine had had four jobs in four months. Yet she wanted to be sympathetic. . . . The coffee tasted like gall.

Lorriane droned on. "I'm not a sue-y person, but I really think I should file. Except that I'd need a lawyer and I don't even know where you start with that. I probably should be out looking for another job, but right now I'm just too down. . . . You okay? You're not looking too good."

"I don't . . . know." Lorraine was the last person in the world she wanted to discuss anything with; still, in her way, she had a good heart. "Sometimes I think the best thing that could happen to me is if I got fired."

"Oh, God! Don't even say that! You have no idea how humiliating it is. And then looking for a new job. It's awful! I'm telling you."

Lorraine poured her another cup of coffee. Claire hadn't even seen her get up. Ugh.

"I can't imagine you don't like your job, Claire," Lorraine said as she sat down. "It's such a great school."

Claire cradled her cup in the palm of her hand. It was warm. "What does that even mean, 'great'? I don't think I even know what that means anymore."

"It's got a great reputation."

No answer.

Lorraine put her cup down and her eyebrows flew together. "Okay, Claire. What's really wrong? You can tell me. I'm a good listener. And it won't go beyond these walls."

"I don't . . . know."

"Did something happen?"

"No."

"Are you sure?"

"Nothing happened."

"Nothing?"

"Nothing, Loraine. Nothing. Nothing."

Now Lorraine's eyebrows flew up. "Ah, I think I'm getting it. You know what you need, Claire? You need what I need. Fun. Fun, fun, fun! Listen: Charlotte told me about this new dating service on the Web for Catholics. She tried it and she said she met this totally super guy. You wanta try it with me? Can't hurt just to try it. Let's try it!"

Suddenly, Claire felt nauseous again, like she did at the convent, in the room filled with incense. "I don't think so."

"I tell you, this is a really super guy!"

No answer.

"Super. Really."

"You know what, Lorraine?" Claire tried to swallow what she was about to say. Couldn't. The words exploded out of her, like a blast from some furnace: "I can't stand 'super' guys. I can't stand 'super' people. In fact, I hate that word, period. Really. Hate it!"

Mean, she knew it. Mean and uncalled for.

Lorraine for the moment seemed unfazed. She just got up and poured herself another cup of coffee. "You know what we ought to do, Claire? I think we ought to pray. Not just words. Some real praying."

Claire acted as if she hadn't heard. Unwittingly, she took a sip of coffee.

"What do you say?" Lorraine persisted.

"Not now."

"Why not?"

"I just . . . I don't feel like it."

Lorraine sat bolt upright, her eyes blazing. "That's just when we ought to pray, when we don't feel like it. That's when a person needs it the most." Then, leaning forward, her voice lowered a bit as if confiding, she said, "You know, there's a prayer that always makes me feel better. No matter how bad I feel. I just printed out twelve copies. For friends, or whoever. We'll say it together. And you watch what happens . . . .I don't know what it is; it's always like a miracle. But it won't work if we don't recite it together; feeling it in our hearts."

What was the use of protesting? Indifferently, Claire watched while Lorraine scrounged around on a paper-strewn desk, eventually coming up with the twelve copies.

"I'll lead," Lorriane said, "I know it so well. *Lord, make me an instrument of Thy peace.*" She prayed loud and vehemently, her eyes upraised. "*Where there is hate, may I bring love; where offense, may I bring pardon. . . .*"

Claire couldn't keep her eyes on the paper. She was watching Lorraine, her pinched face, the thin lips . . . sad. What chance did she have for anything? Attractiveness *is* important. Whose fault? . . .

Lorraine looked up. "Claire," she said in a suddenly querulous tone, "if we're going to pray together, we've both got to do it. Come on, it's such a beautiful prayer. *May I bring union in place of discord: Truth, replacing error; Faith, where once there was doubt; Hope, for despair. Light, where there was darkness; Joy, to replace sadness. . . .*"

Lorraine stopped. "There's no use going on. Claire, tell me honestly, do you want to pray with me or not?"

What could she tell her? "I think I . . ." she replied, "I really pray best alone. Alone – and quietly."

"Then why'd you join the group? The whole purpose is to teach people how to pray together."

Why *had* she joined the group? "I'm not sure."

Despairingly, Lorraine flung up her hands, the prayer rising into the air and then fluttering down. "Claire," she said, "I'm really trying to understand here. Once more – *and this is absolutely the last time I'm going to ask* – why'd you join the group if you didn't want to pray in community?"

"Maybe it's because I was lonely." The words came out without her wanting to say them.

"Yes, well, I'm lonely too," Lorraine snapped. "And we'll always be lonely if we don't get out of ourselves. Whether you like it or not, I'm going to say the St. Francis Prayer, because that's the heart of it. . . ."

Picking the prayer off the floor, she stood in the middle of the room.

"Make me not to so crave to be loved as to love. Help me to learn that in giving I may receive. In forgetting self. . . ."

Claire covered her ears with her hands. "For God's sake," she cried. "stop it! I know the ending." If she could have wept, she would have. "I know the ending!"

"No, you don't. You don't know what love means." Lorraine's chin shot out. "Love means doing things for others; doing things with others. And love is the heart of religion. . . ."

Something excruciatingly hot surged up within Claire. "Religion!" she screamed. "If you want to know the truth, the whole truth, the real truth, I'm tired of religion. I'm tired of religion, I'm tired of the group, I'm tired of . . ."

Lorraine's mouth few open. "Claire, do you know what you're saying? You don't. You must be sick. You must be."

Shakily, Claire got up from her chair. She stumbled over to the bed and picked up her hat box. "I have to go now," she said. "Maybe I am sick. But I know what I'm saying." She went through the door and started slowly, precariously, down the steps. "I know exactly what I'm saying. I'm tired of religion. I'm tired of the group. I'm tired . . ."

Two easy chairs and a green sofa with a retro-shag rug in front. In the corner a bamboo plant. Mondrian's Study of Rectangles, red and yellow, hanging on one wall, a mosaic of brightly colored books opposite. Claire sat on the sofa, in her slip, holding a cat in her lap. Facing her was a half-open window, with half-drawn café curtains, through which the sluggish air refused to move. Her dress, rumpled, was thrown across the arm of a chair.

The cat was black and white with gray-green eyes. When she stroked it, it rubbed against her and purred. "Moses," she said, "you're a good cat and I love you." The cat humped its back. "Of course, you'd love anybody who fed you and petted you, wouldn't you? I'm no fool." Moses meowed. "That's all right. You're an honest cat. And that's good, because if, if . . ." She closed her eyes and laid her head back against the sofa.

How much longer? Oh God, how much longer? Had she fed Moses today? His stomach felt full enough; yet something was wrong. In a few moments, when she got up enough steam, she'd go look at his bowl. When was the last time she had called or even emailed her mother; her sister? The last time they had called or emailed her? Couldn't remember. Funny, she couldn't remember anything today. How much longer? If she saw Moses on the street, writhing in pain, what would she do? . . .

A cold sweat broke out on her forehead. She set Moses down. Room suddenly got darker; clouds going over the beastly sun. Not too many street noises; peaceful and calm. Breeze stirring; not from the window but strangely from an inner wall, coming out of its pores, moving toward the open window. She shivered. Closing the window might help. Afraid to! Heights made her dizzy. Six floors down; six.

Breeze growing stronger now, like a winter draft. She scrunched up on the sofa. Bathrobe? Here, Moses, come here. The cat in her arms, she rushed over to the closet.

Bathrobe warm. How could warm feel so good when the day had been so stifling? Stay away from that draft. Strong enough to suck you out. Close that window. Call someone. Quickly. Tell about that window. Who? Someone from the office? No. To get the day off, she'd called in sick. Couldn't betray herself. An old boyfriend? Danny? No. Too much water under the bridge. Mark? No. Married, with a jealous wife. How about an old apartment mate? Frieda? Hmmmm. Frieda. Yes! Good friend. Had been; is? How could you live with someone for five years, sharing food, thoughts, feelings, without . . . ? But Frieda was married now, too. With a baby. Sharing thoughts, feelings, with someone else. Everything changes. No matter, had to talk to Frieda.

Clutching her robe tight around her, she looked up Frieda's number and dialed. Ring, ring, ring. Why didn't she answer? Frieda, answer the phone! Please, Frieda, please. Wrong number, maybe. Looking up the number again, fixing her eye on it, she hit the buttons slowly, meticulously. This time, after many rings, a woman's voice came on. Please leave a message; after the tone. Nuts! Even if Frieda had answered herself, she wouldn't be wanting to talk. This was August, wasn't it? What was wrong with her memory today? Frieda and Paul always left the city in August. Nobody who was anybody stayed in this furnace of a city during August. Her body drooped. What would she have said to Frieda anyway? Sleepy. Go to sleep! In sleep is peace. Peace. Why this torment? Why, when it is so easy to go to sleep? All you have to do is relax, let yourself go. Let yourself go and the cool, soft breeze blowing off the wall will lift you up and carry you off, off into the dark and peace of the coming night.

"No!" she screamed. Like the shriek of an animal. She ran out of the room and into the corridor of the building. There she stood, panting, her heart throbbing, her fists clenched.

No one to strike, no one to struggle with, to clutch. She moved toward the door of the Gottschalks. They did share the same floor of the building with her.

Rang the buzzer. When nobody answered, she put her ear to the door. No TV, no voices, nothing. They never went anywhere, they must be home, they *had* to be home. With all her might she banged on the door. Then, sobbing, threw her body against it. "Please, let me in," she implored, hammering at the door, scratching, clinging with her fingernails as if she were on a mountainside, falling, sliding, tumbling, grasping for rocks, roots, earth, anything. Finally she let go and slumped to the floor.

Meow. Moses was rubbing against her leg. Meow. Meow.

At first heard him faintly, then more clearly. "Moses," she cried, lifting him up and hugging him. "Yes, I know. You're hungry." She'd have to go back.

Cautiously she moved to the door. Ajar. Curtains hung limp. Breathing easier, she entered and fed Moses.

But when she returned to the living room, a cool finger touched her cheek. She stiffened. Left cheek? Right cheek? Left cheek; it was coming from the wall. And growing steadily stronger, tugging at her, pulling her toward a window. . . .

Threw off the robe and reached for a shirt and a pair of jeans. Wind so strong she had to push against it. Hurry. Grab purse and run.

Wind swirled around the room like a small cyclone, threatening to throw her off her feet, inexorably moving toward the window. Oh God, give me strength! Strength! Not much left. Give up, give up. Let it carry you wherever it will. The wind bloweth where it listeth.

No! Put her head down and flung herself at the maelstrom, piercing it and gaining the hallway. Behind her the door slammed shut.

Down the auxiliary steps she ran, holding grimly onto the railing.

Street deserted except for a single figure walking away from her at the end of the block. The oblique waning light of the day lay like fine dust on the hot pavement. Time for couples and families to be sitting down to their evening meal, those few couples and families still in the city. Happy time . . . the day's work done . . . sitting down to dinner, a glass of chardonnay, perhaps . . .

Had no idea where she was going. She walked, and walked, one building like another, one block like another, until she came to a park with shade trees and a fountain. Benches empty except for an old man who sat feeding the pigeons; a shrunken old man with a narrow-brimmed straw hat perched on top of his head. Rhythmically his hand went in and out of a brown paper sack, scattering morsels of bread on the sidewalk. She sat down.

The old man ignored her. When he had exhausted his supply of crumbs he crushed the sack in his hand and, with a sigh, stuffed it into his pocket.

Silently, while the shadows lengthened, the two sat on the bench: the north pole and the south pole.

The lights went on in the park. It was still hot. Sweat trickled down the old man's face. But he seemed as oblivious of the heat as he was of Claire. Every now and then he would shift his position, and grunt, that was all.

"Do you happen to have the time, sir?"

"Time?" He turned toward her, for a moment. Eyes dim. His hand disappeared into a pocket in his trousers; out came a gold watch. He squinted at it. "Half past seven."

"Thanks."

"Uh-huh." He put the watch back in his pocket.

"I noticed you feeding the pigeons."

"Not much else I can do." Lifted up his fingers. Twisted and knobby.

"I'm sorry."

"Well, lotsa things worse."

Claire nodded.

"Four months ago yesterday my wife passed on."

"I'm very sorry."

"Fifty-five years, we were together. Woulda been our anniversary the last day of this month. Got married in Cleveland." His voice trailed off.

"Any children?"

"Oh yeah." He looked down.

"Grandchildren?"

"Ten. Eleven, I mean. One born last week."

"They live in the city?"

Shook his head. "Only my oldest boy. And his wife. But they don't have children. They travel. Me, I feed pigeons."

Claire sighed. "I don't even feed pigeons. Nothing but my own big mouth."

A grunt. "What's wrong with that?"

"I guess it's like feeding a chicken that's never going to lay eggs."

With some effort he pulled out a handkerchief, wiped the sweat from his face, and blew his nose. "Pointless, you think? Lady, I'll tell you what's pointless. Moldering in the grave. That's what's pointless. And that's the only place I don't long to be with my wife. No siree, I don't."

"What if you were in pain?"

"Pain?"

"Horrible pain."

He fingered his handkerchief, in awkward, jerky movements. "Yeah, pain is horrible."

"Pain you couldn't stand."

"I'd die, I guess, if I couldn't stand it." Snorting; it was half a laugh. "But I'd sure stand it just as long as I could."

"Why? Why?" The muscles in her face were taut; her voice thin and strident, like Lorraine's. The artery in her neck pulsed so hard it was bouncing the collar of her dress.

"Lady, I'll be damned . . ."

Sweat pouring off both their faces.

"You know this song, don't you?" he asked; and in a high, crackly voice, he sang:

> *John Brown's body lies a-moldering in the grave,*
> *John Brown's body lies a-moldering in the grave,*
> *John Brown's body lies a-moldering in the grave,*
> *But his soul goes marching on.*

"I like that song," she said.

"Yeah, well it's hogwash! You think it was John Brown's soul that went a-marching on? Hell, no. It was the Union soldiers! Ha, ha!" A real laugh, a hearty laugh. Then . . . silence. Seemed to have spent himself. Only sound was the chirping of the crickets.

After some time (could have been five minutes, an hour, a month, a year) the old man pulled out his watch again, nodded at it, and, with a squiggly wave of his hand, hobbled away. Strange man! Glad he had gone. For the first time that day, glad to be alone.

. . . .Moses? Dear Moses. He'd have to be on his own tonight, as she was . . . .

Her stomach ached.

An army marches on its stomach. Napoleon? Alexander the Great? Somebody Great had said it. . . . And give 'em steak before the Big Game.

At Ernie's over on First Avenue she could get a good dinner.

Rising, she started to move her feet slowly and rhythmically. More slowly than rhythmically. Hayfoot, strawfoot, one two, one two . . . .

Halfway across the park. Hayfoot, strawfoot, one two . . .

To her side, close upon her path, she noticed a tall, bushy shrub, its leafy branches waving. In the stillness of the evening, waving? It was beckoning to her. A gray-green bushy shrub, its lower branches broad and full like the flowing folds of a woman's skirt. It wanted to talk to her. It looked friendly, hospitable.

Break ranks, talk to it. It knew how tired she was.

She knelt down first, and then – from sheer exhaustion and oblivious to the dangers of a deserted public park – she lay down under the shrub, her body curled in a semi-circle. And for the first time that day she felt good, lying there upon the earth.

Her body only wanted to rest, it needed rest, but her mind kept churning. Almost against her will she found herself echoing the St. Francis prayer. . . . *Where there is hate, let there be love; where despair, hope. Hope. Hope* . . . . But what did she have to hope for? And did she really love God, Who had given her life? Or, in her despair and pain, did she hate Him: How could anyone suffering torture love the torturer? Maybe . . . maybe (God forbid!) God himself was the enemy!

The enemy that nobody's got the guts to challenge. Except maybe the Devil, if we believe the Bible. What guts!

Claire looked up, as if expecting the heavens to open and tell her what she couldn't understand in her tiny, perplexed mind; to let her feel what she couldn't feel without that understanding – but above her loomed only an absolutely black, star-less, silent sky; impenetrable.

Then, suddenly, she thought she saw – no, she was sure of it – the white face of Mother Carolina, like a pale midnight moon, peering down on her from above the Chrysler Building. And she heard the nun address her: "Claire, I've been thinking of you ever since you left the convent earlier today. I'm afraid I treated you badly. Yet have faith in the rightness of things – *in spite of.* If God hasn't given you the calling to be a nun, He has given you your life, to make of it what you will. What a great gift! Love God above all things, and love others as God has loved you. In that love alone will you find what you are seeking."

"Oh Reverend Mother," Claire cried out . . . (she was struggling for words) . . . "you . . . you did me no wrong. You were only telling me what you believed. And you were . . . right. I would have made a lousy nun."

Whether Mother Carolina heard her or not, she couldn't tell. For as suddenly as the nun had appeared, she was no longer there. But where her face had been, shining like a pale moon, there was now, above the crenelated skyline, a bright full moon, large as a pumpkin and brilliantly orange.

Had she, in her exhaustion, fallen asleep, and had it all been a dream?

She closed her eyes, and then opened them again. Not Mother Carolina, but the big full moon was still there. Had to be a dream, or, in her perturbed state, a hallucination. Yet the big moon certainly wasn't a dream or a hallucination – she was wide awake now, fully aware – and how beautiful it looked up there, where only a few minutes before there had been only stark darkness.

The moon, the moon. . . . Hadn't Sister Mary Helena, back in parochial school, once given the brightness and beauty of the moon as a metaphor for God's grace? "The moon, you know, doesn't have any light of its own. It's reflecting light from the sun even though at night we can't see the sun. And so it is between God and the world: He may be invisible to us, but what's great and glorious about the world is a reflection of God's greatness and glory."

But why, oh why, if God's love permeated the whole universe, was it so difficult, so almost impossible, for Claire to overcome her feeling of absolute loneliness? Was it because she herself was incapable of love, as Lorraine had claimed? Was it because there was something inside of her that she hated and therefore, because of that, rejected others? Or was it possible she no longer trusted love itself? If the world was born out of God's love, as the nuns had taught, what kind of love is it that permits so much unmerited pain and suffering in the world – useless wars, brutal terrorism, so many innocent people born into lives of such incredible misery: crippled, deformed, blind, deaf, mentally unbalanced?

Questions, questions, questions – they all seemed irrelevant now. She wasn't even sure that she was still alive. If she were, all those questions she had ever asked, all those books she had read to try to understand, no longer had any meaning for her, no more than the gabbling of geese.

All she wanted now was rest and peace. To be free of that dead weight she'd been carrying around for so long, that dead weight that had robbed her of spirit and life.

If she had a will – the will that Mother Carolina had said she could use to make of her life whatever she chose – she was incapable of using it. She was surrendering her body, her whole being, to whatever there was beyond herself. If there was a God, whether a good one or an evil one, let Him do with her what He willed.

With that resignation, her trembling seemed gradually to cease, and for a long time, she simply lay still, still as a stone, curled beneath the branches of that brushy plant.

She wasn't asleep, she was still aware of lying there, but it was as if she were in a daze, like the half-consciousness of a dream. A state of absolute suspension, neither this nor that, neither past nor present nor future.

Eventually, she became aware of the beating of her heart. It was a faint beat, and somewhat erratic, so faint and erratic that if she was still alive, it might be the last, automatic struggle of a dying body – like a chicken with its head chopped off that keeps flapping its wings and flopping around spasmodically.

She wasn't frightened by it. She was beyond that. It was just that she was conscious enough to be aware that she was aware of the beating of her heart, that heart beating so faintly and erratically, nevertheless beating.

How long she lay there in that state she couldn't tell. Subliminally, she was aware of a growing darkness, that even the silken light of the moon was leaving the sky. That didn't frighten her either. If she had any feeling at all, it was the one of total surrender: Let whatever's going to happen, happen.

It was even possible that she had fallen asleep. Hours may have gone by. Suddenly, her attention was caught again by the beat of her heart. Particularly so because now the beat seemed stronger, slower, and, most of all, regular. Regular as the ticking of a clock.

Almost unconsciously she began to count the beats. One, two, three, four. Too much, the effort was too much. She couldn't keep up. No matter, those stronger, slower, regular beats were comforting, almost pleasant. Eventually, too, with the stronger beat, there was a stirring within her mind.

Was her body trying to tell her something? That, in spite of everything, it wanted to keep on living? Like everything on this earth that's alive wants to keep living. Like the defenseless but nervy cockroaches in her kitchen that scurried frantically this way and that as she chased after them, trying to squash them with her shoe.

Even in her semi-conscious state she could see, in her head, those roaches racing for cracks under her sink. And deep inside of her she couldn't help noting the incongruity of it all. She – five feet, five inches tall, weighing 123 pounds – matching wit and brawn with something hardly an inch long and weighing less than an ounce. And often as not the cockroaches winning!

How funny.

And that inner laugh, as faint as it was, stirred something else in her – even deeper, even more primal.

Life!

Life or death? Doesn't it ultimately come down to that? Particularly if you still have within you the power to choose. And the will.

But having surrendered her will to her body, did she really want to reclaim it now? Did she want to continue a life in which there was a body, but no soul? Did she even have enough life left in her to regain that kind of life?

"Take heart." "Take heart." Wasn't that what Mother Carolina had said to her, just before the nun had whisked her out of the convent?

Was that what the steady beat of her heart was now telling her? For even if she had given up, it obviously hadn't – no more than those roaches scurrying away from her in the kitchen. And for the first time in her life it came to her, like an electric shock: that it might be as hard to die as it was to live, even if you weren't suffering from a fatal illness. Like her parochial classmate Camelia, who had died a miserable death from cancer at age eleven. Life, once created, obviously doesn't give itself up easily. And apparently for good reason: "A live mouse is better than a dead lion," she had read somewhere.

So "take heart." "Take heart."

The words keep repeating themselves in her mind.

Wasn't Mother Carolina telling her the most perfect truth of life? Is there anything better in the whole world than a kind, loving heart? Anything worse than a heart of stone? Is there any better feeling than that of "heartiness"? Any worse feeling than a "broken heart"? (She could testify to that.) Is not all of life engaged in the struggle between the lion-hearted and the tender-hearted? Between the light heart and the heavy heart? The soft-hearted and the hard-hearted? How wonderful it is to do something "with one's whole heart."

She couldn't help thinking of the old man in the park, feeding the pigeons to assuage the ache in his heart. What would it have meant to him if somebody, anybody, her own self, had said to him, "Take heart"? And Lorraine, that lost, beleaguered soul clinging so desperately to the pages of the St. Francis prayer? How cruel she had been to Lorriane, how hard of heart! How could somebody like herself, Claire, herself so hungry for love, be so unlovable?

But what do I do with my life when everybody I've tried to give it to has turned it down? Even a religious order dedicated to God!

A tough question. But, as Claire thought about it, something else came to her – this time like a lightning bolt out of the darkest night! Maybe God hadn't given her her life to give away at all! Maybe Mother Carolina was right: that God had given her her life to use! And use it as she chose! For good or ill!

That sense about her life had just never occurred to her before, given all that she had been taught about the holy virtues of obedience and sacrifice. Or, if it had, she would probably have considered it selfish, self-centered. She even faintly recalled a priest once preaching a sermon on the sin of "personal autonomy."

But where does one find the wisdom to choose? And what was her heart telling her now?

Everything was so complicated in her mind that she couldn't be sure of anything – of anything except that beat of her heart. Thump. Thump. Thump. Thump. Not only regular but so strong. And as long as it was beating, she was still alive, and if alive, free . . . free.

Feelings were racing through her heart now as swiftly as thoughts through her head, one trying to catch up with the other. And though in some ways she felt more alone than ever, deep inside of her, in spite of that aloneness, she could feel something not unpleasant. Something she had not experienced in recent years. The lifeness of life. There was no describing it, no accounting for it. Although it was accentuated by the steady beat of her heart. Yes, somehow, no matter the difficulties or the pain, better to be a live mouse than a dead lion. Coincidentally, there was a slight lifting of the heavy weight she had been carrying around for so long. Slight but definite. And just as her heart was beating now in a strong, regular pattern, she was beginning to breathe easier than before. Slower and deeper. And with a gradual lifting of the weight, energy seemed to be flowing back into her body. Slowly but unmistakably.

How could all this be happening, just when she had almost given up all hope? Everything was so complicated at the moment she couldn't be sure of anything. Yet the reality was that she was feeling lighter and freer by the minute, so definitely that she could no more deny it than she could deny her own existence or that her name was Claire. So much lighter and freer that she almost felt that she could fly.

But free to do what? To *be* what?

The way she had been feeling, maybe it was just free to be free. Like free, when you hear drums beating and trumpets blaring, you don't wait to find out why. You jump up and join the parade.

The new energy she was feeling was already giving her some confidence. For example, to quit her job, something she had been wanting to do for years. Or maybe not to quit her job but to ask to be transferred to a different department. Perhaps the history department where she might research early immigrants to New York: the Germans; the Irish; the Italians; the Chinese; the Puerto Ricans. She loved history, a real love. And if that didn't work out, she would search for something else more true to her nature than writing promos for a university.

Though she had no desire to rejoin the prayer group, most of whom, like herself were lost souls floating in space, perhaps she would try to be a friend to Lorraine (as frustrating as that might be), starting out with teaching her how to hold a job. She had a feeling that Father Joe would now write her off as a lost cause – he had always been skeptical of her – but the priest himself seemed to her to be just another lost soul hunting desperately for the Holy Grail.

She would write her mother and her sister, and she would also write to Mother Carolina and thank her for – well, for being Mother Carolina. Where before she had hated the nun, she now felt only appreciation. What a horrible mistake it would have been for her to have become a nun out of her desperation.

She moved her leg. She still had the power, and the freedom, to do that. Then she moved her arm, and that was the same.

She sat up.

For a few minutes she just remained in the sitting position, breathing deeply, inwardly thankful for that.

Finally, she summoned up the will and the strength to stand up, and though there was some difficulty in doing that – she was somewhat cramped from lying in one position so long – she was able to get to her feet.

Slowly, she began to retrace her way back to her apartment. The lamps in the park showed the path home clearly, and she automatically followed them, pausing now and then, but only for a few moments, each time aware of the steady beat of that heart.

What she would do in the morning, she still wasn't sure. All she knew was that like the rest of the world she was a pilgrim traveling a long, rocky road to somewhere – to somewhere that was only a dim hope deep within her heart, as nameless and indescribable as God Himself.

True, she knew that everything in the world was as it had been earlier in the day – New York's beastly summer; the wealthy gone somewhere else where it was cooler; the sweaty, enduring poor sitting out on their stoops in their undershirts and bras; the President's War on Evil; the chaos and suicide bombings and slaughter and the millions struggling to survive over *there* – yet she could tell that inside of her that everything was not precisely the same.

Moses would be waiting for her, wanting to be fed. Animals, like humans, did need to eat. But though he sometimes snarled and scratched at her, she did love Moses!

A PAIR OF SHOES

New York City, 1959

He spun back toward the door. What a night! February wind screaming down the street, so icy it had edges. Should he forget it? Huddled inside his army parka, he stood with his back to the blow. Four days in that lonely little fourth-story walkup. And down in the bottom of his trouser pocket, gumbo; not much (he'd be crazy to carry around much this time of night), but enough to buy relief.

If he wanted . . .

Fidgets inside, about to drive him nuts, decided it. Putting his head down he plunged into the wind. The jolt set his teeth on edge, but he dug his feet into the sidewalk, kept going.

Eyes lowered, he saw only the skittering of litter down the cement. Bits of paper, cigarette butts, a tattered piece of cloth; flopping and hopping along, wide sheets of blurred, stale newsprint. Made no difference when he lifted his eyes: nothing else to see. Streets deserted. Even of the winos. The lousy sots! Couldn't walk ten feet in this part of New York City, the capital of capitalism, without them swarming around. Bumping into you, hands out, like the beggars of Calcutta. Even on the coldest nights, dozens of bags of rags hugging the dilapidated buildings, huddled around fires flickering in garbage cans, waiting for somebody to stick that hand into.

But this not the ordinary cold night. That rare kind of cold, brittle, fiendish, that would freeze fire itself. Turned into a whiplash by the wind, it'd done what the whole city government couldn't do, driven the panhandlers off the streets, driven them into hiding somewhere back into dark, smelly cracks. Four blocks now, and he hadn't bumped into a single one!

Here and there pale light shone through the frosted windows of some building. A bar, a beanery, a flophouse. Behind their dirty white veils, all looked alike. Most windows dark. Nearly midnight. Midnight? Lot of difference it made, when they'd all deserted, the workers and the drones, the fighters and the queens, leaving the black hulks like corpses to rot themselves away.

Had been thinking recently of moving out of this "neighborhood" himself. He'd had it.

On his mind now, pushing down the street against the gusting, lacerating wind. Where'd he want to move? Hell, where could he afford to move? – an underpaid, underemployed actor (in this city, one of a cast of thousands) with a lousy day-job that paid for a cold-water flat but not much else.

Look, seven blocks and where was anybody? *Anybody?* Not only the winos but every last one of 'em had chickened out.

And the very ferocity of the wind now became something exhilarating. Going right through his heavy coat, cutting into his flesh, twisting him in pain, but he was taking it, wasn't he? He breathed deeply, crossing an intersection against a red light, not bothering to look right or left. Yeah, the very next bar he came to, he'd have a drink. A drink to himself! Maybe two or four!

Didn't see the bum until he'd almost run into him. Looked up and there, as if he'd popped up out of the sidewalk, the man was.

Under the beam of a street lamp, like a fellow thespian under a spotlight. Half real, half unreal. A frail, forlorn figure hunched inside a moth-eaten overcoat, thin gray hair flying in the wind, teeth chattering. Eyes, two bloodshot agates, staring. Liver blotches and swollen red veins scrawled across his puffy face. Mucous dripping from his nose. And his hand was out.

"This is all I got," the wino said, speaking with difficulty, stretching his trembling hand out even farther to show a dime lying in the grimy palm. "I need . . . .more'n this . . . to git . . . something . . . to eat." In the wind his whole body shook and tottered.

Confused. More by the suddenness of the appearance than its ghastliness. He'd been in another world.

The drunkard's lips moved again. "I asked you . . . if you . . ."

"No." Coming out of his trance. He wanted to get on with his walk, back into that other world.

Stepping in a wide arc around the panhandler, he walked on for a short distance; then stopped, rooted to the sidewalk, hands thrust into his pants, the right one nervously fingering the small clump of wadded bills and the few cold, hard coins that rested at the bottom of the pocket.

Three years since he'd given a wino anything. Could still put an "x" on the exact spot. A few days after he'd moved into his little flat; sots-by-the-dozen new to him, their faces tragic, dramatic. Handing the panhandler a fistful of coins, he'd withdrawn a short distance to scribble down some "character" notes – about the man's body language; the expression on his face. "Fuck you," the wino'd screamed when he'd seen the pad and pencil, mistaking it for a sketchpad. "You ain't gonna draw me. You can keep your fuckin' money!"

Keep it? A carpenter couldn't have pried that money loose with a chisel.

The bills and coins at the bottom of his pocket, he was holding them like that now: his whole body a clenched fist. Face growing numb. If he didn't move, they'd have to pry him loose, with a jackhammer. And suddenly the irony of it all struck him. A smile broke through the tautness, then a laugh. Big joke. On everybody. Himself. That poor ridiculous son-of-a-bitch back there who didn't have a dollar to his name, who probably didn't even know his own name anymore. The whole goddamn crazy human race.

One thing he could say about snot-nose back there: the guy had guts.

He turned on his heel and started back in the direction from which he'd come. Half a block away the wino was now moving, slowly, toward the white arc of another streetlight; still wavering like a reed in the wind. About to reach the bum when a mountain of a man in a bulky navy-blue overcoat loomed out of a lighted doorway. "What'd I tell you?"

The wino stopped dead in his tracks.

He stopped too. Watching. Amused by the juxtaposition of the two figures: the towering cop with his head and shoulders trust forward like a grizzly bear, the much-smaller, wizened sot listing dangerously to one side. The bum would have his chance now to show how much guts he had.

"What'd I tell you?" the officer yawped again.

A dog barking at a street lamp!

"Okay, then. You got no opinion on it? Then I guess you don't got no opinion on it if I say that you and me are gonna take a little walk." Grabbing the bedraggled drunkard by the scruff of the neck, the cop started to push him down the street.

He following in their wake, more curious than ever. The bum not much but dead weight. If the cop was booking him at the precinct station for panhandling, it was at least twelve blocks more, upwind. And if they made it: Big Joke. Tomorrow he'd be back again, thirstier and more insolent than ever. Rough him up? Might as well rough up a sack of saw-dust. Like to bet his whole pocket on the wino. Yet the cop was all gristle. To uphold the eminence of the law, not to mention his own self-respect, he'd have to make a pretense. The officer did. For two blocks he kept his charge moving, half pushing half dragging him along. By the third intersection the hunk of cop was stopping to catch his breath. For a few minutes the two of them stood side by side on the street corner blowing out vaporous air: two geysers.

Still betting on the boozer.

And even before he'd expected it he'd won. "All right. Tonight you get a pass," he heard the cop say to the wino, after catching his breath, "But I catch you one more time with your paw out, that's it. You got it?"

The bum let his lower lip droop; a festoon of spit drooled over it. The exasperated cop grabbed him by the shoulders and shook him so violently his head bobbed back and forth like a rag doll's. "Now git!" the cop screamed.

The drunkard didn't git. Remained where he was, mouth agape, eyes befuddled, body weaving from side to side. Instead it was the big cop who took off, heading up the street amid great puffs of congealed air, pulling the collar of his overcoat around his ears as he went.

A great spectacle! The new champ had what it took. Wouldn't have missed it for a million dollars.

A million dollars? Yeah: feeling for them. Still there. Fingers stiff: all this time clinging to the gilt. No matter. The champ had what it took, he'd earned his money. Except that the champ was already so full of juice he probably didn't even know who he was. That's it! Ask him if he knows who he is, and if he can tell you, he needs it. "Hey!"

The wino was shuffling away, wobbling crazily like a top ready to go over on its side. After only a few halting steps, in which he swerved sharply first to one side and then to the other, he lurched into the alcove of a building, bumped up against a wall, and then with his back to the bricks, slipped slowly to the ground. There, his head thrown back, his mouth open wide enough to swallow an apple, he fell into a deep slumber. And there, in the midst of the clutter, the drunkard's shoulder resting against a garbage can, he seemed very much a part of things, at peace.

All of a sudden he felt tired too; spent. Sit down on the curb, rest awhile? No; got the chills, got to keep moving. What's the matter?

Throat's so dry can hardly swallow. Something moist; moist and warm. Plenty of "moist" around, the only thing there's plenty of. Booming business, though where the boozers come from or where they get the gumbo nobody knows: they get it. Could see a bar now from where he was standing, neon light flashing on and off. A bright red light. Get to it quickly!

The place was empty except for the bartender and one customer who sat at the end of the line, slumped over an empty jigger. Radiators hissing madly, the air hot and dry, like a fever.

Took a seat at the counter, keeping his parka on: he would keep it on until his gizzard thawed out. The bartender was a pale, stringy fellow, half his teeth missing.

"Bourbon, straight up. Double."

The bartender eyed him. "You been in here before?"

"I don't think so."

"Thought I recognized you. You got money?"

Eyeing the bartender. "Yeah. Keep the change." Dumping a wadded bill and a number of coins on the counter.

A bottle was on the counter quicker than a rabbit out of a magician's hat. "Didn't mean nothing," the bartender mumbled, pouring. "It's just I got to be careful. Comes outa my pocket if I come up short."

"Yeah, I know." Tossing his drink down.

The bartender wiped the counter with a greasy rag. "See that swill-belly" – pointing with his rag – "one'a my best buddies in the world. But he'd suck me dry, every day, if I let him run a tab. Can't give something for nothing in the business world, ya know."

"Yeah, I know." Throwing a couple of bills on the counter. "Gimme another one. Only gimme back the change this time."

The bartender gave him a dirty look.

Two doubles. Each time the same, disappointing. Tomorrow maybe he'd start hunting around for some other part of town to live in; or, at least, to think about living in, if he could figure out a way to get more gumbo. In some more desirable part of the city. East Village, maybe.

Still another double.

"This one's on the house." The bartender was pouring another drink: into a small house jigger.

Something for nothing, phooey. Drinks watered, no kick in 'em at all . . .

No, goddammit, no: had all the water he could hold. Water in his shanks, in his gizzard, on his brain. Drowning in it. Couldn't breathe any more. Get the hell out of here!

Outside: the jolt brought some life back. Throat and mind clearing. Not the same as before, but something. For a while he stood in front of the bar breathing in in short gasps, feeling the blood race through his body, while the flashing neon sign above him alternately daubed him in a rosey glow. Over there the darkened alcove where the bum was sleeping. Yeah, sleeping. Like a baby. Well, let the stupid son-of-a-bitch sleep; dream his sweet dreams!

But when he started off again, eeny, meeny, miny, mo, it was that way, toward the alcove.

And passing the entrance, eeny, meeny, miny, mo, see the monkey – he looked in; straining his eyes because it was dark, infernal dark, in there. With a start he drew back.

The wino was still there, lying on the sidewalk, as limp as a sack of meal; but no longer alone. Two forms, shadowy yet substantial, were bending over him.

Young men: what kind he couldn't tell: they were on their knees, with their backs to the street.

Eyes adjusting to the darkness, he could make out what they were doing. Taking the shoes and socks off the wino's feet.

Criiiipes! Seeing things? Looked hard again.

Somebody sent by the big cop? A common sight hereabouts, ambulances, paddy wagons, picking up crumpled sots and hauling them off, like the garbage in other parts of town. But why his shoes on a night like this? Where was the stretcher? The long black buggy? Something else. Madness. Midnight madness.

Not until one of the dark figures straightened up and began to stuff the footwear into a paper sack did the fuzz clear. Of course!

His heart pounding, he stepped away from the alcove. Men crapping on the sidewalk, knifing each other in quarrels over nothing, eating out of garbage cans, rolling drunks of their last penny – you name it, he'd seen it on these streets. Nothing surprised anymore. Yet this beat anything. If he hadn't seen it with his own eyes, wouldn't have believed it.

A lump in his chest. Raw and red. Glowing like a hot coal. Then suddenly flaring up, blazing. To the tip of his fingers and toes; his head, his whole body quivering, burning. Ghouls! Worse than ghouls! Rush up to 'em, grab 'em by the necks, knock their heads together and keep knocking 'em together until they were as senseless as the old sot himself.

But they'd stick him like a pig. Puncture him until the blood boiled from his body in a hundred fountains. Had happened once to a friend.

Looking up and down the street in the desperate hope of seeing the hulking form of the big cop. Futile: he knew it. No one in sight.

Run! – as fast and far as he could. Couldn't! Legs paralyzed, helpless. My God!

Maybe they'd go off in the other direction. Maybe, if he didn't look at them, they wouldn't look at him. He cast his eyes downward.

Footsteps, coming his way. Heart pounding harder, so hard he could hear the thumps. They were going to hear it too.

Clop of their shoes drowning out the thumps. Thank God! Keep your head down. Keep it down, you fool. What? His eyes raised. . . . They looked back; a hurried, furtive look. Quickly he hunched his head again, as if against the cold. They passed on.

Only a brief look at them. Light dim, they had caps pulled down low over their heads. Seemed young, between seventeen and twenty, maybe. Punks. That's all. Nothing in their faces to mark them. Not even sure he could recognize them if he saw them again.

But enough. Bestirring himself, starting to follow them. Too much to expect he'd bump into the big cop again, and if everybody else had turned tail before the weather why not the whole constabulary too? Before long the pair would melt back into the squalor and darkness, and that'd be that. Yet wild fire still raging within his breast, his feet being drawn as irresistibly toward the hoodlums as his eyes had been.

Following at a cautious distance, remaining just far enough behind so that if they should look back they wouldn't become suspicious. Wind blowing now harder than ever, striking him with such force that he had already lost sensation in his nose. At any moment going to crack off and fall to the cement, shattering into pieces like a dropped glass.

Two . . . three . . . four blocks. Street one big vacuum tube.

Madness. On a night like this, trailing two ghouls whom he couldn't even pick out of a police lineup if they were standing right in front of him. Because they had stolen a pair of shoes from a wino whom he didn't even know. Two chunks of dirty, smelly, mildewed leather. Which the drunkard probably didn't even need anymore. Sheer, crappy madness! The shoes, the wino, the thieves, all of them together not worth the tip of his nose!

The hoodlums, meanwhile, turning a corner, he lost sight of them. His pace quickening, though inside of him the fire was burning down.

At the corner he saw them again, heads buried in their coats, clumping along with no more hurry than if they were taking a stroll on a warm summer night. The shorter of the pair carrying the paper sack with the shoes, swinging it back and forth like a lantern. So near, yet so far. Wouldn't even have to run to overtake them; yet any time they wanted, in the maze of side streets into which they were heading, could simply pull the walls around themselves and disappear. Hang on, hang on just a little longer!

While he walked, madly rubbing his nose in order to keep up the circulation. One more block; that was it. One more. That was all he and his nose could take.

Coming to an intersection, a blind corner hidden by a squat brick building. Eyes dead ahead, like the headlights of a car. Someone entering from the side street almost collided with him.

The cop! Striding briskly, spinning his night stick first in this direction and then in that as he stalked along.

"Officer!" panting, pointing towards the hoodlums. "Stop 'em! They're thieves!"

The policeman stopped spinning his club. "What'd they steal?"

"Shoes."

"What?"

"Old man back there, punks got his shoes."

"How the hell could they . . ."

"Get 'em! They're getting away! I'm a witness! I saw the whole thing!"

The cop started off after the pair. He right at the officer's heels.

The gap narrowed. The cop putting on the gas. Clomp . . . clomp . . . clomp. The sound of heavy shoe leather pounding down on cement reverberated through the narrow street. The hoodlums whirling around to see the massive blue coat bearing down on them.

"Hold it!" the officer shouted.

One did; the one carrying the paper sack; standing glued to the sidewalk. The other broke and ran, hugging the building at first and then cutting laterally across the street. He disappeared into an alley.

The cop was not about to give chase. Pulled up by the accomplice who hadn't moved an inch. At least they had one! But what a runt! If he was a fish they'd have thrown him back. Even looked like a fish. His eyes, his mouth. If he was afraid, he didn't show it.

"What's in the bag?" the cop asked sharply.

The runt slouched a narrow shoulder. "Nothing."

"And 'nothing' makes a lump like that? I asked you, pal: What's in the bag?"

"Nothing much."

"Yeah, well, let's see what 'nothing much' looks like," jerking the bag out of the hoodlum's hand. The cop reached into the bag. A pair of shoes. . . . Big ones, almost big enough for the cop to wear. Clodhoppers; torn, scuffed, misshapen, without heels, cardboard stuffed inside for soles. Officer looking at the runt's feet. "They sure ain't yours," he said.

"They're my old man's," the hood said.

"Yeah, well, your old man's got stinky feet," snapped the big policeman, stuffing the shoes back into the paper sack. Then frisking the prisoner. A dirty pack of playing cards, two dimes, a wad of string, and a long, thin switchblade, all going into the pocket of the big blue overcoat.

"Okay," the cop said. "Where's the old man he stole 'em from?"

"Back that way. I'll show you."

The thief was given a push. "Move-it!" And with him in front, the three moved slowly back toward the alcove.

"Old guy was passed out," he explained to the officer as they walked. "He was lying on the sidewalk. He's probably frozen to death by now. Dirty bastards!"

Not even a grunt from the cop.

The cop a dirty bastard too. All dirty bastards!

The punk dragging his feet. The policeman gave him a hard shove from behind. Shouldn't have done it: with the shove the hood was off, a rabbit legging it up the street, zigzagging as he ran. Cop off-balance. By the time he steadied himself, the kid had raced around a corner and all that was left was the dying sound of feet beating the pavement.

No move to give chase. The huge navy-blue shoulders shrugged; once, twice. "Ain't worth it." Cop read his thoughts. "I got the shoes back, didn't I?"

"Yeah. Yeah. You did."

"You gonna take 'em back to the stiff – 'r not?"

They walked back to the alcove in silence, only the thick gray stream shooting spasmodically from his mouth bespeaking the turbulence of his thoughts. Fully expecting to find a stiff – an honest-to-God one.

The wino did look like a corpse, sprawled on the cement with his tongue hanging out, eyes rolled back; he wasn't dead, not yet. He was breathing heavily, snoring. That he was lying there in his bare feet seemed of no importance.

"So that's the 'old man'?" the cop said as he looked down on the ugly, swollen face – a face that might have been old; might not have; who could tell? "Sheesh. I know your 'old man' here. He's an old buddy o' mine."

The cop bent over the wino and shook him.

"C'mon, George. Let's git up here. Let's git up and get these god-damn shoes back on you."

The man batted his eyes and then, seeing the blue-coated officer bending over him, began flailing his arms in front of him. After a few feeble efforts he gave up, fell back exhausted.

"Yeah, I know this son-of-a-bitch," the cop said. "He'd yank the gold right outa your mouth if he could stand up. Right, George? Ten to one these ain't even your shoes. You probably stole 'em off some other stiff. That right?" The policeman threw the paper sack with the shoes down beside the wino.

Still looking at the cop. The big hunk of man was slapping his hands together, to warm them. Not satisfied, he flung them up and down, snapping the fingers. Then into the pockets of the great coat. No use looking at him. Not going to look back. Face frozen.

Finally, "I'll put on one shoe."

"You can put 'em on if you want," the cop said, "but it won't make no difference to him if you do or don't."

Gingerly he picked up the paper sack, taking out one shoe for himself while handing the other to the policeman who took it dumbly.

They knelt down beside the wino. His feet were black with dirt, swollen, scabby. Like dead stumps. "Jeezus Christ," the cop said. "You ever smell anything like that?" The officer put on the shoe. He put it on as quickly as he could, then got up, saying, "I'll be damned if I'm gonna tie it for him too."

The other shoe was only half-laced. Fumbling with the strings, he tugged at them, lost them. Starting again, he worked his way up, pulling hard at each pair of eyes, taking up the slack. This time he made it. Interlacing the strings, he looped one and wrapped the other around, putting it through the loop to make a bow. The bow he pulled taut, taut as a sailor's knot.

"Got you a pretty bow here, George," the cop said. "But it won't make no difference." He started off.

A gust of wind caught the paper sack lying on the sidewalk and whirled it around the alcove; another gust of wind and the sack blew out into the street, to join the other litter and become lost in it.

His own head was whirling. Where was the cop going? Bastard! Still on his knees, he reached for an empty bottle by the garbage can and made a tight fist around it. Around and around and around like a baseball, and then he threw – the big whitewashed window in a deserted store a few yards down shattered into ten thousand pieces. He picked up another empty bottle but this time, with a sigh, pulled himself up to his feet and simply dropped it into the garbage can, hearing it clink against another bottle. It too was empty.

MR. COFFEE

Eighteen brown desks. Eighteen gray cubicles. Laid out in two parallel rows – nine desks per, nine cubicles per – in an oblong room with white walls (suite 3134, thirty-first floor). Eighteen figures are hunched over those desks, staring at screens. The big digital clock above the west door reads: 9:12 A.M.

The man sitting at the end of one row, away from the door, stands up. He stretches his neck over his cubicle wall and whispers to the woman below him.

"I brought the coffee today." He hikes a paper sack above the partition. "And a hundred filters."

The woman looks up. "You did?"

"Yes."

"But, Jack, it's not your turn."

"I know."

"Then why'd you bring it?"

"It was on sale."

"But, Jack, it's Deborah's turn."

"Ecuadorian Roast was twenty-five percent off."

"But, Jack, it's Deborah's turn."

> *Stupid girl. It was Deborah's turn ten days ago. But she forgot to bring it. Next time, it was Arthur's turn. Or was it? No. It was still Deborah's turn. The time before Deborah, it was John's turn. Or was it? And so on, and on, blah, blah, blah. Nobody taking their turn. And now Sadie asks me why'd I bring the coffee? I'd tell her, except I'd be throwing pearls to swine. Look at her. Gets her hair streaked blonde every sixth Wednesday – just as religiously as she goes to church every Sunday. And she doesn't wear a bra. But would I give her a second look if she didn't enter my data? How could God have made anything so gross?*

Gross; gross. Married once — she says. Trouble was — she says — he was a Gemini. But she's a Scorpio. Jealous, demanding, sexually over-aggressive. Wow!

"Okay, Sadie, I'll tell you the truth. I brought it because I like good, fresh coffee. All day. If I don't get good, fresh coffee — all day — I'm like a car without gas. I was the Founding Father of this Coffee Club and I'm not gonna pay a dollar-eighty a cup for that stuff from Monty's."

"What's the matter with those single-serve bags?"

What's the matter with single-serve bags? Didn't I tell you she was stupid? A bag is a bag, not a brew. It has no zip. No buzz. No transcendence. Sure, I'll use a bag when there isn't any honest-to-God brewed coffee around. There's my mug on the desk, and — to be honest — this past week I've been keeping a box of those things locked up in my bottom drawer. When I want a cup, I slip a bag into the mug — when nobody's looking — and then go to the men's room and get the hot water out of the tap. But hot, brown tap water? Ugh.

A white-sleeved arm reaches into the paper sack. It pulls out another bag, a smaller one, and a white cardboard box marked "Filters" and carries them to the veneer-topped table on the wall to the left, on which the Mr. Coffee machine is sitting. Water into the bowl. Grinds into the bin. Plug in. Snap on. Gurgle, gurgle; drip, drip. The carafe fills with the steaming brew. Heavenly, heavenly smell!

Not my turn . . . I forgot . . . Nobody reminded me . . . What a bunch of yo-yos. Right up to Charlie in the glass office down the hall. Biggest yo-yo of them all. Puts his feet on his desk and reads magazines about hunting wolverine in Alaska while the slaves in the cubicles toil and sweat. . . .

Heads of hunched figures lift. They sniff the air. One by one, they rise from their chairs.

Let me tell you how big a yo-yo Charlie is. Two weeks ago, he asked K., our data analyst who sits two desks down from me, to run some figures. K. did as he was told. Everybody here does as he's told. But somebody forgot to tell the computer. Heart attack patterns in Minnesota — that's what Charlie wanted to analyze. Stearns Pharmaceutical Co. stuff. But the data that went into the machine had to do with ground meat consumption. National Beef Council figures. Anyway, Charlie okayed the report and went back to his magazine — until he got a call from somebody at Stearns who was hollering. At that point, Charlie called me in to double-check K. Why me? I'm primarily a market analyst — I study moods and trends. My meat's human behavior. But it didn't take me a second. Even from a computer you can't get the right answers if you ask it the wrong questions.

"Ladies and gentlemen, Mr. Coffee's ready. But you'll have to get in line."

Do you think Charlie appreciated it? Hell no. He muttered something about how it's flub-ups like K. who are likely to bring in the union. Then he asked me what I thought about the union. Can you believe it? Used to be, unions were for factory workers and teamsters. Now — it's been in all the papers — the unions are pushing like crazy to corral the white-collar workers. They say we need better job security, a louder "voice on the job." Anyway, Charlie figured he had me there. You see, there's a chance — it depends on a lot of things — that I could step up to division manager when Harold Sueltenfuss leaves for a job in China in September. But blasting labor organizers — even in this day and age — can be dangerous business. So I said to Charlie the only thing I could say under the circumstances. "Charlie, I have no thoughts about the union. Right now, there is no union. What good would it be for me to have thoughts about the union?" But do I have thoughts about a union? Hard call; hard call.

Look at 'em!

Sheep!

It's not my turn, I forgot, nobody reminded me, I didn't know.

But, my, how they crowd in and baa-a-a-a-a-a when the goodies are passed out.

At this point it should be obvious to everyone

that what this company needs

is

LEADERSHIP!

"Right, Madame X?"

Sheep

eat grass

and grow wool

that is useful to human beings.

But sheep don't really know what they're doing.

Only an intelligent being

can answer the question, "Why?"

Intelligence created the great civilizations of this world.

So the formula really is

INTELLIGENCE produces

LEADERSHIP produces

PROGRESS!

(By the way, Madame X's real name is Sarah Jones-Smith. . . .)

"Look here, Jack," Madame X retorts, "if you're trying to pull some stuff on me, you better watch out."

Seems like four or five years ago, before my time, Madame X charged somebody in the company with harassment. He's gone; she's still here. What more is there to say?

"Look here, Jack," Madame X retorts again, "it's bad enough this company doesn't give us free coffee. Where my sister works, the company pays for the coffee. *And* Cokes. *And* bottled water. Anyway, all of us are members of this Coffee Club. It's our right to have that coffee."

"Oh?" Jack wrinkles his face in a feigned surprise. "You're talking about the old Coffee Club, X. The one that went belly-up last week."

"A club's a club. It's all the same."

"Oh, noooooo it isn't. You know who brought the coffee for Mr. Coffee today? Tell her, Sadie."

"Okay, okay, and it wasn't your turn," interrupts Julie Sommers, who sits in the cubicle closest to the door. There was a Monty's paper cup on her desk, but it was empty. "Just gimme a cup, quick. I have low blood sugar. I'm gonna faint."

"Faint?"

"Jack, just gimme a cup, for God's sake. You wanta start the club up again, I'll bring the coffee tomorrow."

> *Tomorrow and tomorrow and tomorrow. This is the United States, beyond the cusp of the 21st century, and everybody's still saying gimme, gimme, gimme, I want it today, right now, I'll pay tomorrow. Don't they know that's what wrecked the economies of the Western democracies during long periods of the century we just left . . . what brought on the Great Depression, galloping inflation, massive unemployment, Communism and the Cold War, welfare cheats, the S&L scandals, Enron, WorldCom, etc. . . .*

"A six-letter word did it," Jack says to the angry, milling throng. "C-r-e-d-i-t. No business, no government, no country, no family, no Coffee Club can be run indefinitely on it. Up to a point, yes. Indefinitely, no. That's where Keynesian economics breaks down. So today I'm going to give you an opportunity to establish a new Coffee Club. A new club based on a principle that's so new it hasn't even been tried yet in our modern economy. . . ."

"Oh, cut out the bullshit," Madame X snarls. "If I don't get a cup of coffee in me soon, I'm gonna scream."

"I'm gonna scream, too," echoes Harriet Reynolds, who sits six cubicles down from Jack.

"Go ahead and scream," Jack says. "Maybe if somebody screamed, we'd get a little work done around here."

From my early education (at St. Anthony's Catholic High School) to my long and intensive study of psychology (four years at the University of Illinois, graduate work at U. of Michigan), I had learned one thing: by the proper system of rewards and punishments, you can condition sheep to do just about anything you want. Why do some people go to church on Sundays and feel charitable toward their neighbor at Christmas? Right. Why are some people afraid to lie and cheat and steal? Right. Not that many people in the business world believe in heaven or hell anymore, but you get the idea; it's been around a long time.

"Let's rush him," comes from a masculine voice hiding in the crowd. "If you do," says Jack, "I'll throw this carafe on the floor."

Everybody except my professors — my psychology professors, that is — thought I'd done a very rational thing when suddenly I shifted my field of study from psychology to business statistics and systems analysis. Ha! That's where the money is!

"S-o-o-o-o-o," Jack goes on, "the *new* Coffee Club will be based on a very new, very modern principle. Here's how it's going to work: I'll be responsible for getting the coffee. I'll get it every week. But before you fill up your cups in the morning, it's going to be cash on the barrel-head."

Murmurs.

"And I assure you that this club has to be administered *with absolute honesty* – "

I had started to say, "with absolute honesty and on democratic principles." But absolute honesty forbade me to say it. Because it wasn't only c-r-e-d-i-t that had brought about the collapse of the Coffee Club. There was also the attempt to run it by democratic principles. Business-like methods are contradicted by democratic principles. "We've got to trust each other." "Everybody takes their turn." "All for one, one for all." You know what it all leads to, don't you?

"I've figured it all out on the computer. It comes to only fifty-five cents a day. That's a dollar and twenty-five cents less than *one* cup at Monty's. And under the new Coffee Club plan, you can drink all you want, because it all figures out statistically. There's only one rule. But it's a hard and fast one. You have to pay up – fifty-five cents – *before* you get your first cup in the morning."

More murmurs.

"Look, this is a good deal. Where else are you going to get a deal like this? Heavenly coffee, guaranteed – as many cups as you want – at only fifty-five cents a day?"

Silence.

"No payee, no coffee. That's it. But let me show you the confidence I have in this new plan here."

He reaches into his pocket, pulls out two shiny new quarters and a shiny new nickel and drops them with a clink into the transparent glass.

"All right, Sandra, you're next."

"No change. I only have a twenty-dollar bill."

"Oh God. All right, Sandra, stand over there and let the others get their coffee, and maybe we can get some change later."

"Here's my fifty-five cents," says Jean Anne, and Jack, smiling, fills her mug.

"And mine," says Rose.

"Change?" asks Mary Lou, holding up a crisp new dollar bill.

"We sure do," says Jack, fingering out forty-five cents.

"Hey, wait a minute," shouts Madame X, who is in the middle. "There's something phony about this whole deal, Jack. I just figured it out."

Jack's hand freezes on the carafe. "What are you talking about? Anybody who wants to double-check my numbers is more than welcome. . . ."

"I'll tell you what's phony," says Madame X. "Okay, you're going to get the coffee all the time. That's nice. But can you tell the rest of us club members exactly how many cups of coffee you drink in a day, Jack?"

"I don't know."

"Will you please *estimate* then, for the rest of us club members, how many cups of coffee you drink a day? On an average."

"I don't know. Maybe six, seven. What's wrong with that?"

"I bet it's more like nine or ten, Jack. But what's wrong with that," Madame X crows triumphantly, "is that even if you only drink six cups,

I only drink two. And Nancy only drinks one. But if you drink six cups, or ten, which I'll bet is more like it – and we all pay the same, that's bogus."   Murmurs.

"Look, X," says Jack, "don't join if you don't like the way it's set up. Nobody's forcing you. If you don't want to belong, keep going down to Monty's. Pay a dollar and eighty cents a cup. It's your choice."

> *My vision certainly*
> > *doesn't end*
> > *at division manager.*
> *When you aim, aim big. The top. Without*
> *LEADERSHIP*
> > *the company is going nowhere.*
> *But division manager's the first step.*
> *My remarks about the union, I'll admit, didn't help.*
> *Now I'm going to have to do some real, first-class, greasy*
> *brown-nosing.*
> > *Next week –*

"He's right, Madame X," says Nancy. "It would cost most of us a lot more."

"Shit, it's bogus," retorts Madame X. "How come he can't run it out on the computer again and figure out how much it'd cost *per cup*? That's the only fair thing."

> *Next week, the Big, Big Boss (they call him "The Team Leader") is coming to town, from corporate headquarters, and Charlie asked me to arrange the seating at the company reception and dinner. I did. Charlie's on his right hand, me (Jack) is on his left, Sueltenfuss is way on down near the end. I'll shout the praises of Mr. Wolverine to Mr. Team Leader in a voice nobody'll miss. Mr. Wolverine's got an ego the size of a mountain.*

"Why can't you charge by the cup?" asks Madame X, a smirk on her face.

"Because, X," Jack replies, "it'd take a cashier and an auditor to run the club that way. Every modern business operates on a statistical curve – and we've got to know how much we're going to take in week to week, month to month. We just can't depend on people's whims, one day you drink one cup of coffee, the next day five. If you want to operate in that kind of slipshod way, you run it."

"I never said I wanted to run it," Madame X declares. "I just said if there was going to be a new Coffee Club, it ought to be run on principles of honesty and nondiscrimination. If it's not going to be that way, I'm going to protest."

"To whom?"

"All I will say is this: I'm going to protest."

At 11 o'clock, O., Charlie's administrative assistant, comes from down the hall. Charlie got a whiff of it when he was going to the men's room.

"Fill 'er up," says O. "He likes it right to the top."

"Hmmmmm," Jack muses. Charlie's mug is one of those Texas-size cups he got at a conference in Houston.

"Something wrong?" O. asks as Jack hesitates.

"No, no," Jack replies. "Only this – Charlie doesn't know this yet, but we have a new Coffee Club now. It's being operated under new rules."

"What 'r the new rules?"

"Everybody who drinks Mr. Coffee has to pay 55 cents a day. They can drink as much as they want. But they've got to pay 55 cents."

"So, Charlie'll pay 55 cents. I'll tell him about it."

"There's one problem," Jack says. "In the old Coffee Club, Charlie didn't have to take a turn bringing the coffee. But he always said he'd pay the equivalent in money. When I went over the records to our old Coffee Club, I found 31 IOU's from Charlie. We can't do that now. If we make exceptions, the club'll go bankrupt."

"Just gimme the coffee," O. says. "I'll tell Charlie the new rules."

At 11:30, O. comes down for another cup. "Charlie says he approves of the new rules. Good business. Only he doesn't have any change on him now. He'll pay after lunch."

By lunch time, everybody's paid in his fifty-five cents except Madame X and Charlie. Jack is smiling. "Cicero said, first wealth, then virtue. With the new Coffee Club, we're going to have discipline first, then generosity."

"Cicero?" Sadie asks.

"Never mind."

After lunch, O. comes down for another mug, bearing an IOU from Charlie. "He says he can't be bothered with small change all the time. Gimme his coffee and he'll pay the whole thing at the end of the month."

"I've never said this out loud before," Jack confides to Sadie, "but it should be obvious to everyone at this point that what this company needs is leadership."

"You're right," says Sadie, "but what I'm waiting to see, Big Boy, is how you're gonna make him pay up."

"All I can say is this: A staff's got to have models, if it's going to be inspired to get things done. No wonder everybody around here's demoralized."

"Jack, he hates his job."

"Of course he hates his job. He's a fish out of water. You can't tell somebody else what to do when you don't know what you're doing yourself."

"Well," says Sadie, "I don't know what I'm doing either, but I do it."

> *Sadie isn't a bad sort. If only she wasn't so gross, and so dumb. Last week, I noticed she had two paper files on her desk with the same heading: One, Miscellaneous, the other 'Miscellaneous.' "Sadie," I asked. "Why's one in quotes?" "Well," she replied. "when you don't know what to do with something, you usually tell me to put it in Miscellaneous, which I do. And when I don't know what to do with something, I put it in 'Miscellaneous.' That way I know where to look for things that nobody knows where to look for."*

At 3:30, Jack still isn't able to make up his mind about the "Charlie Issue." Everything except for *that* is working smoothly. He's found change for Sandra's twenty-dollar bill. Even Madame X has dropped in fifty-five cents and taken four cups of coffee. She'll probably forget all about discrimination when she sees how good a deal the *new* Coffee Club is. But if he knuckles under to Charlie. . . .

"Jack," Sadie whispers, "I know you're bucking for Sueltenfuss's job."

"Oh." His nose wrinkles. "Where'd you hear that?"

"I'm intuitive. But you're not gonna get far if you don't get a clue."

"What are you talking about?"

"Like yesterday, you asked Charlie how his wife was – and then you went on and on about how great she is. That was the wrong question."

"The wrong question?"

"Don't you know he hates his wife too?"

"No!"

"Yes!"

> *Sometimes you have to cut off a mast to save the ship.*
> *Some Pope said that when he disbanded the Jesuit Order*
> *to save the Papacy. I think it was Pope Clement XIV.*

At 3:52, when O. comes down for more coffee for Charlie, Jack surrenders and accepts an IOU. "But don't tell anybody. This new club is going to fold, just like the last one, if we start to make exceptions. Even for Charlie."

"Particularly for Charlie," Sadie, who has overheard the conversation, says later.

By 5 o'clock, the whole office knows that Charlie is giving IOUs again, and Madame X, as she leaves for the day, says to Jack, "I'm definitely going to charge discrimination now."

"Don't bother," he replies. "The new Coffee Club has collapsed. Kerplooey. I'm not bringing in any more coffee."

"No?"

"No. If you want brewed coffee, you can get all you want at Monty's – at a dollar and eighty cents a cup. Or bring in your own coffee-maker and plug it next to your desk."

"Does that include Charlie? You think he's gonna want to bring his own coffee-maker?"

"I have no idea."

"Think about it a second, Jack."

"It's just too bad. It's Charlie's fault the club's gone kerplooey."

"Maybe," says Madame X. "But don't forget, Jack. I know what you're bucking for. If you're smart, I think you'll have some more Mr. Coffee tomorrow morning. By 9 o'clock. That's when Charlie likes his first cup. Without it, he's damn grouchy . . ."

Hmmm.

Gurgle, gurgle. Drip, drip.

THE BUTTERFLY

"What a glorious day!" she exclaimed.

"Um-hmm," said her husband, intent on the speedometer and the interstate. The woman was beside him. In the back-seat sat their son.

"A day like this, and all you can say is 'um-hmm'?" said the woman, reaching over and stroking the man on the back of his neck. "For just a few minutes, could you please forget about work? We're in the country, honey. Just breathe in this air – and be!"

"In about two seconds we'll all not-be!" said the man, suddenly swerving toward the shoulder as a pickup truck cut curtly in front of him.

"Then let's get off this race track."

"Yeah! Yeah! Yeah!" cried the boy. "I wanta catch butterflies!"

"Up there," the woman said, pointing to an exit sign marked "214" just ahead. "Let's take it."

"Where's it go?" the man replied. "We're in the middle of nowhere."

"Nowhere's perfect. C'mon, honey."

"All right," he said, swinging the car onto the exit which carried them round and round like a merry-go-round until it spun off onto a modest, lateral road.

"Now," the woman said, reaching over to her husband and this time patting him on the head, "what I want to find is an old-fashioned country road – a dirt lane! – that'll take us down to a stream. Where we can sit and watch the water."

"And be?" asked her husband. He looked tired now, humped in his seat, one hand limp on the wheel.

"Up there, turn right!" said the woman, pointing this time to a narrower road that seemed to wander in that direction.

The man sighed, but turned.

"Momma," the little boy pleaded, pointing to an array of slots and dials on the car's dashboard, "can you put in Spiderman?"

"No!"

"No?"

"No. Sit back and think about butterflies."

The man let up on the accelerator. The road lazed around gentle hills, through bands of budding trees, past plowed red fields and farmhouses, and finally toward a bridge.

Before they got to the bridge, the man cast a glance toward the rear seat. "I only hope this time he remembers the difference between a butterfly and a bee."

"I'm a bee! Buzz! Buzz! Buzz!" the boy said, poking a finger sharply into the back of his father's neck.

"Ouch!" The man straightened up.

The car rocked with the woman's laughter. "Sweetie, you shouldn't have done that. We could have had an accident."

The boy sat back glumly.

The father's eyes were on the bridge again. Half-way across he stopped. Below, in the bouldery stream-bed, the water churned and foamed. Slender trees lined the banks.

"No, not here," the woman protested.

"This is what you asked for. The boy's getting hungry . . . ."

"Can't you see?" She made another face.

"King's Spark Plugs." "No Fishing." "All-Rite Horse Radish." "No Pikniking." "H.P. Tuttle & Sons Real Estate." "Barnes, McTuffey, Robinson and Jones, Investment Advisors."

"We can park under the bridge," he said. "If you're watching the water, you're not going to see the signs . . . ."

"Just a little longer. I know we'll find the right spot."

He groaned. The car went on.

The road skirted the stream for a while, veered off, then returned as if reluctant to leave it.

"There," she fairly shouted.

He slammed on the brakes. "Where?"

"The lane. Where that fence is down."

"That's a lane?"

"See the ruts? Come on, let's take it."

The man shook his head. But he turned onto the lane and followed the lines. The silver bullet-like car bounced up and down, leaned to one side and then the other. In spots the ruts faded and disappeared; the man got out of the car to scout for them. The trail, becoming more uncertain all the time, led through a valley, up a slight rise, and finally came out upon a broad meadow. "Look, look!" the boy exclaimed, jumping up and down. Instinctively the man cut the motor.

"Have you ever," said the woman, "seen anything like it? Anywhere?"

As far as they could see, the sloping field burned with wildflowers. Red ones; golden; white; brindle ones; blue. The colors massed, swirled and intertwined.

"I'd like to dash right in the middle of them," the woman cried, "and dance and frolic and put garlands in my hair!"

"Ah, the lady's a poet," the man said. But it was clear to the woman that even he had been struck by the beauty of the field.

"Now drive down to the stream," she said. "Please."

They skirted the meadow and went with the lane to the water's edge where the ruts ended abruptly. On the other side trees grew tall and thick, like a wall.

"See," said the man. "We *were* on the road to nowhere."

"Exactly where I wanted to be," his wife rejoined.

"I'm starving," the boy pleaded. "Let's eat."

From the trunk of the car the man took out a portable grill, an ice chest and one, two wicker baskets filled to the brim: hamburger buns with toasted crusts, olives, pickles, cookies, bananas, apples. The food covered the blue plastic tablecloth spread on the ground. Briquettes were stacked on the grill, lighter fluid swished over them. The flames shot up.

The woman walked to the water. Standing on her tiptoes, she stretched her arms skywards. She breathed deeply.

The man sat on the ground and leaned back against a tree trunk.

"Momma," the boy said, stealing a couple of olives out of a bottle, "do we have to wait for the coals?"

"I'm the griller; this is my call," said the father. And soon the meat was sizzling and sending up dense smoke. When he took the patties off the grill they were charred black. Nobody seemed to mind. The boy ate three, at home he would have eaten one. What to have next? Their eyes couldn't decide, their hands reaching out across the tablecloth bumped one another, sending the mother and her son into fits of laughter. No food of the gods ever tasted better.

"I brought way too much," the woman said. "But at feasts the table, like the heart, should overflow."

The husband rolled his eyes, but smiled this time.

She smiled back. She hoped her husband would take his son on a hike. They could jump over the water, rock to rock, and climb the hill beyond. . . .

But the man was so tired; the food had made him drowsy; she could see his eyelids drooping. Sometimes (hadn't she said it herself) he needed to quit the struggle.

"Ants like cookies," the boy said, and he broke a piece over a swarm of tiny red creatures scurrying in and out of a hole in the ground. The ants weren't prepared for it, such manna from heaven, and at first the falling particles threw them into utter confusion. Then, one by one, they came over to inspect a lump here, a crumb there, and before long they were all frantically busy again, carrying sweet morsels much larger and heavier than themselves down into their subterranean home, there to feast too.

"Those aren't sugar ants," the man cautioned the boy. "If you get stung, you're going to swell like a baseball."

"No, I won't!" The boy ground his heel into the ant hole. "There, that'll get 'em."

"Until they tunnel out again," the man said. He stretched out on a khaki blanket. He closed his eyes. "In the meantime, I'm going to become Rip Van Winkle. Don't wake me until my beard reaches down to here" – he tapped the mound at his beltline.

The woman put the leftovers back into the baskets. By now the first exhilaration of the country and a picnic had worn off, the warm sun was working its spell, her own eyes felt heavy. She resisted . . .

The sunlight filtering through the leaves rippled the blades of grass and gilded them with gold. The branches of the trees swayed gently, almost languorously. The air seemed so clean; the wildflowers so fresh, so lively.

"Momma, I want to catch a butterfly," the boy said, breaking into her reverie.

"Well, go out into the meadow and catch one."

"No!"

"You don't need me."

"I'm afraid."

"You're afraid? Of what? There aren't any wild animals around here, sweetie. Now go on."

"A bee might sting me."

"Shame," said the mother. "A big boy like you. They won't bother you if you don't bother them. . . . Oh, well, alright, I'll come."

They walked hand in hand into the field, into the midst of the blooms. He was a handsome boy, with clear blue eyes and curly hair. In her secret heart his mother thought him beautiful.

After they had gone a way into the meadow, the woman said, "You can sit with me, if you're quiet. Or you can hunt for butterflies . . . Look, I see some over there . . . ."

The boy jumped up and down. "How'll I catch one without a net?"

"Wait 'til it lights on a flower, then cup your hands around it. Quickly, like this. But not too hard; they're so fragile."

"It'll get away."

"Go on."

"No, I want to stay here."

A sigh. "Oh, all right. But you must be quiet." They sat down side by side. Her gaily-printed dress – an old-fashioned one; it had once belonged to her mother – made a circle around her, a giant blossom lost in the sheer mass and exuberance of the wildflowers. She stretched out her arms. . . .

The boy did not sit for long. Soon he was on his feet, picking the flowers. He brought her a bouquet. "Thank you," she said, painfully, hugging him. She laid the blooms on her skirt.

He picked more, never going very far.

Suddenly, a large butterfly with black and red wings appeared. It skipped from bloom to bloom, sampling their sweetness, until it settled on a wine-cup. The plant bent slightly.

"Look, Momma," the boy called.

The butterfly was magnificent. She would have loved to capture it herself, holding that flamboyant yet exquisite beauty in the palm of her hand. "Now," she said. "Now's your chance."

The boy crept toward the flower. He raised his right foot high.

"No, no," she cried.

"Why not?" The butterfly lay flat and open.

"Because . . . because," she stammered. Before she could reply, the butterfly rose out of the boy's reach and flew into the distance.

"Darn," said the boy. "I could have gotten it . . . How come you stopped me, Momma?"

"Because . . . because . . ." she stammered.

"Because why?"

"You tell me why," she retorted. "Why did you do that?"

The boy was startled. A scowl came over his face. "Because I wanted to, that's why."

He walked away and stood with his back to her. She felt deflated. Oh well, it would pass. In a few minutes he would be occupied with something else. She tried to return to her own thoughts. . . .

The wildflowers lay wilted on her dress. Sad: he had meant well. But even in the fields they didn't last long; so dazzling today; gone tomorrow. The butterfly too: condemned by its very delicacy to a flicker in the sunlight, little more. Held only in the mind. She would always remember this day. . . .

The boy was picking flowers again, playing games with them, improvising as he went along. He threw the flowers up in the air, one at a time, and watched them fall back to earth. Next he plucked the petals, slowly, pensively, dropping them to earth, one by one. Then he dug into the hearts of the flowers, tearing them to pieces and rubbing the granules between his fingers.

Another butterfly appeared. Completely golden. In the diffused sunlight it looked like a shimmering fairy.

The golden butterfly hovered first over a random patch of blue flowers, then over some firewheels. As it moved it fluttered up and down, and from side to side, as if dancing to unheard music. The boy had never seen anything like it. He watched with awe.

There didn't even emerge in him the impulse to call to his mother, sitting apart.

The butterfly came to a rest, close to the boy, on a low-lying shrub with white flowers. It lay quietly, its wings flared.

The white of the flower next to the butterfly was so purely white that any other color beside it would have seemed a violation, but the gold of the wings was so true that there was no contradiction, the gold enhanced the white, the white the gold.

The boy, his eyes fixed on the gossamer creature, tiptoed toward it. He moved so slowly, lest he frighten it, that he hardly seemed to move at all. Little by little the distance narrowed.

Beneath the flowering shrub a viper stirred. It had only recently come out of its long winter's hibernation. It had shed its skin but had not mated. It was restless.

As the boy approached, the viper slowly coiled.

He was now only a step away from the shrub. The butterfly did not move.

The boy slowly raised his foot. The viper drew back its head.

He stamped down. The viper struck. It struck toward the earth, as vipers strike, its sharp, hollow teeth sending venom into the yielding flesh.

The boy screamed.

The woman, shocked from her dream, screamed too, as she heard the boy scream.

The man, lying on the bank of the stream, heard the screams in his sleep. He jumped up and ran blindly toward the screams.

A gentle breeze stirred the leaves of the trees, causing them to rustle, and swept across the open meadow, making the wildflowers nod. The spring sun cast its soft, golden light over everything.

THE DEER

In the city of Parkhurst there lived a certain William Harris, Ph.D., who loved his wife very dearly. At least, if anyone had asked him whether he loved his wife very dearly he would have thought the question absurd, for he could not imagine living without her. He had been married to her for twenty-nine years, they had brought up three children together, and now, with both sons out of college and their daughter at one of the most elite universities in the Northeast, he was looking forward to the autumnal years – those anticipated years in which he and his wife Katrina could relax somewhat and enjoy the harvest. And why not? They had worked hard, sown well. It was time now for the harvest. He was, if not wealthy, at least secure in his position as a professor of American history at Parkhurst University. He was, if not a famous historian, at least a highly respected scholar, one with a thorough knowledge of his special field: Colonial America. In seven years, if everything went well, and there was no reason to think the contrary, he would be retired and there would be time, even money, for some of the things that he, as well as Katrina, had always wanted to do.

Yes, and Katrina loved him just as dearly as he loved her. There was no doubt about it. Look at the solicitude she had always shown for him when he was working too hard, innundated by research or writing projects, when he needed peace and quiet – and a little time to himself. And how many wives, even very devoted ones, would take the pains that Katrina did to prepare such delectable food? Katrina worked, too, of course (as the assistant director of a children's shelter). And the Professor was not adverse to taking his turn cooking dinners in the evenings because fair was fair, he felt, in modern America. Still, every morning, Katrina ground their coffee beans fresh so their brew would have an indescribable aroma and taste. And this very morning had she not prepared for him his favorite breakfast of fried bacon and buttermilk pancakes?

The Professor was preoccupied as he sat down to breakfast. He was nearly always preoccupied at breakfast – when, as a regular ritual, he went over in his mind, paragraph by paragraph, fact by fact, whatever book chapter or journal article he happened to be working on at the time (on this particular morning, it was an article for *The William and Mary Quarterly*: "Reinterpreting the Influence of West Indies Immigrants on Early South Carolina"). But do not think that this vigorous mental work-out interfered with his appreciation of Katrina's food. Quite the contrary. The Professor never enjoyed food more than at breakfast. And just as surprising, he could never concentrate better than when he was eating, particularly when he was eating one of Katrina's delicious meals. It was a special capacity that he prided himself on – this being able to have both his mind and his senses at maximum activity at the same time. Qualitative Integration and Reinforcement, he called it.

So this morning, though he was running thoughts and notes through his mind at incredible speed, he didn't fail to notice that there was something different about the pancakes. "No doubt about it," he said to himself. Usually the pancakes were so light and fluffy that they fairly melted in his mouth – this morning they seemed heavy and sodden. "Hmmm." He cut himself a piece of bacon. Hmmm. It was soggy, too, not light and crisp as usual. He took a big gulp of steaming hot coffee to wash down the bacon. It tasted heavy and strong, almost bitter, as if it had been overbrewed or made from yesterday's grounds. Hmmm. Highly unusual. Coffee was Katrina's specialty. Nobody could make it as she could – nutty, piquant, lively.

Harris looked over at his wife. She sat slumped in her chair. Her eyes downcast. Toying with her food. There seemed something heavy about her too. Hmmm. Most, most unusual.

If there was one quality which characterized Katrina, it was lightness. Trim and buoyant, she did not walk across a room; she floated. And until a few years ago she was still doing pirouettes and cat-like leaps, *pas de chat*, about the house with all the grace of a young ballerina.

If the Professor had not been so intent upon his paper, he might have said to his wife, "Is something wrong this morning, dear?" Instead, he said to himself, in an aside, "She's not up to herself this morning; oh well, everyone is entitled to an off-morning," then went on thinking about South Carolina.

Even when Katrina looked up, swallowed hard a couple of times, and said, "Will," he did not for a moment stop his munching and mulling.

He did say, "Yes, what is it?" but only by reflex, the same reflex he used to counter ridiculous and inconsequential questions put to him by his under-graduates; not even noticing that there was something different about the way Katrina spoke to him, for she nearly always addressed him, playfully, wittingly, as "Professor"; she hardly ever called him "Will."

"Will," Katrina began, "I don't know how to say this. . . ."

"Say what?"

"Something I've got to say."

"If you have something to say, Katrina, please go ahead and say it." The Professor loved his wife dearly but he did not like to be interrupted in his mental calisthenics.

"What I have to say . . . is very difficult."

"Why so?" – still engrossed – "We're husband and wife, aren't we? What can't we say to each other?"

"That's just it, Will."

"Just what?"

"That we're married. And have been . . . for quite a long time. I think that means something. Wouldn't you say?"

"Katrina! Please say what's on your mind."

"What I'm trying to say is that . . ." Tears came to her eyes. She took in a deep breath. "I'd like a separation."

It took a few seconds for the words to sink in. The mind so concen-trated upon reinterpreting the influence of West Indian immigrants on the early history of our country does not easily shift to one's wife, sitting across the breakfast table, announcing suddenly, starkly, that she would like a separation.

"A what?" he stuttered.

"I said . . . I'd like a separation." She could hardly get the words out. She put her head in her hands and started to sob.

"What in heavens . . .," started the Professor, getting up quickly and hurrying over to his wife's side. "Are you sick? . . . Stop crying for a moment and tell me what's wrong. . . . Here, here . . . let's lie you down on the couch."

Katrina looked up, wiped the tears from her eyes with her napkin. "I don't want to lie down. I want to explain. I . . . I just . . ." she sighed. "I know this is awful timing – with your deadline, and everything that's going on at school, and . . . everything."

"Katrina. What is all this about? I'm utterly and completely con-fused."

"I've been wanting to tell you this for a long time, Will." She swallowed. "But you've just been so busy. . . . And frankly I wasn't sure I had the courage. . . . But when I got up this morning I decided I had to tell you today, no matter what. . . . Another day without telling you and I would have gone mad."

The Professor returned to his chair and sank into it, limply. "But a . . . separation? You want a separation from . . . me?"

A long pause. "Yes."

"But why? Why? Are you unhappy? . . . I really don't understand. . . . You know how much I love you. . . . You know there's nothing I wouldn't do for you. . . . I've always tried to make you happy. . . ."

"I'll try to explain," said Katrina, now twisting her breakfast napkin so roughly that it was falling into shreds. "But I'm not sure I can, really. I just don't . . . I don't know exactly what to say. I'm just not sure what to tell you. And that's the most . . . awful part about it."

"You're not talking sense," said Harris sternly, looking at his wife hard in the face. "I think you need to call work and tell them you're sick and then lie down and let me call Dr. Rodrich. Or is this . . . are you having . . . some sort of . . . woman problem?"

Her eyes blinked. "It's not a woman problem."

"Well, it's absolute craziness, is what it is!" he said, rising from his chair again and walking behind her, laying his hands on her shoulders. "I'm going to get you something to calm you down, Katrina. I think you should stay home today. Work out whatever it is that's bothering you. Tonight I'll cook you a nice dinner and we'll talk this all out. Okay?"

"No, Will. Now that I've told you . . . I can't stay here any longer." Tears were again welling in Katrina's eyes. "We'd just argue and hurt each other. I've hurt you enough already. I know that."

"Yes, you're hurting me!" said the professor, removing his hands from her shoulders and sitting back down. "You're hurting me because there's something obviously very wrong with you – and I can't begin to help you unless I know what it . . ." Suddenly, his brows furrowed. "Is it . . . is there someone else? Is that what this is all about? Be honest with me. Tell me. Is that what this is – you've fallen in love with somebody else?"

"There isn't anybody else."

"Then tell me, damn it all – what in the devil is going on here!"

She buried her head in her arms. "I want to; believe me, I want to. I've been thinking for days what to tell you. But I can't. . . . Believe me, Will."

"For heaven's sake, now you're talking like one of my undergraduates. Stop talking like a silly schoolgirl!"

"Then try to help me. There are some things in life that we can't fully understand or explain. Yet they're there. Can't you understand?"

"How can I understand something that makes no sense? What kind of crazy logic is that? You say there are some things that can't be fully understood. Yet you ask me to understand what you say can't be understood. If I said that to my students, they'd laugh me out of the room."

"You really don't understand. I can see. I feel so stupid."

"You feel stupid! Take a look at me! . . . Now, Katrina, try to pull yourself together. Are you terribly unhappy because of something I've done; or haven't done? You should be able to tell me that at least."

Katrina did not answer immediately. "It isn't that simple," she finally said. "If it were only that simple! . . . I don't know, Will. I feel very mixed up right now."

"Yes, well, you *are* mixed up!" Harris retorted. And with that he rose from his chair again and this time left the room; returning in a few moments with a pill and a glass of water. "Here, take this," he said to Katrina, "and you'll feel better. It'll relax you anyway, so you can at least begin to think clearly again. . . . Now, I've got that damn survey class. Tonight we'll talk things over and we'll get to the bottom of what's bothering you. . . . But get this crazy idea of a separation out of your head. There's not going to be any!"

The Professor leaned over and kissed his wife on the forehead. She did not resist. She did not react in any way.

That morning his lecture was the most chopped-up and incoherent he had ever delivered; mirroring his mind, which was jumping incoherently from one thing to another – an odd state of affairs as he had presented this very same lecture dozens of times before, and it was virtually imprinted on his brain. Moreover, in the midst of today's confusion, he developed a sudden phobia about using the word "separation." Before this it had been strictly a neutral word, one he had neither particularly liked nor disliked – it was just a word that provided yet another ripe opportunity for misspelling by undergraduates (how many dozens of times – nay, hundreds of times! – had he drawn a red circle around the word "sep*e*ration?"). But now this benign word was absolutely the most abominable one in the English language. When he put his whole attention to it, he could avoid using the word. But then his other thoughts would get all jumbled up, causing him to stammer and utter one non sequitur after another. When he would halt to collect his thoughts, forcing himself to concentrate on his theme, out would come that word again, and again, and again – as if it were the most basic and indispensable word in the language; as if he could not describe any fact or concept of colonial history without it. There was, on the one hand, the ever-growing *separation* of the American colonies from Mother England. The same growing *separation* of the colonial churches from the Church of England. There was the *separation* of the colonies from each other. The *separation* of powers (legislative, judicial, executive) within the colonies. The *separation* of church and state. And so on and so on.

It was a terrible ordeal, this struggle for coherence, this ludicrous war against a word, waged openly and nakedly before a class of eighty-five young men and women. Harris felt like a fool. Imagining throughout that his students were laughing at him. (They would be fools if they were not.) With one ear he listened for chuckles and snickers – becoming even more perplexed when he could detect none, even as he went on and on with his disjointed lecture. But the students behaved no differently than in past lectures: Some slouched in their seats and dozed; others gave the appearance of listening carefully but otherwise were completely impassive; still others scribbled furiously in their notebooks, taking copious notes, convincing the Professor beyond all doubt that they would go on taking just as copious notes even if he were talking complete gibberish.

Finally, the ordeal was over. Harris closed his notebook, bracing himself. Half hoping for a flood of angry, derisive students. But none came. Looking out across the classroom, he could see the students falling all over each other in their almost frantic efforts to get out. How could that be? Now Harris felt embarrassed – not for himself, but for his students. Not only embarrassed but vaguely contemptuous – for his students; for all students.

Soon the lecture room was empty – except for the Professor. Empty and completely silent. Though outside of the room – in the corridors, down on the campus two floors below – there were the customary loud noises that spelled the end of class: the shuffling of feet, the buzz of conversation, loud laughter, the starting of cars. Harris was barely aware of the hustle and bustle outside he was so insulated from it by the hollowness of the classroom in which he was standing. (Unlike many of his fellow professors, who welcomed survey classes with about the same enthusiasm as they might have greeted a case of smallpox, Harris actually asked to teach one per semester because he felt that Modern Academia –

as well as democracy and civic engagement themselves! – were suffering dearly from overspecialization and a lack of overarching vision. But, my, weren't those classes huge!)

Feeling tired, he sat down on a chair behind the lectern. And for awhile, staring blankly at the row upon row of empty desks in front of him, he was as still and immobile as everything else in the classroom. Then he became aware of a red dictionary on the desk behind the lectern. He did not want to do it, yet could not resist. He picked up the book and thumbed it open to the section marked "s". Looking for the word "separation" . . . ah, there it was: "separate, v., to draw apart; to go different ways; to divide; to keep apart, as a fence separates two pieces of property."

Panic gripped him. Is this what Katrina wanted? For them to draw apart, to put a fence between them, to go separate ways? Inconceivable! After twenty-nine years of living together and three children! . . . But was it so inconceivable? How about their friends, the Benningtons? The Ryans? The Turners? All three couples had had children and relatively long marriages, yet they had all gotten divorces. . . . True, but in each case there had been serious and obvious reasons: Sarah Bennington had been a closet alcoholic; Bill Ryan, a fellow history professor, had been committing adultery openly with one of his former graduate students; the Turners, after years of almost constant bickering, had gotten a divorce on grounds of incompatibility.

Incompatibility? Hmmm. This was an all-inclusive word. Another word which he had never thought much about one way or the other. Now suddenly it looked suspicious. Very suspicious. He had always thought he knew what the word meant. But did he? Quickly he picked up the dictionary again and thumbed through it. Aha! "Incompatible, adj., incapable of harmonious relations; incongruous."

He breathed a sigh of relief. The word definitely did not apply to him and Katrina. Oh, they had somewhat different natures: She was soft and graceful, playful, even kittenish, intuitive, extremely sensitive; he was more awkward physically but strong, more serious and contemplative, not a genius perhaps but thorough in his work, as a scholar should be. Incongruous traits? Definitely not. In fact, the more Harris thought about them, the more they suggested to him the yin and the yang – the natural feminine and the natural masculine. Different, yes, but not opposing; complementary. And two things that are complementary have a natural unity. If there were no natural unity between Katrina and himself, the Professor reasoned, how could they have lived together so long without violent disagreements? Without mutually destroying each other? True, they had had their differences and quarrels over the years, but every couple, even the most devoted ones, have these. The important thing was that the disagreements had never been so basic that once they were aired and thrashed out, life could not go on again harmoniously. That is why Katrina's request for a separation had shaken him so. . . . And as the Professor thought over and over again of what had transpired at the breakfast table his rage grew. It grew and grew until he found himself, despite his best efforts to prevent it, not only angry at Katrina but actually hating her.

He hated her – until it occurred to him that he still did not know why Katrina had acted as she did. Even Katrina herself did not seem to know. A good indication that her reason, whatever it was, was decidedly irrational. Oh, she was so childish sometimes. Acting impulsively. Purely on her emotions. Perhaps, with her children all out of the nest now, she had been brooding over the loss of her role of mother – a role she had loved so much. Perhaps she was still going through her change of life. Perhaps it was . . . well, whatever it was, it was irrational and given time and patience and understanding, she would certainly see that what she was doing was without real basis. The natural logic which had brought them together in the first place and which had held them together as husband and wife for twenty-nine years would reassert itself. Everything would be fine again and they could, in love and devotion, enjoy the autumnal years, the harvest, together.

He was seized with an impulse to call Katrina. He picked up his notes and books, and hurried to his office on the fourth floor of the University's administration building. Yes, he would call her and act as if nothing had happened. This would reassure her. And tonight he would bring her home a bouquet of flowers as a symbol of his love for her. Doggone it, when he put his mind to it, he could be as romantic a lover as any man! . . . All that Katrina was asking for, in a woman's way, was some unusual display of affection; some positive assertion that even though she was growing older and no longer needed so much as a mother she was still loved and needed as a wife – just as much as ever. How dense he had been not to see it long before this!

He sat down and looked at the telephone sitting on his desk. But somehow could not bring himself to dial. He was trembling all over. Afraid. Afraid that what he had convinced himself was only a nightmare might actually be more than that. What then? What would he say to

Katrina if she answered? He didn't know. If Katrina walked into his office right now he didn't know what he would say to her. What a terrible thing! To want to speak to one's wife and to be unable to do so. To someone who for years had been like an extension of one's very self! . . . The Professor laid down the telephone on his desk.

He was supposed to be at lunch, but he knew that he couldn't eat. Instead he tried to review some galley proofs, just arrived by overnight mail, for an article he'd written that was to be included in a book of essays by some of the most eminent historians in the country. But he was too upset to concentrate. After re-reading the second paragraph of the essay four times he gave up, shoving the proofs aside, wondering why he had been so excited yesterday about his inclusion in this book. How we deceive ourselves! He had thought it would bring prestige both to himself and to Parkhurst; that Katrina would be proud of him; that his students would accord him a new respect. But now he knew that the book really meant nothing to Katrina. Nor to his students. And why should it? This semester they were in his class, the next they would be in somebody else's. So why should this book mean anything to them? Or to Parkhurst? For reasons of prestige (and grants!), the University wanted its teachers to write essays, journal articles, reviews, books, and more books, but what beyond its own selfish interests would this book mean to Parkhurst?

Suddenly the Professor found himself hating Parkhurst. That which before – next to Katrina – he had loved more than anything else in the world; that which he had loved even longer than Katrina, having done most of his graduate work at the University and having taught there for exactly twenty-six years – only three less than he had been married to Katrina. He hated Parkhurst and everything connected with it, including its stupid students.

At two o'clock the bell rang for the Professor's afternoon class – a smaller, upper-division class: "The Ecclesiastical Origins of Constitutionalism." But it too was a disaster. Whereas in the morning period he had boggled over his material and become the fool out of sheer distraction, he turned this afternoon class into a farce deliberately – out of sheer anger. Hurling one incongruity and absurdity after another at his students. Taunting them. Daring them to be intelligent and alert – to challenge him, laugh at him, or better, walk out of the room and leave him to himself. Yet in spite of his best efforts the afternoon students reacted not much differently than the morning ones; that is, some listened impassively, some dozed, some took copious notes. Goodness knows what they thought – if indeed they thought anything at all. He imagined that a few sensitive ones among them might be saying to themselves, "Something's a little off with Dr. Harris this afternoon – but then everyone has an off-day now and then." That would be very tolerant of them. But who gives a damn!

The lecture over, Harris headed for home. He could hardly wait to get there, to find out whether Katrina was there, the storm abated, everything exactly as it had been. Yet he was also afraid – even more afraid than he had been at noon. Not afraid of standing speechless in front of Katrina. But afraid that she would not be there at all. Or if she was, that something terribly profound had happened in their lives that would make it impossible for things ever again to be as they had been. He wanted to know the truth – as all men in some way want to know the truth and are angry when they are deceived. Yet he also knew that sometimes the truth is too awful to hear: He did not know whether he had the courage to hear it.

At the front door he paused. Listening intently for some sound of life inside. The sound of radio or television. Of Katrina talking over the telephone. Or simply footsteps. But he could hear nothing at all. The house seemed as silent as a tomb.

He tried the door. It would not open. He pushed hard on it, hoping it was only a jammed lock and that if he pushed hard enough it would give. To no avail. He grasped the brass knob and turned it frenziedly back and forth. But still the door was unyielding. His hand went limp on the knob.

Finally he opened the door with his key. The whole house was dark and empty. No motion, no sign of life anywhere. Not even a flutter of curtains to greet him. Not even a stirring of air – for the windows were all shut tight.

He walked through the house into the kitchen. There everything was neat and clean, everything in its place, so much in its place that it looked like the kitchen of a model home in which no one lived. The Professor looked up at the electric clock on the wall. It was running, the second hand spinning around and around, smoothly, silently, relentlessly. Ugh! Who ever invented electric clocks anyway? Clocks were meant to tick. . . . He walked over to the refrigerator and opened the door. There was food in it – cheese, a bottle of milk, eggs, some apples and grapes. A reassuring sight, after everything else. For where there is food, food consciously assembled (even if it is nothing more than the gathered nuts of the squirrel) there is some kind of life. Harris had not eaten anything since breakfast and now, confronted by the provender, he realized that his stomach was empty, achingly empty. Still he had no appetite for it.

He climbed up the stairs to the master bedroom. Looking to see if there were any significant differences. The queen bed was made up neatly, impeccably: That was normal, to be expected. Katrina's bureau? He dreaded to look into it. Touching the knobs of the top drawer, he could feel the blood throbbing in his finger tips. . . . The drawer was empty. He opened the other drawers, one after another, in rapid succession. They were all empty.

With a heavy heart he went into his study. Heading instinctively for his pipe which lay on a stand next to his easy chair. His pipe – something old and reliable, that he could always depend upon for relaxation and solace when he was troubled or pent-up. Flopping into the easy chair, he reached for the pipe and for the bag of tobacco which lay next to it. Under the pouch was something white. A piece of letter paper, folded up, with his name – Will – on the top fold; written in Katrina's hand. He unfolded the paper. Knowing even before he looked at it what it was all about. He read the note quickly; then slowly reread it. It said, "Dear Will, I have gone to Emily's. Please believe me when I say that I am sorry to the bottom of my heart for what has happened. This is the saddest day of my whole life. If it could have been otherwise, I would have had it so. Despite what you may think, I have not acted rashly or impulsively. It was only after the most intense soul-searching and anguish that I spoke to you this morning. I know that I owe you a fuller explanation. I shall try to give it to you when I collect my wits. For this I must have time, particularly time to myself. I do not want to cause you pain; and yet it seems that in living we hurt even when we do not want to hurt. Please forgive me. Katrina."

The Professor flung the note to the floor. "What nonsense," he exclaimed. Now he really hated his wife – for insulting and humiliating him like this. His own wife, whom he loved so dearly, walking out on him and leaving such a note! Pretending to be contrite, but superciliously so, treating him like a child or some inferior. "Oh, she's so sorry to have hurt me!" What tripe! What arrogance!

He thought of going immediately and directly to Emily's, demanding that Katrina cut out all this nonsense and return home; bring her home by force if necessary.

But while the idea of carrying Katrina home over his shoulder gave the Professor a kind of vicarious satisfaction, he could not really see himself in the role of the forceful, truculent male. Force never decided or settled anything. It would only exacerbate the situation. Perhaps he should talk to Emily, to see if she had any clues to Katrina's abrupt and tragic behavior. Everything might be readily explained by some relatively simple cause, which Katrina might have confided to her sister, a member of her own sex, in a way that she could not confide to him. So why not talk to Emily? . . . But would it be fair? Hmmm. Would Katrina construe it as an invasion of her sanctuary? Could Emily, as Katrina's sister, really be objective?

One moment Katrina was a she-devil, mendacious, despicable; the next moment she was desperately sick and in need of his help. One moment he himself felt small, mean, inconsequential; the next, large, understanding, magnanimous. If only he had the facts, he would know how to feel and act. But what were the facts?

Suddenly he felt weak and faint.

He must eat something; so he went into the kitchen and made himself a cheese sandwich. He munched on it and drank a glass of milk. Staring again at the telephone. If only it would ring; it or the doorbell; his dilemma might be resolved. For it was just possible that in her present irrational state Katrina might have another change of heart and want to return home as suddenly and impulsively as she had left. He strained his ears – as if by straining he could set bells to ringing, as if by straining he could produce a change in Katrina's heart. But the silence was so complete that all he could hear was his own hastily-filled stomach rumbling and grumbling.

He needed sleep. He fell into bed.

Soon lost consciousness.

He saw a deer . . . a beautiful deer . . . of tawny color, with slim, graceful body and long, curving antlers . . . grazing peacefully in a woodland meadow . . . of which it seemed a part, as much and as naturally a part as the grass and trees . . . even in its color, the deer itself being only another shadow in the variegated scene, merging with it, hardly distinguishable from it.

Then, suddenly, the scene was rent by a pack of eager, sniffing, baying hounds; ferocious animals belonging to a hunting party. The startled deer lifted high its head, fled; pursued by the hounds.

On and on went the chase. Across open, sunlit meadows. Through thick, dark woods. Over fallen logs and over fences. The deer always going over the hurdles with an easy, graceful, floating motion; without ever losing its stride. The huge hounds clearing them, too, but only with much greater effort.

Eventually, however, the deer's energy began to flag. It was fleeter than the hounds, but it did not have their rugged, driving, relentless endurance. Going over a barbed-wire fence, it tripped on the top strand of wire. Falling, rolling, sliding. The hounds on it at once. Torn, bleeding, the deer thrashed about. Shaking off its assailants. Struggling to its feet. Then, with antlers lowered, it thrust and stabbed. With one last, great burst of energy it rammed an antler point into a black, hairy chest. Even as bared teeth grabbed its jugular vein. . . .

The Professor awoke, clutching at his throat.

When he came to his senses, he said to himself, "Thank God; but oh, what a horrible dream."

For a long time he could not get back to sleep. His throat pained him awfully. Of course it was only his imagination playing a trick on him. What else could it be? And yet he felt the pain so acutely that he got up, turned on the light and looked at himself in the mirror, just to make sure. Then he was able to doze off. But the rest of the night he slept fitfully.

And the next morning, preparing his breakfast, he could not get the dream out of his mind. "It was obviously an anxiety dream," he kept telling himself. Perfectly understandable, considering the strain he was under. At the same time he could not help wondering about it. Hmmm. He had often thought – until this week – of Katrina as deerlike. Not only because she moved with the same kind of easy, floating grace but because of her gentleness and innocence. How many times had he called her, "My little deer," and had fun making puns about it? "Katrina, my dear, my little deer, my dear deer" . . . Katrina the deer . . . Dear Katrina. . . . The deer leaped over the fence; the deer leaped lightly over the fence; the deer tripped the light fantastic; the deer tripped over the top wire. . . . The deer gored the dog through its heart . . . gored the dog; through its heart. . . .

"Dear me! Oh dear!" The deer in the dream, for all its beauty and grace, had antlers – long, curving antlers. It wasn't a female at all. It was a male!

The Professor chewed and stewed over his dream right through breakfast. Achieving nothing, for he could make no sense of it. It was like all nightmares, non-logical – as non-logical as the nightmare through which he was actually living.

So preoccupied was he with the dream that he was almost at the University before he realized that he did not have any classes that day.

Thank God! Thank God! He could not have gone through another ordeal like yesterday's. If he had had a class, he would have simply dismissed the students, pleading illness. He was sick, in a way.

He must confide in someone.

The most logical person he could think of was a fellow professor, Dr. Henry Stern, chair of the biology department. Stern knew Katrina well because he and his wife and the Harrises often saw each other socially and had even taken three vacations together. (Although it was fairly unusual for professors in such different departments to form close bonds, Harris had befriended Stern many years before while researching a journal article on the cross-Atlantic transport of European livestock – cattle, goats, sheep, swine – into early New England and the Chesapeake region.) At any rate, Stern had a good analytical mind, one of the university's best. Moreover, he was discreet.

Of course, it was going to be embarrassing. And so Harris found himself walking up and down the wide red-brick path that paralleled the science building several times before actually screwing up his courage and going *into* the building. He found Stern in the small lab that adjoined the biologist's office, where the rank odor of some sort of chemical (formaldehyde, perhaps?) almost took Harris' breath away. His fellow professor was gingerly holding a tiny dead frog with a pair of tweezers over an open specimen box. "Well, well, good to see you, Will," Stern said, smiling broadly when he noticed Harris standing gingerly in the doorway. "Come in and have a seat. Somebody just brought me this little fellow from South America. A rare one."

Stern seemed so relaxed that Harris relaxed himself and before he knew it, to his own surprise, as soon as the frog was ensconced in his little box, the history professor was telling the entire story to the biology professor, bringing in the most minute details: Who, at this point, could tell what was significant? Harris even described to Stern his dream about the deer and hounds which was still very much on his mind. Yes, he wanted Stern to know everything, no matter how far-fetched or embarrassing. Besides, he felt a great need to unburden himself.

Stern listened with furrowed, sympathetic brow. "It's a strange story, and, to be completely honest, Will, I'm just not quite sure what to say," he said when Harris had concluded. "If there's one thing I've learned after all these years of living, it's that one really ought not to be surprised at surprises. Look at the coelacanth. We thought it extinct; that it had become extinct millions of years ago. And then a fisherman catches one east of South

Africa. What about that? A wonderful surprise! Yes, life is full of surprises."

"Well, this surprise was not at all wonderful, I can assure you of that," Harris replied, smiling at his colleague wanly. "And it's just absolutely out of character for Katrina. Can you make anything of it at all? Even the slightest clue? I'd be most grateful for even the tiniest of clues."

"It's just so hard to say, Will." Stern kneaded the loose, flour-white skin of his forehead with long slender fingers. "I mean, it certainly represents some radical change of mind or heart or body. I myself have never noticed any signs of . . . " he paused, ". . . of illness of any kind in Katrina. She always appeared to me – and to Helen – to be just about one of the healthiest persons we knew. I've always thought of her as the one person who was with it, you know. . . ."

"With 'it,' maybe. But was she with me?"

"Hard to say. You know, you look at a tibia and a femur and they look like perfect fits. But when you put them together, *nein*. Nothing wrong with either bone. Both good specimens. They just don't fit. Try the tibia on some other femur and it works."

Harris' lips twitched nervously. *This* was logic? "Henry, just indulge me for a minute. Please. From your perspective, and I realize – of course – it's only from your perspective, but do you think Katrina and I were . . . are . . . a good fit? I've got to know."

Stern shrugged his rather wide shoulders and smiled. "I would have thought so, Will. I honestly would have thought so. But it's an extremely complicated thing, you know, all this business of human man and woman. Not predictable, like the mating of fiddler crabs. Or gecko lizards. Or elephant-shrews. No, some days Helen and I swing along wonderfully, and then other days, *Gott in Himmel*, I get one of the damndest surprises."

"With all respect, Henry, are you not contradicting yourself?" Harris said. "I mean, first, you say the bones either fit or they don't. Now you say one never really knows whether they fit or not."

Stern smiled. "You're taking me too literally, Will. Really, the only ones who can know the answer to your question are you and Katrina. What do *you* think?"

"What does it matter now what I think? What matters is what Katrina thinks. And how can I find that out – when she disappears . . . takes off like a . . ."

Harris didn't finish his sentence; neither did Stern attempt to finish it for him. They both knew where it was going: Tail up. Gone . . . Gone.

"The manner in which Katrina left you does explain something, I suppose," said Stern. "Not much perhaps, but something. In your dream, Will, why did the deer leave?"

"You're not intimating. . . ."

Stern shook his head. "I'm just trying to understand a very enigmatic situation."

"But you were intimating. . . ."

"No, no, no. Henry, now it's your turn to indulge me. It was male, right?"

"Male?"

"The deer."

"Yes. But when somebody's world turns upside-down, everything else in it is turned upside-down too. Males seem like females, females like males; black seems white; animals seem like humans, and humans like animals. So, it's not surprising, I guess, that friends should also seem like enemies. . . ."

Stern's eyes blinked. He ran his hand over the pate of his bald, bony head. "You know, Will, you and I could stand here all day – all night – all year – speculating about what's going on with your wife, when you and I both know what the most logical thing to do is. Go talk to her. Ask her directly. And if she dances around your questions, well, pin her down."

"She doesn't want to talk to me. She made that very clear. But if you want to know the real reason, I think it's because she doesn't have the courage. I truly think that's why she left as she did."

"Well, I suppose I could go see her for you. Or Helen could. But I would imagine that we're both too close to be good mediators. What would be best is someone neutral."

"Like whom?"

"I don't know. There are a number of good counselors in town." Stern again ran his hand over his head. "You know what? Now that I think about it, why don't you try that new chaplain? McLain, I think his name is. Seems to me Charlie told me he has a background in couples' counseling. Which makes you wonder what he'll do here with the barely post-pubescent." Stern nodded and smiled. "Actually, he'd be a perfect third party, now that I think about it. Katrina's a believer, isn't she?"

Harris' jaw tightened. "All I want at this point are some questions answered, Henry. If one were to see a reason for something, one can perhaps learn to accept it. But when there's no apparent reason. . . ." He shook his head. He shook Stern's hand. "Thanks, Henry. Thanks very much for listening."

Harris left Stern's office more frustrated than when he had entered. He was disappointed in his fellow professor who hadn't really helped any; in fact, had done nothing but hand his problem right back to him. He was also miffed at Stern for intimating. . . . Though he wasn't too sure what Stern thought now. He didn't really care; that was the least of his problems. Of course, Stern had given him one last straw to clutch: Reverend McLain. But wasn't that a pretty fragile straw? Instinctively he disliked the idea of using clergymen to pull chestnuts out of the fire. Neither he nor Katrina attended any sort of church regularly, though Stern was indeed correct: Katrina was something of a believer (in her own unimposing sort of way). And perhaps, *perhaps*, she might not resent a chaplain as much as a psychologist. Still, Harris had a helpless, hopeless, feeling that there was something final about Katrina's departure that nobody, not even the most astute and respected clergyman in the world, could do anything about.

One, two, three, four, five days went by. Every waking hour, on the hour (except for the few times he was in class or conference), he eagerly checked his computer for incoming emails, hoping to find one from Katrina. There were none; not even a message from his sons or daughter. Each day, as soon as he returned from the university, he would look eagerly in the mailbox, hoping to find a letter from her there. There was none. Each evening he would listen eagerly for the doorbell to ring; but there was not even a call from Stern to inquire how he was. It was almost as if the whole world had joined in a conspiracy against him – to torment and torture him. But how silly even to imagine such a thing! What did the world care about him? What did it care if he, William Harris, professor of American Colonial history at Parkhurst University, had lost his love; been abandoned; forsaken?

Day by day, in large, bitter doses, the Professor learned what Katrina had really meant to him. For until now he had only thought of his life being empty and meaningless without her; now, for the first time, he was actually experiencing it – feeling what it was like, not to think about emptiness, but to be empty. And how total and all-pervasive it was, that void! Looting and stripping and draining everything of its substance and richness. During the day, while he was at the University, he would wonder what he was doing there. He would yearn to be at home. His home – with the bust of William Penn on the mantle, the facsimile of the Articles of

Confederation hanging on the living room wall, the 17th century Spanish candelabra on the dining room table – belonged to him, and he to it. It was his castle, his fortress, it was himself. He longed to be home – when he was at the University. But no sooner he passed through the door, it was all different. Then everything – the house, its comfortable furnishings, the once-cherished mementos – seemed strange, alien, superfluous. What good was it all, what need did he have of it all, without Katrina? Even the books in his library meant nothing: Yesterday each one of them had been like a living person to him, but now they all stood still and mute on their shelves, nothing more than printed pages between covers.

In the evenings, after dinner, sitting in his easy chair, smoking his pipe, he would get more and more nervous. So much so that he would have to snuff out his pipe. Might as well. It had a bitter taste anyway. But it was even worse sitting and staring at the walls. They would start closing in on him. And he would have to rise quickly and leave the house. If he walked, walked, walked at a fast pace, the tensions would subside – somewhat. But only for a little while. After walking a number of blocks, he would long more than ever to be home.

On the sixth day – that is, on the sixth day after his visit to Stern – Harris called Reverend McLain. He did not want to see the minister; he really didn't think it would do any good; no more good than his visit to Stern. But if not McLain, who or what else? He was desperate.

An appointment was made, and the next afternoon, following his graduate seminar, he went to the chaplain's office. Reverend McLain received him very courteously, nodded his head amiably when the Professor insisted the chaplain call him "Will," and then listened to Harris' story patiently and sympathetically. In fact, Harris felt so much at ease in the congenial presence of the chaplain (similar to the relaxed way he had felt, initially at least, with Stern, the biology professor), that, to his own surprise, he went on at length.

"I imagine I'm somewhat old-fashioned about marriage," he told the chaplain, leaning forward in a rather overstuffed chair, "but I'd like to believe that the marriage vow means something. And when husband and wife disagree, I believe they ought to be able to settle their differences reasonably. With reason and good will. . . . Yet my wife, when she left, gave absolutely no reason at all. That's what baffles me. And, to be honest, that's what makes me suspect her good will." Harris attempted a smile. "I know the heart has its reasons which reason knows not. Still the heart does have reasons – even if reason knows, or pretends to know, them not.

. . . I imagine that my wife may have had trouble articulating her reasons. I'll grant that. But she could have at very least given me some sort of hint. At the very least, she should have tried. . . . Don't you agree?"

Reverend McLain smiled back agreeably. "Well, you've certainly covered a lot of ground, Will. I wouldn't want to comment upon all your points at this time. Particularly since I make it a firm practice never to form any conclusions until I've heard both parties. . . . But we certainly have some common beliefs. The Church, too, takes an old-fashioned position on marriage – if you want to call it that. To some it's a pretty hard, uncompromising position: 'What God hath joined together let no man put asunder' . . . this is what God Himself has commanded. And He hasn't commanded it arbitrarily. For the sake of the children, for their own sakes, it's highly desirable that husband and wife commit themselves to each other, body and soul, without reservations – be one in flesh and spirit – until death do them part. Of course, human nature being what it is, differences do develop. . . . But still, in the great majority of cases, couples who vow to live together until death do them part should be able to do so. At least within a tolerable degree. If reason and good will are employed, as well as – here is where the Church differs from you; or adds an extra dimension – the grace of God. Now you may not. . . ."

"Oh, I believe absolutely in grace. Absolutely," Harris said. "Perhaps not as you mean it, Reverend, but I believe that graciousness is an extremely important ingredient in the implicit social contract between civilized people."

"Well, graciousness is indeed one human expression of grace," said Reverend McLain, still smiling amiably. "But what I mean by grace, in this context, is that God just doesn't create man – and woman – and lay out the 'rules' and then leave things on their own, to fall into chaos. He helps us to do what He has asked us to do. First, by giving our wills a prod in the right direction, so that we desire the right things and are willing to work for them. Secondly, by giving us the power to accomplish what we might not have the power to accomplish if left to ourselves. Naturally, for grace to be effective we have to cooperate and do our parts too. . . . Even then, it's not easy to keep God's commandments; there's no such thing as cheap grace. . . . So I want to warn you that even with grace and cooperation on your part it may not be easy to resolve your dilemma."

Harris blinked his eyes a few times, and then, finally, nodded. "Perhaps if you see Katrina she'll agree to getting together with me. If we can only talk things out. . . ."

"Would you like to call her first and ask if she'd like to meet with me?"

"Actually, no. I think it would be best if you called her directly."

"You're absolutely sure you don't want to call her first?"

"Absolutely."

"Well, all right then, Will," Reverend McClain said, standing up and extending a strong and straight hand to Harris. "I'll get in touch with your wife sometime today, if I can. If she'll consent to see me we'll at least be on the road. I'll keep you informed."

Harris left the chaplain's office feeling almost elated. He had some real hope now – for the first time. Hope – and help – at last to accomplish what by himself he knew he could not accomplish. Reverend McLain, he felt, was a man of intelligence and good will, who could, if anybody could, win Katrina's confidence.

And he would do his part. If Katrina had acted impulsively, he would be understanding and forgiving; let bygones be bygones. If the trouble turned out to be more serious, he would be understanding about that too. Even if it turned out that he himself was somehow at fault. After all, everyone has blind spots that would not be blind if the person saw them. He determined that if, through the intercession of Reverend McLain, any blind spots were brought to his attention, he would look at them – no matter how painful, no matter what the cost to his own ego or pride – and correct what needed to be corrected.

After all, despite his deep hurt and sometimes hatred of Katrina for having hurt him, he wanted her back. For he could not bear to think of living the rest of his life without her. He needed her desperately. He had to have her! . . . He would get her back, if only the minister would arrange for them to talk freely to each other. He would take her to dinner at their favorite French restaurant and they would sit by candlelight and each sip a glass of chilled Cheval Blanc; he would hold her hand, and they would talk. He was certain that she would be his again when he told her how much he loved her; better still, when he demonstrated to her, by actions, how much he loved her!

It was four days before the Professor heard from Reverend McLain. Days not of sheer emptiness, as before, but of charged, mixed emotion, of alternating hope and despair. One moment he was on top of the world, convinced that everything ultimately turns out for the best, that after this brief crisis and absence from each other he and Katrina would be closer than ever. The next moment he was in the lowest depths, wondering how he could ever again have implicit faith in her. If she betrayed him once, she might just as well do it again. Look how his friend Stern – in a crisis, just when he needed him – had disappointed him. And Reverend McLain might too. So why not Katrina again; and again. It was a terribly sad thought. A life in which there is no complete trust. Is such a life worth living?

During the interval of the four days Harris got an email from one of his sons, Will Jr., and another from his daughter Martha. But he left them unopened. Suspicious even of them. For how could he know whether they were for or against him? Besides, without Katrina, his sons no longer seemed his sons, nor his daughter his daughter.

Finally, on the fourth day – while he was dawdling over his breakfast at home – Reverend McLain called. Could he come to the chaplain's office at this earliest convenience? Yes, he would be there in a couple of hours, right after his morning lecture.

Harris did not know whether he could stand the strain and anxiety of waiting even that long. He was relieved to know that the clergyman had something to tell him, yet there was something in the man's voice that he did not like.

Reverend McLain was not smiling when the Professor entered his office. He was courteous and friendly as before; but still not smiling. Harris had a feeling that it was rare that the chaplain did not smile. His heart sank.

Yes, said the clergyman, he had talked to Katrina. Once over the telephone, later at her sister Emily's. At first she was hesitant about seeing him but finally consented. The meeting took place last night. And they talked for nearly three hours. Katrina courteous and gracious throughout. Answering all questions put to her – with feeling and earnestness. Still, all in all. . . .

Harris broke in anxiously. "And did she tell you what's bothering her? Why she wanted a separation?"

"Well, before I go any further," said the chaplain, "I should stress that what I like to do – ideally, and as a matter of course, actually – is to bring two people together in the same room so they can talk to each other directly, in my presence but without my trying to translate their feelings as a messenger."

"But . . .?"

"She asked that, at this point, anyway, I relay to you my conversation with her."

"So did she tell you what it is that's bothering her?"

"Well, yes and no."

"What do you mean, yes and no?"

The chaplain drew in a rather long breath. "To be frank, Will," he said, "your wife has a very enigmatic way of talking. I mean, she talks in an idiom that isn't always easy to understand."

"Well, I certainly never had any trouble understanding her," said Harris, pinching his nose with his right hand and pulling his fingers down over his top lip. "But you should be able to answer this one: Is she willing to talk about all this with me at some point?"

"Again I'm afraid I have to answer yes and no," replied McLain.

"I don't understand," said Harris. "Either she is or is not willing to talk with me."

"She said she was willing to talk with you – if you really wanted her to. But she wonders whether you really want to talk to her."

"She wonders what?" Harris sputtered.

"Whether you really want to talk to her."

"For God's sake, what does *that* mean?"

"I'm afraid I can only repeat what your wife told me," the chaplain replied.

"Reverend. This is all rather confusing to me. Let me ask you this, very directly: Don't you think that my wife has an obligation to return to her home and to settle whatever differences she has with me amicably. . . . And at this point God only knows what these differences are; I surely don't. . . . Now could you please answer me yes or no?"

Reverend McLain drummed on his desk with a pencil. "Will, not all questions can be answered with a simple yes or no. I'd say both you and your wife have certain obligations in this matter. Certain obligations and certain rights."

"I recognize that. But maybe we're not talking about the same things. Could you be more specific please? Let's start with 'the rights,' for example."

"Well, we come into the world alone and we go out of it alone, so even though a person is married, he or she is still an individual with all the rights of an individual. Like the right on occasion to the privacy of her or his own person."

"The right to privacy, yes. Of course. Of course. But not the right to break up a marriage of twenty-nine years with absolutely no explanation!"

"My friend, at this point I don't know what your wife is or is not try-ing to do. So until I have evidence to the contrary, I must assume that she is acting in good faith – just as I assume you are acting in good faith. When I have talked to you both at greater length and have learned more about your marriage, perhaps then I can begin to make some judgments. Until then I have to confine myself to general principles."

The Professor was fidgeting in his seat. He reached into his coat pocket, brought out a handkerchief and wiped his forehead – though he wasn't perspiring in the slightest.

"Don't misunderstand me, Reverend. I have complete confidence in you. I'd also like to give my wife the benefit of all doubts. But until she indicates a real willingness to sit down with me, my doubts about her good will aren't going to disappear, just like that. I'm sure you can appreciate that. . . . I'm curious. Did you discuss with my wife the necessity for both parties to show their good will? As a general principle, I mean?"

McLain nodded. "I certainly did."

"And what did she say?"

"In summary, I would say she agreed wholeheartedly. Though she did ask, after we had pretty well exhausted the topic, whether I thought good will was enough."

"Now, honestly, does that kind of question in itself show good will?"

The chaplain shrugged. "Depends on what she meant by it. As I said before, your wife said a lot of things that needed translating. But I gather that what she meant by her question was that good will was only one of many factors in a problem. On that I'd have to agree with her. The road to Hell, as they say, is paved with the best of intentions."

"And with bad ones too."

"That's right. But good will, by itself, isn't the answer to everything. All the good will in the world, for example, isn't going to make oil mix with water successfully."

"Maybe not, maybe not," replied the Professor, sighing. "But unless a wife – I mean both husband and wife – take their obligations to each other seriously, there's no chance of anything. None at all. What I'd really like to know is whether my wife's vow to be loyal and true to her husband, for better for worse, for richer for poorer, in sickness and in health, until death do them part, means anything to her at all. Do you think it does? . . . No, I don't want to put you on the spot again. Let me put it this way. Did you happen to discuss this vow with her?"

McLain nodded. "I did. In fact, she brought up the subject herself."

"Yes, and what did she say?"

"She said that she had not forgotten her vow. That she was only too aware of it."

"And that was her only comment?"

"No, when we talked about it further, she became very emotional and started to cry."

"The old feminine trick – when you've got them cornered and they don't have a real answer. I hope you didn't let her get away with it."

McLain's face blanched. "I didn't go there as a prosecuting attorney, Will. I went to see your wife as a third party trying, with the help of God, to bring peace to two people."

"But crying is no answer. It's an irrational response to a rational question, that's what it is. I'm surprised that you let her get away with it."

"I didn't let her get away with anything, to use your own words," replied the minister. "But I certainly didn't want to alienate your wife before I had even heard her side of the story. Later on, in fact, I made the point again – that this solemn vow 'until death' meant just what it said."

"And I suppose she wept again?"

"Not right off. First, she looked up at me kind of quizzically. Then, she asked, 'What is death?' And started to cry again. I saw there was no use in belaboring the point, so I dropped it."

The Professor grimaced. "But that was no answer! 'What is death?' What the devil kind of answer is that? Answer me that, Reverend! What ridiculous kind of an answer is that? How could you just 'drop it,' without asking her to explain!"

"Will!" exclaimed Reverend McClain. "You're letting your emotions get control of you!"

"Perhaps I am, perhaps I am," said Harris, wiping his forehead again. "I'm sorry if I said anything offensive to you. I didn't mean it that way. Not at all. I am wrought up, I'll admit it."

"I know how you feel. And I'm not unsympathetic. . . . But I'd like to remind you that you were the one who insisted from the beginning in discussing this problem in a friendly, objective manner. . . . I also told you right from the beginning, if you remember, that it wouldn't be an easy thing, resolving this matter in the best interests of both parties. . . . And when I say both, I mean both – both you and your wife."

"I'm very sorry," said Harris. "But as you yourself have just said – it isn't an easy thing; particularly when one is so deeply involved, as I am."

"And as your wife is, too. I trust you are beginning to see that it isn't at all a simple matter of good will."

The Professor sighed again. "I never did say it was just a matter of good will. I said good will and reason. You yourself admitted that my wife spoke to you in an enigmatic way."

"Yes I did. And that's exactly why we can't draw any conclusions or make any judgments until we know precisely what she meant. Reason can't be applied to something until one has something to apply it to. There are so many things we've got to know first. Whether there are financial problems, psychological ones, whether there is a question of basic incompatibility, and so on. That will take time."

Again the chaplain began drumming the desk with his pencil. He looked at his watch.

The Professor's lips trembled. "Did Katrina say . . . or indicate . . that the femur didn't fit with the tibia? ! . . ."

"I'm sorry?"

"The trouble was incompatibility? That we weren't – aren't – a natural fit."

McLain laughed. "She didn't say she thought the trouble was incompatibility. But that's always a possibility in cases like yours."

"Well . . . well, suppose it was a problem. Would there be no hope?"

"Oh yes," said the chaplain, smiling. "Because while incompatibility is a most serious problem, it's not an impossible one. Provided – provided grace is given an opportunity to operate. . . . You have no idea what a wonderful gift of God grace is! It moves mountains; it heals the most serious wounds; it brings the dead back to life. In short, it does the impossible. Now let me ask you something. Do you think that God would ask men and women to remain married until death do them part if He knew this were absolutely impossible? It may be impossible for some men and women, given their particular natures. But it's not impossible for God – if these people ask for His grace and cooperate with it. For grace transcends nature, transforms it and perfects it – without destroying it. It's miraculous, I'll admit. . . . But do you understand what I mean?"

"Not exactly," Harris replied. "I'd like to believe you, because I do want Katrina back. More than anything in the world. But somehow it all sounds to me – if you'll permit me to be completely frank – a little too much like some . . . I don't know . . . some fairy godmother. And as much as I'd like to, Reverend, I'm afraid I just can't believe in fairy godmothers."

McLain was looking again at his watch. "I'll admit that it's a difficult concept to grasp. In fact, it can't really be grasped by the mind at all. It's essentially a matter of faith. . . ."

Harris looked now at his own watch. "Oh, for God's sake! I've taken enough of your time. Besides annoying you no end. But I'm very appreciative of what you have done. . . . It's a real mess, isn't it?"

"Don't despair," said McLain, rising. "Why don't you think over what I've told you and then maybe in a couple of days or so – after you've had a chance to mull things over – we can decide on our next step. I know it may not make much sense right now; may even seem hopeless. But if you're willing to keep trying, I am too."

"I'm willing," said the Professor. "I will think over what you've told me."

"And you'll get in touch with me again in a few days?"

Harris nodded.

"That's the spirit," said Reverend McLain. He was smiling again as Harris rose to leave. But the Professor no longer had the confidence in that smile that he once did. It was just a smile. Nothing super-human or magical or miraculous about it.

The days went by.

What happened to them? – Well, for awhile, the Professor continued to batter at things. Almost impersonally. Because he could not stop. Though he was no longer sure there was anything behind the walls.

He battered so hard that his hands – his hands first, that is; then the whole body – actually grew numb. So numb that he could pinch himself on the arm and feel nothing. He couldn't even feel his heart beat. Occasionally he would hear a groan or a grumble from his stomach but that was all.

Otherwise, nothing of much consequence happened. The Professor went on living by himself in a silent, empty house, trying to live as normally as possible. Cooking his own breakfast and dinners, or picking something up from a nearby deli. Perfunctorily preparing his lectures. Perfunctorily delivering them. Not inspiring or challenging or disturbing his students. Not expecting to. Just getting by.

He received no communications of any kind from Katrina, though he did receive both emails and letters from his children and from friends. The emails he left unopened. The letters he put in a neat stack on the living room table. What was the use of reading them? They would not – and could not – tell him anything. Only Katrina could do that herself.

If he could have convinced himself that Katrina was a liar and a cheat, he might have felt anger. Also some kind of hope. Not much. But at least a glimmer. Hope that Katrina would repent of her ways and come back to him on her knees – the Prodigal Wife. But he could not convince himself of that. . . .

He didn't even feel despair. He might have, if he still had any hope of Katrina's returning. But he no longer had any hope of that; and so because he no longer felt any hope, because he no longer felt anything, he could not even feel despair.

How he had once wanted Katrina to talk to him, give him some kind of explanation, prove that logic and order had not gone out of the universe. But now, little by little – and what was surprising to him, not even painfully – he was coming to realize that talk would do no good; no good at all. That any explanation Katrina might try to give would really be superfluous. That what he had once thought possible was, in reality, impossible.

Because he now accepted it as impossible, he did not go back to see Reverend McLain. Why should he?

Sometimes he would see the chaplain in the hallway, smiling. He would smile back – with oh, how knowing a smile. But neither one, beyond exchanging greetings or some impersonal comment about University matters, said anything. Certainly not about Katrina. It was sort of a gentleman's agreement.

At first he avoided Henry Stern, the biology professor. If ever Harris saw Stern coming down a corridor or down a walk, he would change his path and go another way. But gradually he began to exchange greetings with him; and one day, when the occasion arose, he even inquired about Helen and the children.

Little by little, uncertainly, obscurely, the numbness in his body began to disappear. He was hardly aware of the change, it came about so gradually. The faint beat of a heart. Then he could feel blood coursing through his arteries, then warmth coming back into his body.

He still, for days and days, could not imagine living without Katrina, as a very small child simply cannot imagine living without his mother or father.

Yet, as other days went by – though it still seemed impossible that he could live without her – he now began to feel, even to know, that it was possible. First only as a thought. Then as a feeling. And finally as a reality.

He was, after all, still a father to his children. . . . (He would answer their correspondence). . . . He would deliver his paper at the annual conference of the Organization of American Historians and then start on a new book. . . . He had at least a handful of bright undergraduates who responded every now and then to his teaching, and three or four graduate students with refreshingly exuberant passions for history. . . . The others – though not as bright, nor so responsive, nor even appreciative – still needed him, or someone, or something. . . .

And there was more than autumn. There was spring and summer and winter. There was spring and summer and autumn and winter. Spring and summer, autumn and winter.

THE ARTIST

Red and yellow streaks: Vulcan's tongue lifts up
and licks the sky . . .

– Peter Augustus Fairfield
Born Sheffield, England August 12, 1842

Peter Fairfield: Big, robust, always moving, like restless rock; large eyes straining in their sockets; veins dilated and hot, setting fire to the face.

When he built his house in Piedmont, Pennsylvania, he built it like himself, a massive structure of imported red granite he chose over the protests of wife and architect, so that it not only loomed large in the eye but burned itself into the mind. Once you saw it you never forgot it, though Peter Fairfield hadn't built it for show. His was a particular kind of a dream – of many children living in the big red house, racing along the corridors, running up and down the long stairways, laughing, taunting, shouting; of expanding his interests beyond Piedmont into a conglomerate of different kinds of enterprises, one child for each enterprise, one enterprise for each child, hopefully, for as he remarked to his wife, "All anyone can give his children is a foundation to build on – and some kind of a choice. It's too much to expect that any of them will be exactly like you or me."

Diana Rene Fairfield
Born Piedmont, Pennsylvania March 24, 1872

Me! Look at me in the mirror! I am four years old. I have green eyes, red hair, and freckles on my nose. I look pretty in a white dress with a big bow. Papa and Mother love me very much. More than anything in the world, Papa says.

Don't, child, don't! Why, Mattie? *Because you'll come to love your-self too much.* Is it wrong to love me? *I said, too much.* Why? *God doesn't like it. He's a jealous God.* How do you know? *I just do.* Does God ever look at Himself in the mirror? *Heaven's no: He's a spirit.* Then I can do something He can't do, yah, yah! *Diana, you stop that! Someday your face is going to stay that way.*

"You've got to spank her," Mrs. Fairfield said. "She's been going up to the fourth floor, where I've forbidden her to go. And today she spit at Mattie."

"Can't you punish her?" her husband asked.

"I've tried to, but it's done no good. This afternoon, after Mattie told me what she did, I locked her in her room and ordered her to stay there the rest of the day. A few minutes later we heard a loud crash, like the splintering of glass. My heart stopped, and I couldn't have opened the door if Mattie hadn't done it for me. And what do you think we saw?" Her hand to her head. "One of the windows smashed with a stool, and Diana trying to climb out through the grill. It was terrible. The glass could have cut her to pieces. You must give her a spanking she'll never forget."

Peter Fairfield called his daughter. She came running up the stairs, two steps at a time, leg muscles straining: firm, well-formed legs that running and jumping would some day (he could see them now) make long and lithe and beautiful. She came up to him, pink and breathless.

"Why did you spit at Mattie?" he asked.

"Because she was trying to turn me into a witch."

"Without your doing anything?"

"Not really."

"Not really?"

"I was only making faces at myself in the mirror."

"At yourself?"

"Yes. I wasn't hurting anybody."

"You were hurting Mattie when you spit at her. And you broke the window in your room."

Diana hung her head.

Her father gave her a spanking that stung like fire. But later that evening Peter Fairfield said to his wife, "I don't know that I did right in spanking her so hard."

"We've got to discipline her, Peter. She's getting more spoiled all the time."

"She may be a little spoiled, but not much. It's spunk she's got. And she's lonely. She needs someone to make faces at; even to spit at sometimes. She needs brothers and sisters."

Beatrice Fairfield was silent, her lips drawn and tight. This was the way it always was, when he brought the subject up. She turned her head to the side, away from him.

"I said she needs brothers and sisters." This time in a louder voice.

"Please don't shout. I heard you."

"I'm not sure you did."

"Peter – please, let's not go into it again. You know how much I love Diana; how much I'd love to have others. We will – in time."

"In time!" he mocked. "How much time?"

"How do I know?" his wife said, beginning to tremble. "I wish I did. You don't know how I wish it! But I still haven't recovered my strength yet; from her."

"It's been almost five years now," he said. "We don't have that much time. Listen: I've talked to the doctors. And there's no reason why we can't have others – if we're careful."

She started to cry.

This time, he didn't sit down beside her, didn't put his arm around her reassuringly. He stood rigid; the arteries in his forehead throbbing, his eyes bulging and red as hot coals.

Automatically, without looking, she reached into a bureau drawer and groped in it until she brought forth a handkerchief. A dainty white one, into which she continued to pour her tears. His eyes only burned all the more: she was always reaching for handkerchiefs, little, flimsy, embroidered ones, always dabbing at her eyes or her nose with them – or clutching them in her hands, crumpling them. The dresser tops, the tables, the beds were forever littered with crumpled handkerchiefs!

He would have spit out his fury at her, if she had been a man. . . . A seed to grow and multiply needs the right kind of soil; an arm to become strong must commit itself to something; even a bird, to fly, must have solid air under it. But what could he do with her? Poor, pitiful creature. Sitting there hunched up to about half her normal size, her sobs subsiding into short gasps, like a small, sick rabbit.

He went into his own room. And all that night he paced the floor, grinding his teeth, swallowing his anguish, silently grieving over those who would never be; who, in his mind, were the same as murdered! . . .

Beatrice Stewart Fairfield
Born Montgomery, Ala. June 5, 1850
Died Piedmont, Penn. July 23, 1888
Requiestat in Pace

A sickly woman, pale and frail – that is the way Beatrice Fairfield had always seemed to her daughter Diana. But Diana preferred to think of her mother as she looked in the daguerreotype on her dresser, an exceedingly beautiful young lady with golden curls, petite, exquisite, flawlessly feminine; as Beatrice must have looked when Peter Fairfield first met her, when he fell in love with her at first sight and proposed to her within a week. Was Diana, the daughter, as beautiful as that? In her mind she saw herself now beside her mother. Taller by two or three inches, slender rather than petite; her hair straight but long, flowing down behind her like a glimmering waterfall. . . . Had Edward Kent fallen in love with her at first sight? It was two weeks since they had met. But Edward Kent was different than her father, shyer. . . . So proper. Not even deigning to hold her hand. Yet a special kind of light and alertness in his eyes when he looked at her, a special tenderness when he held her coat for her. . . .

When the last guests had left, and the servants were still cleaning up, she suggested that they take a stroll across the grounds of the estate. A large, gleaming ball had appeared high in the sky, casting a warm light over everything; there were dim, ghostly shadows on the ground and the air was perfumed with the scent of spring roses. They walked beneath a row of tall, cascading elms; talking in low tones; he for the first time of his ambitions and dreams, of his desire to make the best use of his education, to be somebody; not to become famous or to make a lot of money but to be someone of substance and authority. "Like your father is, in the business world. "

"That's a great compliment," she said. "But how about your own father? He's a man of substance and authority too. Don't you want to be like him?"

"A minister? I don't know. My father would like it. He wants me to go on to theological school. It's a worthy, satisfying life, I suppose. But so restricted. So many things you are not to do because you're a minister. I really can't see myself as a minister. Can you?"

Diana laughed. "No, I really can't."

"Of course, although I admire your father, I can't see myself in the business world either – so driven, as men have to be in the world of commerce. Can you see me as a man of commerce?"

Diana laughed again. "No, I can't see you as that either. You're too sensitive."

He reached over, as they walked, and took her hand. Her heart raced.

"I can't go on being a tutor much longer," he said. "I've got to make some big decisions. Soon."

"It's difficult, I know," she returned. "If I were a man I really don't know what I'd choose. Life is so dull these days compared to, say, the days of Richard the Lion-Hearted or Napoleon. When men wore clothes with color in them. When they rode horses with spirit and charged across continents – swords gleaming, pennants flying."

"Oh, I don't know," he said. "It sounds so much more exciting, looking back, then it was probably. Don't forget men were more brutal in those days too. . . . Yet you may be right. Mediocre minds; drab clothes! And the great men of today, as Nietzsche says, make clothespins and hosiery. No, I could never be a businessman or a manufacturer. . . . Your father, of course, is different. A most exceptional man. And he manufactures steel! If I had to manufacture something, it'd be steel too."

"He manufactures hosiery as well – in one of his plants, somewhere."

"I didn't know that."

"The people of this town don't really have any idea of all he does."

Their hands had become warm, moist. Then Diana could feel his grow cold again, as if his heart had stopped beating. He dropped her hand and put his arms around her. His body pressed firmly against her breasts like no man had ever held her before.

They were standing at the edge of the tennis courts. Behind them loomed the big red house, lit up like a huge fairy castle. Here, there, the lights in the windows blinked and went out.

Little things, the way she parted her hair, assumed great importance. Food tasted better. She became more solicitous about the servants and their problems. Her father got an extra hug in the evenings. Peter Fairfield was not one to overlook such things. But he said nothing, and finally, at the dinner table one evening, Diana brought up the subject herself.

"Papa, what do you think of Edward Kent?"

He put down his fork. "What do *you* think of him?"

She blushed. "Your opinion means a lot to me."

"Not as much as yours."

"All right, if you want to know, I think he's very intelligent and kind."

"Admirable qualities."

"Is that all you've got to say?" A sudden chill in her voice.

"I don't know much about him. I only hope he's not a ninny like his father."

"Papa! How can you say something like that about Reverend Kent! I'm surprised at you. What do you mean – a ninny?"

"The way he comes asking for money for the church. Hat in hand, as if he were apologizing for living. Either he believes in the church, or he doesn't. If he does, he oughtn't to apologize for it."

"Well, it isn't easy." Lips quivering. "Money's an embarrassing subject."

"Not for me," he said. "St. Paul did a great disservice to humanity when he talked about money as if it were a curse. Actually, it's one of mankind's greatest inventions. What makes the whole modern world possible. If I didn't talk about money, want it, borrow it, make it, I couldn't make anything. Nor could anyone else. No sir, I don't apologize for living."

"It's not the same. You give people something for their money. He has to ask for it; beg for it; giving nothing in return."

"Giving nothing in return? You think he believes that?"

"I don't want to talk about it any more," she snapped. "I'm sorry I brought the subject up." Tears were in her eyes. Pushing her plate from her, she raised her napkin to her lips, held it there for a moment, brushing her lips, then set it back on the table.

He was glad she hadn't raised the napkin to her eyes. She had Beatrice's soft green eyes, and sometimes when he looked at her he flinched. But she had his bones, his jaw. She hadn't raised the napkin to her eyes; he was glad.

He got up, walked over to his daughter and put his arm around her. "Please forgive me, Diana. I was talking about the father, not the son. I really don't know Edward. It's your opinion that counts – and I trust your judgment. Only never, never apologize for yourself – if you think what you're doing is right for you. No matter what it is."

"Thank you," she said. Her father had an arm like Samson. Reassuring. Yet he didn't fully understand: she determined that if Edward Kent asked her to marry him, to flee with him to some distant part of the world where they could live as they wanted to, she would do so.

But Edward Kent, though he kept coming to visit her several times a week, never once suggested that they marry or flee together to some distant part of the world. Not even remotely. He was always affectionate and tender; yet he seemed detached whenever she tried to bring their conversation down to immediate, practical matters. Like what he would do if he gave up tutoring.

"If you want to be a tutor for the rest of your life, that's fine," she said. "I've had some wonderful tutors! Tutors who widened my eyes and sharpened my mind – through history, art, music, philosophy, literature. So if you want to do that for the rest of your life, don't apologize for it! Just be a good one! The best you can be!"

"Now, Diana, that's not fair! How many times have I told you that I don't want to be some mousy, ill-paid tutor for the rest of my life. But it's not easy for someone, like that" – snapping his fingers – "to change the whole course of his life. Someone, furthermore, with no means."

"I grant you that," she declared. "But sooner or later one has to choose, to decide what one wants. You'll never find the means to get there if you don't know where you want to go. My father started out with very little."

Such talk flustered Edward Kent, made him ill at ease and peevish. He tried to change the subject, "Interestingly, something reminded me of 'Candide' today. . . ."

But she didn't want to talk about Voltaire, or de Tocqueville, or Nietzsche; she wanted to talk about Edward Kent. She would tell him bluntly that it would be better if they didn't see each other anymore. The thought had come to her the previous day. She had quickly repressed it, hoping that, like a nightmare, it would never reappear. Now she blurted it out, as water breaks through the mightiest dam when it has built up enough pressure.

"Why, why . . . " he stammered.

On Diana's twenty-fifth birthday her father bought her a handsome blue silk dress. Imported from France. Soft and lustrous, as if it were reflecting sunlight. She kissed him, thanked him, but demurred at his suggestion that she try on the dress at once. "I want to see how pretty you look in it." "After dinner," she begged. And at the dinner table, while he joked about this and that and toasted her with a glass of sparkling Moselle, she sat slumped and taciturn.

As they rose from the table, he took her hands. "What's the matter, honey? Why so sad – on such a special day as this?"

"Papa, I've got to do something!"

"Do something? I don't understand."

"I've been idle long enough."

"Idle? You're not idle. You're the mistress of my home; you spend hours each week in charity work; and you're the most eligible woman in Piedmont."

"That's not enough. I want to do something more. Like you're doing."

He roared. "I'll make you my vice president."

"I'm serious. I'd appreciate it if you'd take me seriously."

"I am taking you seriously. But you're a woman. . . ."

"Yes, I am a woman," she exclaimed, eyes dilating. "A woman! That's why I've got to do something more."

"Listen, Diana," he said, "nature didn't mean women to dig coal or run factories. But that doesn't mean they aren't important. All the things that men do, everything they build or accumulate, is for their women. Their women – and the families these women bring into the world. Someday this whole house is going to be yours. And you'll have children, lots of them, chasing each other down the corridors, running up and down the stairways, laughing, taunting, shouting. And if you have six, seven, eight, nine or even ten children, I'll have an enterprise for each of them. Two or three enterprises. . . .So you see, though it's men who spin the world, who do all the hard work, it's really women that the world revolves around."

She forced a laugh. "Papa, we're not living in the sixteenth century; and I'm neither a princess nor an axle!"

"You'll know what I mean; someday. When you have a family of your own."

Another forced laugh. "Papa, spinsters don't produce families."

"Oh ho, so that's it!" This time the father laughed – his leonine roar. "Now we're getting to the bottom of things. I knew it all along. Your trouble is, you're lonely. I know it, because I know what it is to be lonely myself. But don't worry, my dear. You'll have a husband, all right. When the right man comes along. Someone who's not a ninny or a jellyfish. And you'll have a family. A big family. I know, because I know you. That's what you really want; and that's what I want for you too. More than anything else in the world."

"And what do I do, in the meantime? While I'm waiting for this 'real man' to come along?"

He stroked his chin; rubbing his fingers back and forth across the cleft that divided it. That's what he always did when he was trying to solve a very hard, complex problem.

"Paint!" he replied.

"Paint?"

He nodded. "Yes, paint. You're a good painter, an excellent one. And yet you haven't painted in months. . . ."

"And what shall I paint that I haven't already?" She was looking out of the window. "I've painted everything that my eyes have ever seen; inside this house and out. People, dogs, cats, horses, trees, landscapes, clouds – even my old dolls."

He stroked his chin again, looking now hard into her wistful green eyes which reminded him so much of his wife, startled to find his own image reflected there; looking now above them to the russet stream which flowed backward across her head and then downward in a great sweep. "There's one thing you haven't painted yet. The most lovely, wonderful thing I can think of."

"What's that?"

"If I tell you what it is, will you paint it for me?"

She hesitated. "I'm tired of painting, Papa. But all right – if you wish it. What is it?"

"Yourself!"

"I . . . me?"

"Yes, you! Paint me a portrait of yourself. Not glum, as you look now. But as you look when you're the prettiest – smiling. A big picture. One I can hang in my office where everybody can see it. A remembrance of your birthday; one I'll never forget!"

The easel was set up in her bedroom in front of a full-length mirror where artist and subject could confront each other. It was not, as she anticipated, an easy or happy confrontation. For except to fix her hair or to powder her nose she did not like to spend time looking in the mirror. And women who dallied in front of mirrors, preening themselves like birds, admiring themselves, disgusted her.

Now, to please her father, she had to do it. Looking in the mirror, she tilted her head to one side, like a cockatoo, and smiled. How silly! Ridiculous! Repulsive! Smiling so artificially and falsely. Now, without smiling, she examined herself in the mirror. Hair; nose; chin; finally daring to look into her own eyes. How sad they looked. They were the real mirror, not the silvered glass into which she was staring. Why should she be so sad? Was life so terrible that she couldn't even smile from the heart? *Smile, Diana, smile!* But instead of smiling, she stuck out her tongue and made a face at herself. *Don't, Diana, don't: Your face will stay that way.* How funny! And how funny she looked, sticking out her tongue at herself. Now she smiled, and this time from the heart.

But when she picked up a pencil to sketch the outlines of her face from the image in the mirror, the smile vanished. It was unsettling, looking at herself so intensely. She put down the pencil. And turned away from the mirror. Immediately she felt better. But every time she looked back and picked up her pencil she would have that same uneasy, queasy feeling all over again.

Finally, in desperation, she moved the canvas away from the glass. Her hands came back to life. She could paint. She painted with abandon, using broad, vigorous strokes. She painted all that afternoon and late into the night. The only break for a cup of coffee that old Mattie brought up to her. No longer sad, but exuberant; more exuberant than she had felt in years. When she finished the portrait at midnight, she was exhausted but happy.

"But it's not you," admonished her father. "Maybe I just don't understand about art, but to me it's not you. I want something I can point to and say, that's my daughter; exactly as she looks, down to the finest hair. So will you try once more – for me! I know you can do it. And it'll please me no end. But this time, set yourself up a mirror and look into it, and keep looking into it, until you finish. Honey, paint yourself as you really are; truthfully, without false modesty; beautiful and fresh as a May flower."

She promised to try, promising nothing further. For her father she would try, even if it made her ill.

A clean canvas was brought in front of the mirror. This time there would be no dissembling; no making of faces either. Only an honest examination of the subject by the artist, insofar as it was within her to be honest, and to judge. Again she looked into the mirror. Was she really as beautiful as her father believed? Or pretended to believe; since she was sure that her father, as much as he loved her, would never believe anyone the equal of her mother. Perhaps rightly so. Examine the evidence. Features: Neither grotesque nor distorted. So why not pleasing? Too, she had the fair skin, the kind that elegant women are supposed to have, with only a slight trace of her old red freckles. And hair that was as dazzling as a sunset. Pleasing too? Why not? Of course, beauty is in the eye of the observer; yet not only there; and if in her father's eye, and in her own eye, honestly, why not in the eyes of others? She turned her head slowly, from left to right, from right to left, to observe her features at different angles, watching the highlights in her hair sparkle and jump, as in a moving crystal. She fluffed her hair, which was as pleasant to touch as to look at.

It took her four canvases. But this time the woman in the painting was an almost exact reproduction of the one in the mirror. A slight trace of wistfulness, yes, but not much: Hidden behind the smile, her father would never find it.

He hung the portrait in his office in Piedmont and each night, for weeks, reported on the reactions of people who saw it for the first time. "It's right behind my desk, so they can't help seeing it when they come in. And after the introduction they're lost. I know it, because I watch them: All the time I'm talking, their eyes keep coming back to you. It makes me feel very proud, and it ought to make you happy too; it's a great gift to be beautiful. . . . One of these days the right man is going to come along. . . . Only today someone from American Steel – an old business acquaintance – came in and before he'd discuss anything he wanted to know who the goddess was. 'Somebody as homely as you couldn't have a daughter like that.' I told him you got your looks from your mother, and if he thought the girl in the painting was a vision, he should see the original. I would have brought him home to see the original, too, except he's too old for you – and has half a dozen children of his own. . . ."

"Mr. Phillips, my daughter Diana."

Mr. Phillips, tall, well-built, coal-black hair, square face. "Yes, definitely, I think we're in for a period of prosperity, and our company is preparing for it." "Red, please; I like a robust wine." "Red hair too. I've never seen any like yours, Miss Fairfield." "You're right, Mr. Fairfield, absolutely right" – but eyes, dark eyes, upon the daughter, gleaming. Her eyes, trying to be natural and casual, involuntarily upon him too. Peter Fairfield retired early, leaving the two to entertain each other.

She listened to him talk for two more hours.

Sorry. Heartbroken. Not for him. For herself. Selfishly, she thought. She felt mean and small for being so selfish.

Peter Fairfield was sorry too. But no use fretting about it. There would be others. Lots of others. In the meantime, "there's only one answer for loneliness of the heart. Work. The kind you're so good at. In fact, I want to put in an order right this minute. Another portrait. Exactly like the other one. For my office in Philadelphia. To be delivered to me on your next birthday. Will you do it for me – please?"

She really had no heart for another. If she had not already given her father the first one, she would have destroyed it. Yet she knew her father really wanted another, that he wasn't playing tag with her. His escutcheon, his flower. She would do it for him.

This time without a mirror, though. She knew every line, every tint. She had Jeremy bring her easel up to the fourth floor and set it up by the window, where she could look out as she painted, where she could be completely private without old Mattie or the other servants looking over her shoulder. The fourth floor, which had so many memories for her – the four floors of the big red house being too much for her mother but not too much for Diana the daughter of the moon, the whole mansion her playhouse, at least one doll and one secret in every room, loving the upper two floors the best because no one except herself ever went up there and she could stand at the grilled window and spit, hoping the magic moisture would land on somebody's head down below . . . or look far off across the roofs of Piedmont to the dark green forests beyond. . . .

It became something of a ritual; every year. As her birthday approached, Peter Fairfield would ask Diana for a portrait of herself for one of his offices – Harrisburg, Washington, Boston; and every year she complied. From time to time he would bring home a young man who like Paul Phillips had been so taken with the painting that he would insist upon seeing the original. Each time there would be the excitement, the anticipation, the dashing around to get things ready, set her hair, do her nails, hoping and praying that this one would be different, would be the one. Each time the inevitable letdown.

To console herself she took trips. To California, Paris, London; to Florence where she spent most of her time visiting the art galleries. Once, depressed, she moved out of the big red house and took up residence in New York, occupying a suite overlooking Central Park South in The Plaza, then a brand-new hotel on Fifth Avenue. It was against her father's wishes but he knew better than to forbid it. "If I had locked the door," he told friends, "she would have flown through one of the windows. And if I had locked the windows she would have climbed out through the chimney. So let her go. She'll be back." He was right. Within six months. "What can an unbetrothed woman do in New York, other than join some women's guild or choral group? Learn shorthand and become a secretary? Sew in a sweatshop? If I had needed the money I'd have become a secretary or a seamstress. But unfortunately I didn't. Money *is* a curse."

Was something wrong with her? There must be. At the dinner table one evening she confessed her misgivings to her father. "I'm glad you brought it up," he said, "because it's something I've been worrying about myself. There's nothing wrong with you, count the number of men you've enchanted. But I do think you're looking for something that doesn't exist. You've read too many romantic novels."

"One can't force one's self to fall in love."

"No, but falling in love isn't all that mysterious. Maybe it is when you're very young; not so much as you grow older. Now every one of these young men I brought home I screened myself. Every one was a real man: character, brains, ambition. Else I wouldn't have brought him home for my own daughter. Can you tell me what more a woman could want?"

Diana could only shake her head sadly. "I don't know. Except none of them was what I wanted."

"Diana," her father said, "you know I want the very best for you. But sooner or later you're going to have to face some facts of life. When we can't have what we want, sometimes we have to want what we have. What's been offered to you has been something very good – in my opinion; so one of these days you're going to have to want what's been offered; or do without. Most other women, if you ask me, would have given their eye teeth for one of these men."

"Did you marry Mother because you loved her – or because you made yourself want her?"

"I thought I loved her very much. But I was young. And it was prob-ably a mistake – marrying when I was so impassioned. As it turned out, she wasn't really my kind. . . . I'm sorry to have to tell you this, Diana, but it's the truth, and you're old enough to know it. You ought to know it, so you don't make the same mistake."

Diana lowered her head, eyes blurring. Then the blur cleared and her eyes became dark – darker; dark almost to the point of blackness.

As her thirty-fifth birthday approached, her father did not make his usual plea for a painting. Puzzled, she couldn't tell whether the matter had slipped his mind – or perhaps he had changed his mind. She assumed the first, since she could not imagine the latter; she painted the portrait as usual. As always he seemed delighted with it, but left it on the easel; and a few days later said to her, "Diana, my dear, I already have one of your paintings in each of my main offices; so why don't we hang this one up in the house. We don't have a single one of you here in the house, and we ought to. What do you say?"

She stood shocked, speechless. She had anticipated it, felt it, feared it, as a bird anticipates and trembles at the approach of winter, yet could not believe it, now that her father was saying it. How could he!

She hung the painting in a room on the third floor, where no one ever came. He never asked her for another.

Peter Augustus Fairfield
Born Sheffield, England August 12, 1842
Died Piedmont, Penn. December 2, 1911
Requiestat in Pace

Diana Rene Fairfield
Born Piedmont, Penn. March 24, 1872
Died Piedmont, Penn. May 12, 1948
May She Rest in Peace

Her two servants and her gardener were in the kitchen having a cup of tea when the attorney, Mr. Van Clyde, arrived. Mr. Van Clyde read them the will in which, as he put it, "all three of you are well taken care of," though the great bulk of the estate, including the big red house, had been left to the Fairfield Trust for Charities. "I'll have to ask you not to take anything off the property until we've made an inventory."

"We haven't touched a thing," the housekeeper said. "Everything is just as it was when Miss Fairfield went to the hospital."

"Good. Now, if you please, would you give me a tour of the house."

They went from room to room, Mr. Van Clyde jotting down notes on a pad. On the second floor, in Diana Fairfield's bedroom, he picked up a copy of a book that was lying open on the dresser. He paged through it. Nearly every page had comments written in the margin in a fine, even hand.

"She was reading that the morning she was taken ill," the house-keeper said. "I know, I took it from her hands and laid it on the dresser."

"A rather strange book for an elderly person, a gentlewoman, to be reading," Mr. Van Clyde mused. "*Beyond Good and Evil?* Odd, really. I thought the comments in the margin might be of a personal nature. But they're about the book."

"She did a lot of reading," the housekeeper said. "You saw the book-shelves on the first and second floors. But she used to like to take her books up with her to the fourth floor, where she could read by a window and look out across the town and the countryside. You can see ten miles or more from up there." The housekeeper gave Mr. Van Clyde a quizzical look. "Miss Fairfield was a most remarkable woman. Not like anybody I've ever known."

"She must have been, indeed. Now could we see the rest of the house?"

The housekeeper led the way up the staircase to the third floor. In the middle the steps were white and worn.

They entered a long hallway, with doors to the right and left, all closed. The housekeeper opened the nearest one and groped in the dark for a light switch. When the light went on she stepped aside to give Mr. Van Clyde room. He blinked.

It could have been a library or parlor, except there were no books or tables or furnishings of any kind; not even drapes. Only yellow shades, pulled down.

"I'll be damned!" Mr. Van Clyde exclaimed, looking around the room. "Please excuse me . . . but I really don't know what else to say."

"I told you," the housekeeper said. "No matter where you stand or look, she's looking back at you."

Indeed she was. Dozens of eyes, returning Mr. Van Clyde's stare, from all four walls of the cavernous room. The determined green eyes of a young woman, beautiful and fresh, with a bountiful and curving bust, flaming hair, a wisp of a smile.

"For a moment, I thought I was in a hall of mirrors," Mr. Van Clyde said, circumambulating the room, examining the portraits more closely. At first glance they had seemed identical. But as he looked more carefully, he noticed slight, subtle differences. In some of them the young lady appeared somewhat younger, in others somewhat older, yet none revealed a woman beyond her early thirties.

"Unbelievable," the attorney repeated. "Absolutely unbelievable."

"She painted very well, don't you think?" the housekeeper said. "She did all of them."

"All of them?"

"Yes; and there are others. Come, I'll show you."

She showed him, in every room of the third floor, large and small, a repetition of the same spectacle, the same comely, staring, smiling face emerging out of almost identical portraits covering every foot of every wall. And the same with the rooms of the fourth floor, none of which had any furnishings or decorations beyond the dozens of similar portraits covering the walls.

The paintings were all signed "D.F." – and dated. Mr. Van Clyde read off the dates as he passed by the paintings, year after year, like a litany, the years of Diana Fairfield's life, three of the portraits done in the last year of her life, executed as precisely as the others, the subject just as girlish and coquettish, with only that slight touch of wistfulness.

"She was a beautiful woman, don't you think?" the housekeeper asked.

When the inventory was made, the appraisers did not give a final count of the paintings of Diana; only listed them as: "Numerous. Similar subject." An art dealer came to look at them. "They're very competently done. A lot of talent. But not even Rembrandt could have done one subject indefinitely. . . . Their only value, in my opinion, is sentimental."

"Sentimental!" the chairman of the board echoed. "Why, of course, we'd like to remember Miss Fairfield and her generosity by keeping one or two of her portraits. But dozens upon dozens! We'd have to build a museum."

Eventually the big red house was sold to a company that planned to convert it into a sanatorium. The officers of the company asked that the contents be removed as soon as possible. The directors of the Fairfield Trust felt they had no choice. All but two of the paintings were stacked in a pile well to the rear of the mansion – where the tennis courts used to be but where the earth was now cracked and overgrown with grass and weeds. On top and around were dumped all the other possessions of the original Fairfield family (father, mother, daughter) that had no commercial value: old clothes, bundles of old letters, canopied beds and other furniture that had gone out of style. The plan was to apply a torch and destroy it all in one gargantuan bonfire.

A local minister intervened. "Why not first allow the townspeople onto the property," he asked, "to take whatever they might want or be able to use from the piles, after which the rest can be burned?"

So on a bright, sunny day in November, for the first time since Peter Fairfield had built his big red house, his estate was opened up to the curious public. They came in swarms. The clothes, most made of expensive materials, and furniture disappeared fast, carted off to the last piece. The paintings of Diana Fairfield were picked up and looked at, usually with wonderment, but only four or five were taken, not more.

Early the next morning what was left of the pile was doused with kerosene – "though why I don't know," said Mr. Van Clyde, who was in charge of the operation, "because there's enough oil on those canvasses to burn down the state capitol" – and a torch thrown upon it. Flames shot up and the last earthly possessions of the Fairfields burned, the biggest, most dazzling bonfire Piedmont had ever seen, the tongues of fire reaching almost as high as the top turret of the old red mansion.

Gray ash, light and swirling like snowflakes, rose above the billowing black smoke, and floated away across the town toward the woods beyond.

The *Piedmont Herald*, reporting on the event in a front-page story, quoted one local citizen as saying, "It's too bad the paintings of Miss Fairfield had to be destroyed," but that he had looked at them and passed them up "because if I wanted a painting on my wall I'd hang up a mountain or a meadow or a lake."

LIVE AND LET LIVE

The thing I was after lay at the edge of a stream-bed. It was unmistakable, stretched out full-length on some chalky-white stones – long and black and fat and stub-tailed.

I could feel my heart beating at my chest. I was in the kind of mood that, like flood water, overasserts itself until it finds its own level. Nervously, I began to look for the right kind of rock. Heavy enough to crush the skull. The locus of life. The vulnerable part.

There were plenty of rocks around; the creek bottom next to where the thing was sunning was nearly dry, except for one deep pocket of water. In May, when my family and I had come down from the city to spend our summer in the country, spring rain had filled the gravelly channel. The water moved slowly along, picking up speed where the land dropped away, until it plunged over the boulders with a frothy roar. But now, after a long summer's drought, there was only a trickle, barely enough to keep the stream alive – except for occasional pools.

The pocket of water in front of me was small, though likely the largest for a stretch of several miles. Which is precisely why *it* was here. A snake, too, has to eat.

At the pool's center it could have been four or five feet deep, maybe six; the clear, crystal-green water was deceptive. Within these bounds lived what might be considered a nice mess of fish – bass, catfish, perch, with enough minnows, if the tiny lifeline of water continued to flow, to sustain them until the heavy fall rains.

Within a few minutes, I found what I was looking for – a large gray stone, flat on the top and flat on the bottom, so it would land squarely. Grasping it firmly in my hand, I headed back toward the thing.

As it sensed my approach, it reared up half a foot. Devilish, that forked, sizzling tongue. Taunting me to come closer? Then it tilted its head back and popped its mouth wide open. Who said that black was the color of evil? Oh, yes, the body was black but that wasn't what gave the scene its horror. It was the white of the gaping mouth – the cottonmouth. Looking down that fibrous throat, rendered even more white by contrast with the dark body, I could almost see the milky-white venom dripping out of those white, curved fangs. That venom, injected into a leg, through those fangs, could kill one of our children. Or me or my wife.

I fingered the rock.

But why was my heart thumping so? What was so horrible about smashing a snake's head with a rock? Unlike my wife and children, all city-bred, I'd grown up in the country – snake country. As a boy, I had killed snakes innumerable times, hurling rock after rock until the job was done, with no more feeling than if I were throwing at a tin can. Back in those days, there were "good" snakes and "bad" snakes, just as there were "good" and "bad" people. A king snake was a good snake, primarily because it killed bad snakes. Coachwhips were also good snakes; one lived under our house and was a better mouser than the cat. Grass snakes were good snakes too – good for throwing at girls. The bad, meanwhile, were the pit vipers: rattlesnakes, copperheads, cottonmouth moccasins. And back in those days, everybody – even the kids – would kill a bad snake on sight, just as in the earlier days everybody would join in to hook up a horse-thief. The bad snakes all had fangs with deadly venom in them and unlike humans they didn't make distinctions between good and bad people, or even between animals and people: If you were walking along a well-worn animal trail, hunting for a milk cow, and a rattlesnake was coiled up waiting for a pack-rat to come bouncing by – well, my 10-year-old cousin died from a rattler bite on the calf of her little left leg. And the echo was still there in me, somewhere far down at the base of the brain: *You kill a bad snake on sight.*

I fingered the rock again. No question, I was going to kill this one if I could. Not necessarily with relish, but with a kind of righteous anger (was that the rub?) that I couldn't completely explain to myself if I tried and that might even have had a certain pleasure mixed up with it.

But a snake doesn't deliberate. I had waited too long – and even before I could raise my hand, the cottonmouth was gone. Somewhere into the weeds.

I suppose I should have felt relieved. I didn't. I felt let down, cheated. Still, I wasn't about to plow into the underbrush after the snake. If there is anything that bothers me more than a bad snake, it's a bad snake in the grass. Instead, I trudged the half mile back up the dirt path that led to the house we'd rented for the summer, and I told my wife that I had almost killed a cottonmouth. Almost.

My wife was noncommittal. She didn't like snakes, any kind, bad or good. But even more she didn't like to see anything killed. Still, I knew the big cottonmouth would be back. It was as tied to those glistening fish within the pool of water as they were to the trickle of water coming from springs into the channel. It would be back, as certainly as the sun would rise the next morning. And so would I. The very next morning.

I set my alarm for 5:30.

I set the big, flat rock at the leg of our bed.

It was there, all right. Even in the faint pink of dawn, I could see it coursing slowly through the water like a giant arrow, sending diagonal ripples away from its body. But I wasn't about to enter the pool. No more than I was about to follow it into the weeds. This I know about cottonmouths: they can bite *in* the water, and they can bite *under* the water.

Then, as I was standing there deliberating, the most amazing thing happened. Out of the corner of my eye, on a crescent of land arcing out into the stream-bed, I saw two smaller moccasins slithering toward the water. They could have been the big one's children, or, if the big one was a male – which I certainly couldn't tell, but only hazarded a guess that he was by his size – one could have been his mate and the other his child. Makes no difference, really, except in the light of what followed. No sooner had they entered the water then the big one charged at them, first one and then the other; his mouth gaped open, flashing white.

I was spellbound. I had never seen anything like it in my life.

Facing the wrath of the big cottonmouth, the two smaller snakes then whipped around in the water and fled back onto the rocky shore where – sensing the danger over, I suppose – they stretched themselves out and began basking in the rising sun.

But that didn't suit the big one either. Shooting out of the water onto the shore himself, he approached the smaller snakes and again raised his head up and popped his fanged mouth wide open, this time also feinting lunges at them, as if to say: "This is only a warning. This is my territory! . . ." Well, they didn't like that at all, who was he to order them off? – and so, rearing up themselves, they popped open their own mouths and lunged back at him – flashing white – and for a few moments it looked as if I was going to witness the damndest cottonmouth tangle anybody could imagine.

The two smaller ones, if they had understood teamwork, could probably have won. But apparently that's not how it works in the cottonmouth pecking order: I'd never seen a snake more angry than the big one, and by the sheer ferocity and power of his lunges he let the smaller two know that he wasn't taking any sass. He soon had them intimidated and crawling away.

By this time it was clear even to me that Big Daddy had staked out this pool with all the fish in it and all the frogs around it as his private pantry, and woe to anybody else, big or small, even of his own species, who disputed him! The drought, of course, had made it possible, and perhaps even necessary, looking at it from his point of view.

Though I still had the rock in my hand I had become so absorbed that I had almost forgotten about the weapon. It was only when the big cottonmouth slithered back to the edge of the water and lay there motionless, as if waiting for a big frog to come along that he could grab and swallow, that I remembered what I had come down to the water to do. It was a relatively easy target, stretched out with its stub-tail toward me. I raised my right arm.

No.

The damn thing had won my respect, if not my admiration. And if this were his private preserve, he'd be there again tomorrow, and the next day, and the day after that, performing no telling what extraordinary feats. For the time being, the simple wonder of it that was stirring within me surmounted my other feelings. I walked back home.

My wife said she was glad. "None of us are swimming down there now," she said, "so just let the snake be."

"That's not the way nature operates," I said back, reminding her that I had said my quest was over "for the time being." "If I don't get him eventually, something else will," and I told her about the time I came upon a turtle with a water moccasin in its mouth: The snake was writhing and twisting in a desperate effort to get its fangs into the soft, vulnerable part of the turtle, but it never did. The turtle bit him in two.

I thought my wife would be horrified by the story, but she wasn't. "That may be nature's ways," she said, "but that doesn't have to be a human's ways. Why kill when you don't have to? Just for the sake of killing? Do you find all this fun? Is that what this is to you – fun?"

"Sometimes," I argued, "when there's too much of something, man's got to help nature along. That old-timer who lives over at Horn's Bend told me there's more cottonmouths now than there ever was. He says everybody's 'citified' and nobody's killing the bad snakes anymore."

"Oh, how does that old man know if there's more snakes," my wife said over her shoulder as she left the living room for the kitchen. "You think he counted them?" Her voice was faint now, separated by a wall, but I could still hear her. "Remember how Mr. Thorndike used to swear a hundred times over that there were more deer way back when," she was saying, "and then we read that story in the paper where the Fish and Wildlife man said just the opposite. I don't know, but I wouldn't put too much count in one old man's memories."

She had a point. In fact, I began to remember certain people in my younger days who didn't kill snakes, even bad ones, on sight. There weren't many such people. Only a few. They were the exceptions. But there were some: men and women who lived so close to nature, among dogs and cats and horses and cows and owls and coons and bees and snakes, that they had acquired almost the senses and instincts of animals. If a single chicken was missing from their yard, they knew it at once, and whether a hawk or a coon had gotten it. In the mornings and evenings they never walked the animal trails where rattlesnakes were apt to be coiled and waiting. Even at night they walked through the wild grasses and weeds, knowing that snakes, at the sound of an approaching human, are likely to follow their instincts with regard to something larger and more powerful – that is, to keep moving. An old cowboy on our ranch, named Pablo Cruz, was one such person. On Saturday nights, because Pablo disdained bathtubs, he would walk half a mile through rattlesnake-infested grass and weeds to bathe in the stock tank. Never once was he bitten. What's more, the stock tank at night was usually chock-full of cottonmouths, but this didn't bother the old cowboy, not at all, he would have thought something was wrong with the water if it didn't have moccasins in it. He'd simply take off his shirt, swish it in the water several times to let the snakes know they better get over to the other side of the tank, then he'd sit down in the muddy water among the cow turds and enjoy himself infinitely more than if he were in a suite at the Waldorf-Astoria. . . .

Pablo did kill snakes, but only if and when they were an actual threat to him. My wife had a point. . . .

And yet the more I pondered it, the more I could see it wasn't all that simple. When I was a boy, we killed every bad snake on sight because we assumed they were all a threat: The one you killed might be the very one that would get you later, if you didn't get it first. Would the Big One make exceptions, or distinctions?

Tomorrow I'd do it! One more, one less, it does make a difference.

My wife was sweeping the porch. I asked her to come with me. "Sooner or later, you're going to have to get over your squeamishness."

She gave me a look. "*My* squeamishness?"

"Just come with me."

"If I thought there was really a reason for killing the thing," she said, "I'd go down there. But I don't."

"You want it to bite one of the children?"

"The children aren't going down there anymore. So you're the only one it could bite. I think you're asking for it, if you want my opinion."

Touché.

And so I puttered around the yard, digging up around the marigolds, looking for a rattlesnake under every plant. The children did play in the yard, and if there was a rattler in the yard, there was certainly a possibility it might bite them. Let her deny that!

After awhile, in the warm sun, the good earth crumbling between my fingers, I began to relax. It had been that way at the beginning of the summer. First, a kind of apprehension at the thought of living for three months with three relatively small children in the midst of poisonous snakes. ("Now, remember," I told them over and over again, because being kids, and city kids at that, I knew they'd forget it, "don't put your hands where you can't see. Stay away from the bushes. Swing a stick in front of you if you go out walking in the fields.") Then the panic at the boy's discovery of a rattler – two inches thick – coiled in the grass under a swing that hung from an oak limb right in front of the house, where the kids often played. For several days neither my wife nor I would let the children out of our sight. But, as nothing happened, as nobody got bitten, as the family became accustomed to the sight of snakes, as we fell into the easy rhythms of cool mornings and nights and soft breezes and green trees and tall native grasses swaying with the wind, all of us began to relax. . . . And after two months, and reading a dozen books on the life and habits of mockingbirds and bobwhites and armadillos and rattlers, we all began to feel a part of it. . . . The strangeness, the alienness, began to disappear. . . .

Still, as this particular day wore on, I began to brood, avoiding my wife by lying in the hammock and pretending to read. The house, an old rock one with big rooms and two fireplaces, sat on a rise overlooking half a mile of grasses and trees, the eye eventually stopping at a high limestone cliff at the base of which the stream ran. Lying in the hammock, eyes half-closed, lulled by breezes which came up a draw from the southeast, free from the customary pressures of work and social obligations, I could easily imagine how Adam and Eve must have felt living in the primeval Garden of Eden supposedly at peace with all creation. But weren't there serpents even then plotting to destroy their peace and joy and freedom? . . .

All a myth, my wife would say; particularly that part about the apple and God's condemning the serpent for his craftiness to crawl on his belly forever. Where's the good or evil in nature? Is the rattlesnake any more evil for eating the rabbit than the rabbit is good when eaten by humans (particularly as hasenpfeffer)? Are not good and evil simple human terms by which we separate that which supports us from that which threatens? Yes, a rattler is dangerous if you step on it: But so are we! I thought of that early American flag: the one with the coiled snake and the words "Don't Tread on Me." My wife could have designed that flag.

But then, while I was lying in the hammock, having these secret thoughts, the front door of the house squeaked open and out came my wife, holding in her hand a tall highball glass. She began to move in my direction. Ah. Nothing I like better on a hot summer afternoon than a gin and tonic with a lime slice in it, smeared around the rim of the glass. . . .

Though didn't she know that the juice of that tree was reserved for the Gods?

"Thank you very much," I said.

"What are you reading?" she asked.

"The Bible."

"The Bible? Doesn't look like the Bible to me."

I took a sip. Delicious. How good it is! Except for somebody with cirrhosis of the liver. "There's always an exception," I said.

"What are you mumbling about?" she asked.

"Mumbling?"

"I hope it isn't more about that cottonmouth." And she took a handkerchief out of her shorts pocket and wiped the perspiration off her brow. I took another good sip. It was loosening my tongue. "Think about this," I said. "If you splash in the water a cottonmouth generally goes the other way, right? And if you walk through the grass and let a rattlesnake know you're coming, it generally crawls on out of your way, right? But not always; right?"

"Please. I'm going back in the house."

She did go back. But that didn't stop me. I was going to keep on talking, if only to myself. "It's the exceptions that cross you up. With snakes, with human beings, with everything. There's no absolute certainty."

A long sip this time.

In the late afternoon, as the shadows were lengthening, I went down to the pool, armed with my rock. I had wanted to take the boy with me, he was old enough now to know, and being a boy might understand without a lot of explanations. But I decided against it. He really wouldn't understand, and it would be too complicated to explain. He'd think it was just another snake. One more, one less, what difference would it make?

The big fat cottonmouth was there, lying on the rocky bank, undisputed lord of his domain, and at my approach, as usual, he reared up and opened wide his white jaws. . . . Did I say, Undisputed Lord of His Domain? Well, I should have said, Undisputed except for me. Anyway, whatever was happening inside of him (adrenalin to the nervous system, venom squirting into the fangs), the adrenaline was certainly gushing inside of me, for my heart was beating wildly. . . .

Except now I knew why it was! . . .

And there was no way out. I had to take the risk!

I came to within a few feet of the thing, so frightened I could scarcely move, and it, sensing that the issue was no longer make-believe, no longer feinting and lunging and camouflage, but life or death, reared up to almost a third the length of its big body. It had power too!

Poison from those little sacs that sit right at the hinges of the snake's jaws, injected through the curved, hollow fangs into a main artery. . . .

But then . . . having reared up one fraction higher than the complicated laws of gravity permit – that is, one fraction beyond that invisible point where force and counter-force produce stability – it fell forward.

It landed flat, the mouth closed, the head exposed on the sun-bleached sacrificial stone . . .

I hurled the rock – with all the power and fury I could summon.

It landed squarely.

The body twisted and writhed. It rolled over and over on the ground, as if the coils were all in a knot and it was trying to untie itself.

But it was only the reflexes playing themselves out. The vital center, the locus of life, had been destroyed.

With a splash it convoluted into the water.

Immediately, in the crystal-clear liquid, I could see the long, contorted form surrounded by pinkish perch, yellow-bellied bass, whiskered catfish, hundreds of tiny silver-flashing minnows, the entire congregation of the pool, all pressing their noses against the black flesh tipped by the bloody-red head which now was beginning to color the water.

That night I writhed on the bed, and in my nightmare I saw a big fat cottonmouth, an exact duplicate of the one I had killed, pursuing me with its fanged mouth open; it went around and around the house, through one room after another, back into the city, along one street and down another, into my very bed, where I flailed futilely with my arms to ward off those hypodermic teeth. Hadn't I read story after story of how snakes always travel in pairs, like husband and wife, and if one is killed the mate will pursue the murderer forever, around the world if necessary, to avenge its death? Pure myth, I would have said in the daytime. But in the turmoil of troubled sleep, beware! The pursuing cottonmouth became retribution embodied, and I was consumed with guilt, not moral guilt but a kind of metaphysical guilt which kept asking me over and over again: Do you think you are God, to whom only belongs Absolute Knowledge, to whom only belongs the Absolute Power of Life and Death? . . .

No, no, I cried out.

Early the next morning, when the sun was just rising and casting its pink glow across the mirrored surface of the water, I was back, drawn there even in death by the fascination of the power that had once been in that long, black, stub-tailed form. But when I looked down into the water, glazed now by the slanting light of the rising sun, it was no longer that. I mean, no longer a black, full-fleshed form. Not even one with a bloody-red crushed head. All that remained was a long white skeleton – absolutely white; whiter I tell you than any white I have ever seen, with equally white ribs radiating from the spine like the thin, tiny wires of an electronic circuit. And along both sides of the long skeleton huddled dozens of tiny, silver-flecked minnows, their mouths pressed close to the vertebrae as they nibbled the last few remaining morsels of flesh.

How ironic! How just, I was tempted to add, in a nature where there is no good and no evil, where the big fish simply eat the smaller fish, the smaller fish eat the still smaller, and on down the line to the inconsequential tiny minnow which must wait in order to gorge itself on what is by nature beyond it, on the fortuitous exception to the rule....

I shuddered at the sight of the calcified skeleton which only yesterday in the flushed flesh of life had held the power of life and death over those others imprisoned within the encapsulated pool. It was awful. Yet bewitching.

I couldn't resist racing back home to bring my wife and children back down to see it.

And my wife shuddered too, at the horror of it, but had to agree. It was a beautiful thing. The exquisite symmetry of the skeleton and the absolute whiteness of the white, if nothing else.

The boy got a long stick and wanted to fish it out so he could take it back to the city when school started again, and show it to his teacher.

"No!" I exclaimed, with more emotion than I knew I had left. "No, let it be."

Then my girls begged: "C'mon Daddy. Please. It's so pretty."

"No," I said. "It belongs here."

Belongs here, I said.

The next morning when I went down to the pool, still drawn by the vision of that white skeleton, the two smaller cottonmouths that had been driven off (at least, I presume they were the same) were there, stretched out full-length on some flat rocks at the edge of the stream-bed, with all the insouciance of ownership. At the sound of my approach they both reared up and popped opened their mouths, flashing white. . . .

One less, two more.

My God, I whispered to myself, what *is* the Law?

My heart suddenly went back to thump-thumping, thump-bump, thump-bump, so hard against the wall of my chest that I could actually hear it – and it only quietened when I turned around and headed back toward the house, resolved not to go down there again until we return for a weekend visit in autumn, when the rains have refilled the channel and restored the stream to its springtime vigor.

SOME PEOPLE CAN

She had three husbands.

Then came unto Him the Sadducees, which say there is no Resurrection; and they asked Him, saying, Master, a certain woman had seven husbands, all of whom died, and last of all the woman died also. In the Resurrection, therefore, when they shall rise, whose wife shall she be?

Sam and Chester were both cads; Bertha didn't care if she ever saw them again. Solomon she had married more out of loneliness than love. But he was a kindly man and, in this own way, a wise one. He never asked her if she loved him.

And Jesus answering said unto them, Ye know not the Scriptures, neither the power of God. For when they shall rise from the dead they shall be as the angels.

Solomon was ill for almost a year before he died. Bertha nursed him like a mother. Often in the evening, when the weather was right, they would sit together in the backyard and listen to the rustling of the leaves in the tall sycamore. And they would laugh at the big, chesty mockingbird that lived in the tree and thought it belonged to him, screaming like a fishwife at the cat. Sometimes Solomon laughed so hard that tears shook from his eyes and streamed down his cheeks. Bertha wished Solomon would talk more than he did but that was the way he was and when he didn't feel like talking it was better, she had learned, to let him be. It was so peaceful, so soothing, sitting out in the yard in the cool of a summer evening that sooner or later Solomon's head would nod with the leaves and he would fall asleep, to awaken with a start and a smile at the mockingbird's loud, resounding, "Tcack, tcack, tcack, tchair, tchair, tchair."

For when they shall rise from the dead they shall be as the angels.

Once, when she was a little girl playing in the woods near her home, she saw a band of Indians riding down a trail toward her. In her fright she almost swooned. "But they can't be real Indians; they must be from some circus." Hiding behind a tree she watched, entranced, as they rode by. Led by a chief wearing a bright feathered headdress, they moved in single file so closely that the feet of their ponies seemed to belong to one body, like a giant centipede. Their faces were smeared with paint and they carried long lances which nodded with the prancing of their ponies. When they were gone, swallowed up by the brush, Bertha ran breathlessly home to tell her mother. "Circus? There's no circus in town. Child, what's the matter with you?" But she had seen them. She'd ask her teacher; Miss Clifford would know. "That's strange. There was a camp of Indians in those woods once; a long, long time ago."

"Do you believe in things you can't see?" she asked Solomon one evening. They were sitting in the yard looking at the sycamore.

"I don't know."

"Well, look at those leaves. Can you see what's making them sing and dance?"

He was silent for a moment. "Caterpillars," he said finally. "Fiddlefooted caterpillars. There's one kicking up his heels behind every leaf."

"I'm serious," she said.

"I'm serious too," he said, laughing.

Living joyfully with the husband whom thou lovest all the days of the life which He hath given thee under the sun; for that is thy portion in this life.

In August, in the fullness of summer, Solomon died. It wasn't a difficult end. He had had a restless night, then shortly before dawn he fell into a sleep, a deep sleep from which he never awakened. "God of mercy, God of grace, show the brightness of Thy face." Bertha was holding his hand and singing in a low voice as he breathed his last.

Outside, the air was clear. The sycamore stood as still as a tree in a painting, the mockingbird was silent.

Feeling Solomon's hand grow cold in hers, Bertha beckoned the doctor who sat across the room, patiently waiting. He had come about an hour before although he knew that he could do no good. Now he did no more than look at Solomon's blank, graying face.

Bertha's heart swelled up within her until she thought her ribs would snap. But she couldn't cry; the tears were too deep within her. She could only shake her head.

The doctor patted her gently on the shoulder and went into the next room where her sister Ida and Solomon's friend Albert were waiting.

They, too, had come that morning at Bertha's call. Receiving the news silently, they waited for a few minutes before going into the bedroom.

The doctor stood behind them. "I'll be going now," he said, clearing his throat. "I'm very sorry about Solomon."

When the doctor had gone, Ida said to Bertha, "We're going to stay. We don't think you should be alone."

"I'm not alone," Bertha replied.

"I know," said Ida. "But Solomon's dead, Bertha. Do you want me to call the funeral home?"

Bertha didn't answer. The last time she had talked to Solomon was shortly before midnight, when he had asked her for a drink of water.

Jesus answereth, If any man walk in the day he stumbleth not, because he seeth the light of this world. But if a man walk in the night, he stumbleth, because there is no light in him. These things said He: and after that He saith unto them, Our friend Lazarus sleepeth; but I go, that I may awake him out of sleep.

Once more. Oh God, just once more!

"Bertha, I tell you Solomon's dead!"

For that which befalleth the sons of men befalleth beasts; even one thing befalleth them: as the one dieth, so dieth the other; yea, they have all one breath; so that a man hath no preeminence above a beast; for all is vanity.

"I tell you, Bertha, if the Lord ever breathes on Solomon again it will be on Resurrection Day; not now."

"You don't know what you're talking about."

"As much as you do."

"No, you don't."

"Bertha, we're all the same. You and me and Albert – and Solomon, too, when he was alive. But he's not one of us anymore."

Bertha stared out of the window. A slight breeze quickened. The sycamore leaves were quivering.

"Please leave for a while," she said. "Come back tonight."

"We'll be back shortly," Ida replied. "It's not good for you to be alone."

When they had gone, Bertha sat down again by Solomon. She looked into his face. He was resting so peacefully; why should she feel so sad?

Reaching over, she took one of his hands. It was dry and leaden but she clung to it.

There was a clock on top of the bureau. An old clock in a mahogany-veneer case. Solomon had bought it at an auction. He liked it because without any noise it let you know that it was keeping time. The big minute hand moved with a sharp twitch. While Bertha waited, the big hand jogged slowly from four to ten. An airplane droned overhead.

Bertha leaned forward. "Solomon, honey," she said, "speak to me."

The hand on the old clock twitched. Several minutes passed.

This time in a more urgent tone, "Solomon, speak to me; please."

No response.

"Solomon," she demanded, "now you speak to me!"

Nothing.

Anger mingled with grief for a moment, before a smile came slowly to Bertha's face. "That's Solomon, all right," she said. "Best-hearted man in the world, but he won't be ordered about. He'll speak to me, I know he will, when he gets good and ready."

Standing up, she lifted Solomon's hand and laid it on his chest. Then she folded the other over it, the way he had often done himself when he was thinking about something.

She would wait for as long as he wanted her to.

Outside, in the stillness, a bird twittered. Bertha's heart leaped. Tchair, tchair, tchair. High notes. Tcack, tcack, tcack. Low and deep-throated, mournful-like. Tchair, tchair, tchair. High again, brilliant, exultant. Bertha's heart was lifted with the song.

"You hear him, Solomon? The mockingbird; your bird is singing. Singing for you. Tell me you hear him."

There was no answer.

Bertha was tired, exhausted, for she had been up most of the night and many nights before that. She slumped into a chair and in a few minutes, though she fought against it, her eyelids began to drop.

She was asleep, her legs sprawled outwards, her hands folded like Solomon's.

The mockingbird stopped singing.

How long she slept she didn't know – when suddenly she heard a familiar voice cry out.

"Bertha. Bertha."

She was on her feet. Holding his hand again. "Yes, Solomon, what is it? I'm here. Here, right beside you."

Solomon's mouth was open. Wider than before. She was sure of it.

"You called me, Solomon! You called me! What is it you want to tell me? Are you happy? Are you sad? Tell me, so I'll know."

Her lips kept moving. She would speak the words for him if he wanted her to, if only she knew what he wanted to say. "Tell me, Solomon, tell me. But you've got to speak louder. Much louder. "

The big hand on the mahogany clock danced forward but in the room there wasn't the slightest sound.

She waited. Waited. Waited for as long as she could stand it. And when she could stand it no longer she put her face into her hands and groaned. And now the tears were loosed. She wept. Wept until she could weep no more, until her body was drained of all tears and all feeling.

When Ida and Albert returned, she was sitting in the chair, her face pale and drawn though without the trace of a tear.

"Shall I call the funeral home now?" Ida asked.

Bertha didn't answer.

"I said, shall I call the funeral home?"

Bertha looked up.

"You can call them."

Her eyes lowered, and she looked down at her hands.

"Yes, you can call them. Solomon's ready to go."

MORNING GLORIES

"M orn-n-ing, Mister Montgomery."
Oh-no! That shrill voice: the last person in the world he
wanted to see today. He kept his eyes closed.

She screeched it this time. "Morn-n-n-ing, Mister Montgomery!"

He'd have to do something. Otherwise, there'd be stories again. One
eyelid fluttered open.

"Looked like you was in a trance or something," she said, her neck
arching over the fence.

"No, no, nothing like that. Just taking a little catnap. Sun was shining
so bright, the morning glories all a-blooming."

"You can see all that with your eyes closed?"

Mister Montgomery opened the other eye. "Is there something that
you're wanting to tell me, Missis Jackson?"

"Nothing specific. Except I think you oughta know, Jarvis is pretty
mad."

"So what's new about that?" His elbow slipped off the arm of his
hard-backed porch chair. "Jarvis is always mad. He was born mad."

"What I'm saying is, he's mad at you. Boiling over."

"Boiling over? At me? What did I ever do to Jarvis?"

"You never said you was gonna tell the police about him and that
hokus powder?"

He sat bolt upright. Some kind of a trap. He shouldn't have opened
even one eye. "Who said that? Was it Mary?"

"I really can't tell you." She began to sing. "*Mary. Mary. Quite
contrary. How does your garden gro-o-o-o-w?* . . ."

Now he was boiling over. "It's a lie! A fat bald-faced lie!"

"Well, you better tell that to Jarvis," Missis Jackson came right
back. " 'Cause he's so mad he can't see out of his eyes. I heard him myself,
over at the market. He said: 'I'm gonna get me a baseball bat and break
both his legs. And then, when he's flat on the ground, I'm gonna do it to
both his arms. And then I'm gonna stomp on his stomach, and spit in his

face . . . .' Oh me, times a-passing. I got to go now. Good morning, Mister Montgomery. You're sure right; it sure is a pretty day."

Ta-di; ta-do. Missis Jackson turned and walked away, humming. It *had* been a pretty day – the morning glories on the white picket fence all wide open and bright blue; rent money coming in. . . . Break his arms and his legs with a baseball bat? He shuddered. Stomp on his stomach and spit in his face? It was too much! That old busybody! No, she was only the finger. It was that bitch Mary. Incapable of telling the truth. That is, unless somehow it hurt. Hurt? Hurt! . . .

He walked out in the yard. Everything peaceful up and down the street. Kids jumping over the potholes. . . . They'd be filled up by August 1. "Dear Mister Montgomery, We received your letter dated the 14th of June concerning street repair on 136th Street, SW. We appreciate your bringing this matter to our attention. Please be assured that the condition will be corrected within the next six weeks, or by August 1. Yours respect-fully, Thomas J. Cobb, Inspector of Streets and Drainage, Third Precinct."

His chest swelled. So what if August 1 was election day. Who else on 136th Street, SW, would ever have figured out how to get the job done? His Beulah would have been proud.

"Hi-ya, Mister Montgomery!" Ezra Brown cleared the pothole with an arching broad-jump that must have measured at least six feet. What legs! Someday, the New York Yankees or the Green Bay Packers. He waved back. Ezra might not appreciate the potholes being filled up. But at least the kids could play baseball without stumbling into a hole and breaking a leg, breaking a leg . . . Jarvis was fully capable of it! Didn't he almost kill his first wife with a baseball bat? Aggravated assault. Five years. Suspended, so he could beat her up again . . . Mister Montgomery shuddered. He had seen a bird once with two broken legs and a broken wing.

"Morning, Mister Montgomery."

"Morning, Missis Jackson." His eyes flew wide open.

"Your petunias could stand some fertilizer. They're looking a little peaked."

"Fertilizer? Yes ma'am, well, you tell me where I can find a cow and I'll give 'em a shot."

"Cow? What you need a cow for?"

"Best kind of fertilizer. Farmers have been depending on cow patties for fertilizer since before the time of Noah."

Missis Jackson squinted. "Your wife didn't have no cow; how come her petunias was so pretty and big?"

"That's something you wouldn't understand. All Beulah had to do was throw the seeds on the ground and spit on 'em, and they grew like Glory . . ."

Missis Jackson wasn't listening. She was humming. *"Mary, Mary – quite contrary. . . ."*

"You have something you want to tell me, Missis Jackson?"

"Only what I think you ought to know. Like Mary's telling everybody between Central Avenue and the Expressway that Jarvis is too scared to do it. . . ."

Mister Montgomery gulped. "You know Mary. Always talking about something."

Missis Jackson sniffed. "Yeah, I know Mary, and I know Jarvis too, and that's why I'm telling you about it." The way she bent over the fence, he could tell she was going to carve the whole goose. "Ordinarily Jarvis don't care what people say about him – like about him drinking; or playing the numbers; or not doing right by his family; or getting put in jail; but there's one thing he won't tolerate, no sir" – and she looked around her, as if almost afraid to say it – "and that's for anybody to think he's a coward! So when he heard what Mary was telling everybody – that he was scared to do it – well, I tell you he's seeing red, white, and blue! . . ."

"How many times do I have to tell you, Missis Jackson, that it is all one big fat lie!"

She looked at him with a squinting eye. "You never said you was going to do anything if Jarvis didn't pay you back the money he owed you?"

Mister Montgomery gulped again. "Oh, that? All I said was that I was going to turn the matter over to a lawyer."

"Oh-no!" Missis Jackson scrumpfed. "Don't you know that to Jarvis a lawyer means the law, and the law means the po-lice?"

"No connection at all," Mister Montgomery protested. "A lawyer is somebody who handles business matters and things like that according to the law while policemen handle people who break the law. Next time I see Jarvis I'll explain it to him. It's all a big misunderstanding."

"Next time you see Jarvis?" Missus Jackson cackled, looking up and down the street as if expecting Jarvis to show any second. "If I know him, he's not gonna give you a chance to see him . . . Well, time's a-passing. Good day, Mister Montgomery." She shuffled off, humming, *"Mary, Mary . . ."*

Mister Montgomery rose from his chair and shouted at her: "The only garden that that whore Mary ever grew was thorns and thistles. Pure thorns and thistles! Good thing I got rid of her when I did!"

But his day was ruined. Damn that Missis Jackson! Damn that Mary! Damn that Jarvis! Why couldn't a man who wanted to live in peace, live in peace?

Nervously he looked up and down the street, seeing nothing any different than it ever was: neither better nor worse. The potholes still there (it was five weeks to August 1), Ezra Brown broadjumping, his own house sitting straight and proud on its foundations – a shiny clear white with blue shutters, whereas there wasn't another house on 136th Street, SW, that wasn't peeling or sagging.

What would Beulah have done? Damn sure, if she was alive, he'd never have gotten mixed up with Mary. Nor loaned Jarvis a hundred dollars. . . . Beulah never seemed to think much about what she was going to do, or why. At the right moment she just did it, like the time she was over at her sister Katie's house, cutting up meat, and Katie's husband George got drunk and went on a rampage, chasing Katie around the house with a butcher knife, and Beulah, without blinking an eye, picked up the meat cleaver and let George have it across the side of his head; thirty stitches; after which George never so much as raised his voice at Katie!

Mister Montgomery flexed the muscle of his right arm. Not bad for a sixty-seven-year-old man. Though he hadn't done much physical work recently, he hadn't dissipated himself in alcohol or hokus powder. So let that Jarvis come. Swish! A right to the nose! Swash! A left to the jaw! . . .

All in his mind. He wasn't a fighting man. Never had been. When he'd given Jody a bloody nose back of the school, he had brooded about it for weeks. Senseless, hitting your best friend in the mouth; for no reason. Though Beulah claimed that people didn't hit each other in the nose for no reason. "Somebody, or something, is always there, urging them to do it. If that's not so, how do you explain that everybody says they want to live in peace and yet they're always fighting somebody about something or other?"

A darn good question. Except that Mister Montgomery didn't really believe in the Devil; not in the way that Beulah did, anyway. Jarvis might look like the Devil, with his high-raised eyebrows and drooping mustache, his bloodshot eyes rolling in their sockets, but Mister Montgomery knew very well who it was urging him on.

All he really had to do to clear the matter up, he thought as he sat on his front porch, looking up the street, down the street, half expecting Jarvis to come charging at him with a baseball bat, half chiding himself for getting so upset over a sheer rumor, was to pay her the money. It wouldn't break him.

But, blackmailed by a whore! He wasn't going to do it!

"Oh, Mister Montgomery! Mister Montgomery!"

Missis Ophelia Smith, who was built like a big rubber ball, came bouncing down the sidewalk.

"What is it?" he asked, though in the pit of his stomach he already knew what it was.

"You better get in the house, quick, and lock the door!"

"Why?" he asked. "Why should I go in the house and lock the door when it's so pretty outside, the sun shining so brightly, the morning glories all open and bluer than the sky?"

"It's . . . that . . . rascal Jarvis," she panted between wheezing breaths. "I heard him . . . with my own ears . . . at Sammie's Store. That when he gets . . . his hands on you . . . he's gonna cut your heart right out . . . with a butcher knife!"

Mister Montgomery gulped. "Whoever heard of such a thing?" he said to Missis Smith as calmly as he could. "Jarvis is just talking to hear his head roar."

"No, he isn't!" Missis Smith cried out. "He meant it. I could tell it in his eyes. They were all big and bulging. And that's not all he said. He said that after he cut your heart out with a butcher knife, he was gonna kick it . . . like a football . . . all the way down 136th Street."

Something in Mister Montgomery's throat was keeping him from swallowing. Something big shaped like a football. He could almost see Jarvis kicking it down 136th Street, past the kids jumping over the pot-holes, past the Shamrock Pool Hall, all the way to the dead-end at the Expressway. Who'd ever think of such a fiendish thing, except . . .?

"He's been taking that hokus powder, that's what he's been doing," Missis Smith went on. "And you know how he gets when he takes that stuff, he goes completely out of his head, like a crazy man."

Suddenly Mister Montgomery could stand it no longer. Up on his feet, he strode back and forth across the porch, pounding his fist into his hand. "No, no, Missis Smith, it ain't just the hokus powder – and it's not just Jarvis. If it was only Jarvis, I'd know how to take care of him."

Missis Smith squinted. "You mean Mary, don't you?"

"No. Mary's only the instrument. Like Eve was only the instrument in the Garden of Eden. It's the Devil."

"The Devil?"

"Yes, the Devil. Like a lot of people, I 'usta not believe in him. But now I do. Who but the Devil stirs things up, and causes trouble, when there's no real cause for trouble? I done nothing against Mary. I done nothing against Jarvis; except loan him a hundred dollars when he was broke. And if it was only Jarvis, I'd sit down and explain all that to him, and that'd be that. But you can't reason with the Devil, the Bible says not even Jesus could reason with him."

Beads of sweat had formed on Mister Montgomery's face. His eyes stared.

"You know, Missis Smith, and you're the only person I've told this to so far – I had a dream last night. Maybe it was because I been thinking of Jarvis . . . and all the things he's been saying about me . . . I don't know – but, anyway, I had this dream . . . and in it I saw the Archangel Michael . . . "

"The Archangel Michael?" Missis Smith's mouth flew wide open.

"Yes, the Archangel Michael. And I said to him, 'Michael, what am I gonna do about Jarvis?' And Michael said, 'Mister Montgomery, the Devil's got hold of Jarvis and there's nothing you can do about him. Absolutely nothing. Me and the other angels and archangels have been fighting the Devil for more than a trillion years, and we still haven't licked him yet, and we are beings with supernatural powers. So do you think that you, a puny human, can do what we have not been able to do?'"

Missis Smith cocked her head to one side. "Mister Montgomery," she said, "have you been taking some o' that hokus powder?"

"Me? You know better than that."

"Then, was it a dream, or in one of them trances, that you seen the Archangel Michael?"

"Trances?" Mister Montgomery was still shaking from the emotion of his speech. "What'da you mean, 'trances'?"

"You know how Beulah used to go into them trances, and see things. And now people passing by your house, they say they see you sitting up there with your eyes closed, like Beulah used to do, and they speak to you and you don't answer."

"Missis Jackson told you that, didn't she?" he asked, pointing his finger at Missus Smith. "I don't answer her because she's a gossip, and every time I talk to her, she passes on what I say to somebody else, along with a lot I didn't say. That's one of the reasons I'm in trouble now with Jarvis, because there's too much talk in this neighborhood."

"Well, that dream sure sounds like a trance. People see other people in dreams, but they don't usually see angels and archangels."

"I told you it was a dream," Mister Montgomery insisted. He was sorry he had said anything to her. No telling what the story would be by the time it reached Sammie's Store.

"Well, if the Archangel Michael said there was nothing you can do, what are you going to do?"

"Nothing. Absolutely nothing. Like he recommended."

"You're not going into the house and lock the doors?"

"No! So go back to Sammie's Store and tell them that. And tell it to Jarvis too!"

Next morning, when Missis Jackson shrilled "Good morning Mister Montgomery" at him, he quickly replied, "Good morning, Missis Jackson. I've got a lot on my mind these days, so if there's anything you want to tell me, please save it for next week." She harumpffed and strode on. His resoluteness surprised even himself, and the next few days, to keep his mind on constructive things, he weeded the flower garden and did things around the house that he'd been putting off for months. It was at night, when he was asleep and couldn't help himself, that his tormentors returned. Night after night he dreamed of Jarvis, grinning fiendishly, charging into his house with a baseball bat in one hand, a butcher knife in the other: Swish, he'd slam the door shut in Jarvis' face, only, swash, to see the rascal coming at him through another door! In one dream he'd be lying helplessly on the floor and Jarvis would be hammering him with the bat. In another, he'd be strapped to an operating table and Jarvis, with great obvious glee, would be standing over him with a long, shiny knife. One night he lay in a coffin, a large gaping hole in his chest, and a solemn-faced undertaker in a long black frock-coat was saying to his daughter Rose, "Ma'am, I'm afraid we're gonna have to fill this hole up with sawdust 'r something, 'cause we can't have his shirt sagging in on him. I've got too much pride in my work to leave things like that." Mister Montgomery woke in a cold sweat, pushing the undertaker's clammy hand away.

It got so he hated to go to sleep at night. As he puttered around the house after dark, too fidgety to read or look at TV, putting off bed as long as possible, he came to the unhappy conclusion that he was, in spite of all his pretenses, a coward! Yes, a coward, for not once in his dreams did he stand up to Jarvis; all he did was slam doors and run. . . . He could do something. Even Beulah, who had a mortal fear of the Devil (the only thing in the universe she was afraid of), had said that a person had to stand up to him and wrestle with him, "and hope that somehow with the grace of God you get two falls out of three."

But more and more he stayed inside the house, even on beautiful sunny days. More and more, he found reasons for keeping the doors locked.

One day, while he was having his lunch of a bowl of soup (he hardly had appetite for that) he heard a loud knock at the door. The knock was so unexpected and so insistent that it literally jarred the spoon out of his hand. He sat frozen in his chair, all kinds of wild thoughts racing through his mind. . . . Perhaps it was only Rose. Yet he couldn't bring himself to go see. Rose never came in the daytime.

Again the knock, louder and more determined than ever, as if Death Itself were at the door, demanding to be let in. Inside him there was an answering knock, a fist hammering at the wall of his chest, harder and harder. He felt faint; as if he were going to pass out.

"Daddy, Daddy, you in there?"

When he opened the door, after fumbling with the lock for an interminable time, he wanted to hug Rose. How beautiful she looked!

"Rose, Rose, what you doing here this time of the day?"

"What you doing with the house all locked up, this time of day? And what's the matter with you? You're trembling!"

He was too ashamed to tell her.

"Daddy," Rose repeated, "what's the matter with you? I met Missis Jackson over at the drugstore this morning, and she said she hadn't seen you on the porch or in the yard for three straight days, and she thought you might be sick or something."

Finally he told her, feeling a great relief. Rose looked enough like Beulah to have been her twin sister. Her eyes, they never wavered.

"Well, if you want my opinion," Rose said, "I think you ought to call the police. They know how to handle somebody like Jarvis."

Mister Montgomery shook his head. "That'd be falling right into Mary's trap. They'd lock him up for a few days, then let him out, and that's when he'd come charging over here for sure."

"Then I'm going to move in here with you for awhile. And if Jarvis so much as shows his face, I'm gonna let him have it with my flatiron."

"No, Rose,' he said, "no man ought to hide behind a woman's skirts."

"Don't be silly, Daddy. Jarvis is crazy even when he's not taking that hokus powder. And nobody tangles with a crazy man, if he can help it, except another crazy man."

"I know, I know," her father replied. "But it's more than Jarvis, more even than that bitch Mary. There's Missis Jackson and Missis Smith and all the rest. They're like the Romans that ran to that old Coliseum so they could watch the lions eat somebody. And if they don't get a show they're gonna be mighty unhappy."

Rose came over and put her arm around her father. "Forget about Missis Jackson, Daddy. Forget about all of 'em – particularly that Jarvis. Jarvis's more like a mad dog than a lion. And the best way not to get bit by a mad dog is to stay out of his way." A light came into her eyes. "When's the last time you visited Joshua?"

"I don't know. Maybe five years ago. Why?"

"It's high time you visited him again. You oughta be seeing your favorite cousin more'n every five years! I think you ought to leave tomorrow morning."

"Tomorrow morning. He lives in Florida!"

"So? It'd be a nice vacation for you. And while you're away, if I know Jarvis, it won't be long before he's in trouble again. Except it won't be you. It'll be Mary, or one of the others. It just stands to reason that anybody who plays around with a mad dog is gonna get bit sooner or later."

"I don't know, I don't know." He wanted a little time to think it over. But when Rose insisted on staying and cooking him his supper, he didn't protest. That night he ate three helpings of liver and three pieces of green apple pie.

"You'll need them in Florida," Rose said. She'd gone to the store and bought him a pair of those big round sunglasses. Monstrous things, zippy, you used to see them on the old-timey movie stars in magazines. He put them on and looked in the mirror. Hardly recognized himself. But Beulah probably would have liked them. Like that big wide-brimmed straw hat she wore on Sunday mornings in the summertime when she strutted – not walked, strutted – down 136th Street to church.

Honk! Honk! Honk, honk, honk! The cab driver outside was getting impatient.

"The damn fool! He's gonna have every dog and cat in the neighborhood running this way." Mister Montgomery adjusted the glasses on his nose and kissed Rose on the cheek. "Goodbye, my honey. I'll send you some postcards." His stomach felt like Epsom salts.

Down 136th Street the cab went slowly, avoiding one pothole and plopping into another. Bumpety-bump; bumpety-bump. As Mister Montgomery turned in the seat to wave to Rose, bumpety-bump, he hit the ceiling of the cab and the sunglasses flew to the tip of his nose.

"Damnedest street I ever seen," the driver growled out of the corner of his mouth.

"You come back August 1 and you won't see a pothole in it," Mister Montgomery said.

"How's that?"

"I took the matter up with the street and drainage inspector and he assured me a completely new pavement by August 1, or shortly thereafter."

"Or shortly thereafter?" The cab driver roared. "Don't you know that August 1 is election day? Them old politicians'r gonna promise you anything and everything right before election day!" Haw! Haw!

No use talking any more to him. Bumpety-bump! He grabbed for his hand strap.

Then suddenly the bumpety-bumps changed to thumpety-thumps; the cab swerved. "Flat; damn it!" the driver grunted.

"How long will it take to fix it?" Now the bubbles were in Mister Montgomery's head. "I got to be at the airport in forty minutes."

"Won't be seven 'r eight minutes."

"Make it five and I'll add a five to your tip."

The driver went to work. Mister Montgomery pulled the brim of his straw hat down over his bespectacled eyes. Something eerie about this flat. All he needed to know that Something was behind all this was to see Jarvis coming down the street. Highly unlikely this time of the morning. But what a sitting duck he'd be! Nervously he began to count to himself. One . . . two . . . . . . three . . . . . . four. Noises and grunts from the rear of the cab, the jack kept slipping off the bumper. He'd be the laughingstock of the neighborhood if Street and Drainage Inspector Thomas J. Cobb was soft-soaping him about the potholes. Maybe he'd be anyway, when they found out about his trip to Florida. Coward! Coward! Coward! But Beulah must have seen something in him or she would never have married him. Never did anything she didn't want to. . . .

"Goddam this jack!"

Forty-eight, forty-nine, fifty . . . . . .

Beulah wasn't afraid! Looking out the window at the gathering dusk she had said, "It's Death coming, and Beulah's going to sleep like those morning glories fold up and go to sleep when it gets dark. . . . But then one day the sun is gonna come up and stand still. . . . And all the morning glories in the world are gonna open up and stay open. . . . And all the graves are gonna open up too. . . . And the dead people are gonna wake up in that shining light. . . . And then they're gonna rise and bloom just like those morning glories. . . . And when that happens, you're really gonna be living! Hallelujah!"

The jack was clicking now, he was rising with the back seat. But he felt worse than ever. Those dark glasses he was hiding behind – they took all the glow out of the world! If only he could be as sure as Beulah that if Jarvis cut him up into small pieces he'd come back together someday and blossom like the morning glories. . . . Just couldn't believe it, and no use making out that he did. . . .

He leaned out the window to see whether the new tire was on yet, and instinctively glanced up and down the street. Oh my God! Jarvis!

Coming down the sidewalk toward the cab; lean and loose-jointed, moving slowly and cautiously in a kind of gliding lope, like a hungry cat on the prowl, his long thin mustache drooping down beneath his chin, his eyes darting this way and that for sign of prey.

Jump out of the cab and run! – Mister Montgomery couldn't if he had wanted to. He sat rigidly, looking straight in front of him, hoping with all he had that Jarvis wouldn't recognize him and would pass on by. Maybe with those monstrous sunglasses on, he wouldn't!

Each step, each second, brought Jarvis nearer. . . . Anyway, if it were really the Devil inside of Jarvis, there was nothing he could do except pray. . . .

And there was no prayer in him.

Now he could hear footsteps passing the cab. Though he didn't dare to turn his eyes to look at Jarvis, he could almost feel Satanic eyes piercing like X-rays through the steel body of the cab and through the dark lenses of his glasses.

He held his breath . . .

The footsteps continued on past the cab and retreated into the distance. If there had been a pause, or recognition of any kind, it wasn't noticeable.

He breathed again, slowly, deeply. The driver was putting the lugs on the wheel; he could tell by the grunts as he tightened up. . . .

"Where you going in that taxi?"

He almost jumped through the roof.

"When I first passed you by," Jarvis said, "I didn't recognize you . . . with them owl eyes. Then as I kept walking, it come to me like in a dream."

Like in a dream; Jarvis had his face right up to the window, and there seemed to be the trace of a grin on it. Though with that drooping mustache and low-slung jaw, it could have been a scowl: If a grin, it was the grin of a cat about to pounce on a mouse.

"I didn't see you either." Mister Montgomery smiled weakly. "My mind was on a lot of things." Like: Did Jarvis have anything in his hands when he passed the cab? Was he hiding something now, the way his body was pressed up against the side of the car?

"What you wearing those big glasses for?"

The cat toying with the mouse?

"I got weak eyes."

"Weak eyes?"

"I been having a awful lot of trouble with 'em last few weeks."

Jarvis' own bulging, bloodshot eyes went round and round in their sockets like racing cars. "Oh."

Mister Montgomery steeled himself for the pounce.

"I got troubles too," Jarvis said.

"Yeah?" Mister Montgomery straightened up in his seat. "What kind o' troubles?"

"Bad troubles."

If it wasn't all a trick, it was the best bad news that Mister Montgomery had heard in his entire life! But watch out!

"I'm bankrupt," Jarvis went on. "Downright bankrupt."

"Bankrupt? That *is* bad trouble." Mister Montgomery shook his head gravely. "Almost the worst thing that could happen to a man."

"I gotta get $100 to my landlady tonight or she tells me she's gonna get the sheriff to evict me. Me; my furniture; my wife and my kids – we're all gonna be out on the street. . . ."

Maybe it wasn't a trick, after all; maybe. "Maybe the bank could loan you some money."

"She-e-e-t, man! They wouldn't loan me five cents. That's how come I was on my way to see you. You're the only person I know that's got money."

"People think I got a lot more money than I do." He was watching Jarvis' eyes closely. At the moment there was a kind of distant, melancholy look in them, they didn't seem murderous. "You know I haven't worked for some time now. . . ." He wasn't going to drop his guard. "Besides, you already owe me a hundred dollars; for more than a year now. . . ."

"Yeah, yeah, I know that," Jarvis said. "But lemme tell you what – what I can't do is, I can't let that old sheriff evict my furniture and my family. You'll get it back by Christmas. I swear it on the Bible."

The Devil swearing on the Bible? But maybe it was worth it. "No use bringing the Good Book into this," Mister Montgomery said. "Tell you what I'll do. I'll let you have the hundred – if you promise me you'll never, never ask me for anything again."

The distant, melancholy look was suddenly gone. "I swear, man! I swear to anything you want me to swear to!" Jarvis raised both hands.

Empty; Mister Montgomery sighed. He took two crisp $50 bills out of his wallet and fingered them briefly – now *he* could be the cat if he wanted to; what power money had, within a few seconds turning mice into cats, cats into mice! – while Jarvis looked on hungrily. When he handed them over, the money was thrust quickly into a pocket and the low-hanging jaw listed somewhat. And as Jarvis turned to go, Mister Montgomery thought he detected a grin on his face – the same grin he had on when he first came up to the cab. . . . Face to face, and now it was all over! . . . As he watched Jarvis disappear into the distance, striding along again like a slinking leopard, his head turning this way and that as if he were afraid somebody would come up and grab the crisp $50 bills out of his pocket, Mister Montgomery slumped into his seat.

The tools went clinking into the trunk. "We'll still make it in plenty of time," the driver said.

"You know what? I've changed my mind." Mister Montgomery slumped back even farther in his seat, his shoulders limply falling forward. "What I want you to do is just drive up and down Central Avenue a couple of times. I think I need some fresh air."

The driver shook his head uncomprehendingly.

Mister Montgomery took off his glasses. Monstrous things, they really didn't suit him. Didn't want to hurt Rose's feelings but . . . there'd been too much deceit already. The Father Of Lies: Isn't that what the Bible called the Devil? And not only a coward but a sucker! He was ashamed to go back and face Rose.

The cab cruised up and down Central Avenue twice, three times, four times, Mister Montgomery too sunk in blackness and humiliation to say anything except, "One more time please. One more, one more."

Then it came to him like a revelation. Beulah had no choice! . . . Well, not really. It was inevitable, all men born of women, like the coming of night and the falling of leaves. . . . But he had had a choice, and like Rose said, nobody tangles with a crazy man *if he can help it*, except another crazy man. Not cowardice after all, he just wasn't crazy!

He sat up in his seat, his chest out again.

Then slumped back. Jarvis crazy? – Like a fox! A hundred dollars now, and next month, or next year, another hundred. Then another. And another. The only way to beat a fox is to outfox him. . . . Wasn't he a lot smarter than Jarvis? Maybe. Had he outfoxed Street and Drainage Inspector Thomas J. Cobb; or had Street and Drainage Inspector Thomas J. Cobb outfoxed him? . . . Okay, he'd lost this fall to Jarvis. But there'd be another chance. You could count on it. . . .

"Would you drive me home, now, please." And as the cab went bumpety-bump, bumpety-bump down 136th Street, he waved to Ezra Brown jumping over the potholes: Everything as it was, and as it was likely to be tomorrow: The potholes, Ezra, Missis Jackson, Mary, Jarvis, The Devil. Yeah, the Devil too. Ho-hum. La-ti-do. He hummed to himself a little ditty, one they used to sing when he was a boy. *Oh, hang the Devil on the washline. And wrap him round and round with twine.* This afternoon he was going to take some flowers out to Beulah's grave; it had been a long time and tomorrow was always tomorrow.

PEACE AND JOY

Texas Hill Country, 1938

The cemetery was quiet and peaceful, as it's proper for cemeteries to be. On this hot summer day, even the air seemed to be resting; not a leaf moved on the big sycamore and oak trees whose limbs reached out over many of the graves, shading them from the blazing sun. The cemetery was an old one, with neither order nor regularity. Over some of the graves towered huge, richly-ornamented monuments of marble and granite, while others had only simple weather-worn wooden crosses; and since the rich dead are often forgotten as quickly and conveniently as the poor dead, weeds and tall clumps of uncut grass crowded as tightly around the huge hulks of stone as around the tiniest, most humble wooden cross.

Into this peaceful if somewhat unkempt old cemetery, on this hot summer day, walked a young woman, carrying pink garden roses, and a boy. Both were comfortably dressed for the weather, the woman in a short-sleeved blue dress and straw hat, the boy in knickers and a sailor cap. They walked slowly down the main gravel path, turned into an over-grown side-path, and stopped finally at a family plot of some half a dozen graves. The plot was one of the few in the cemetery still being trimmed and tended.

"Grandpa's over there," the woman said, pointing to a gray stone about three feet high in the center of the plot. It was the boy's first visit to the cemetery.

"Are all those flowers for your grandpa, Momma?" he asked.

"Yes. I told you. It's his birthday."

"I know. Can I go run around now?" He stood up on one foot and spun in a circle, arms outstretched and waving at nobody in particular, as boys of seven or eight are wont to do.

"No," said the mother, "I want you to stay close by. Why don't you see if you can read what it says on some of these other gravestones while I get some water for the flowers."

And so the boy began looking at inscriptions while the woman cut the stems of the roses she had brought out and put the flowers into a jardiniere, filling it with water from a faucet.

"Momma! Here's one that's falling over!" the boy called to his mother. He was crouched in front of a small, weathered tombstone, leaning slightly to one side.

The woman set the jardiniere on her grandfather's grave and walked over to the boy, who was now tracing his finger over the eroding words cut into the stone.

"Ah, this is Grandpa's father. Your great-great-grandfather," she said.

"Let me try to read it out loud!," the boy exclaimed with some excitement. "'Daniel . . . Jos-*iii*-ah . . . Josiah Williams,'" he read haltingly, "'Born February 20, 18 . . . 1810. Died June 6, 1905. May he rest in peace.' Was he a soldier, Momma?"

"I don't think so. What makes you think he was a soldier?"

"I don't know. I just asked. Did you know him?"

The woman shook her head. "He died before I was born. But I did see a tintype of him one time. He had a very long beard. In fact, his beard was so long it went right out of the picture. Oh, and I seem to remember that he was very tall for his day. Like Abraham Lincoln."

"He looked tall in the picture?" the boy asked.

"No, actually. The picture was just the top part of him. But Grandpa told me he was tall. What I could see in the picture was that his shoulders were stooped, like he was carrying the whole world on his shoulders. He was a very hard worker, Grandpa told me. He was a black-smith, I think. Oh, and he was wearing a pair of those little wire-rimmed glasses. And his eyes were squinting. Maybe he wore them out because Grandpa said he liked to read books. Like you do. And I guess he must have read a lot of books because he lived to be very old."

"Ninety-five. Right?" said the boy, who had been calculating from the dates on the stone.

"I think that's right. Yes. Ninety-five."

"You're damn right I was a hard-working man," said Daniel Josiah Williams. "Have you ever seen a blacksmith work – with a sledgehammer; tongs; a heavy, red-hot bar of iron? That's hard work, I tell you – and that's what I did for a good part of my life, blacksmithing. Also, I was ambitious, and if you wanted business to come your way, you not only had to work hard but you had to work harder'n the next fellow. You're right, too, when you say that I liked to read books. At night, on Sundays, every moment I could spare from my work and my family, I read. I read every book I could get my hands on. I read the Christian Bible six times, and besides that the Bible of three or four other religions. How smart reading all those books made me I don't know. There were a lot of important questions I couldn't find the answers to anywhere in 'em. But when I couldn't find out something that I wanted to know in a book, I asked people questions. Too damn many questions, some folks would say. Brother Ben, the Presbyterian preacher, was scandalized. . . ."

"Momma," said the boy, who was still crouched in front of Daniel Josiah Williams' tombstone, again tracing a finger over the weathered letters. "How come they say on here 'May he rest in peace'?"

"That's just something they write on tombstones, sweetheart."

"How come they write that?"

"I guess they hope that whoever died won't have any more worries."

The boy stood up and laid his hand on the top of the tombstone, then patted it, like you might pat the head of a dog. "What kind of worries did my great-great-grandfather have when he was alive?"

"I don't know, exactly." The mother smiled faintly at her son. "But I do think he had a very sad life, from what little Grandpa told me. So if anybody deserves to rest in peace, I imagine it's Daniel Josiah Williams."

"There's truth in that, all right," said Daniel Josiah Williams. "The Christian Bible says that man that is born of woman is of few days and full of trouble. Now I lived a long time compared to most folks . . . and for that I suppose I ought to be thankful. But how many people would choose to live such a long life if it was as full of trouble and griefs as mine was? Don't get me wrong. I'm not complaining. I'm just asking one of those damn fool questions again."

"The question seems to embarrass you more than it does me," said Brother Ben.

They were sitting on the front porch on rocking chairs made of raw oak by Daniel Josiah Williams himself. Though the Reverend had just said he wasn't embarrassed to be talking as they were, Daniel Josiah could tell by the way he sat in his chair that he wasn't feeling very comfortable. In Brother Ben's eyes, he knew, he was one of those cloven-hoofed goats that were going to be separated from the faithful sheep on Judgment Day and sent right to the crackling fires of Hell. Yet he also knew that Brother

Ben had told his wife who had told others who had quickly told Daniel Josiah that if he never did another thing in his life he was going to get "that stubborn old goat" to accept the Lord.

"Now let me ask you a question," said Brother Ben. "Do you mean to say that in all of your many years of living you never had any happy moments, any moments when you thought life was worthwhile after all?"

Daniel Josiah pulled on his beard. "Oh sure. And more than once I was successful in my business, you might even say prosperous. But what I mean is that if I could put the happy and successful times on one side of a scale, and my troubles and griefs on the other side, I think that the troubles and griefs would far outweigh the happy and prosperous times. There were many times, in fact, when I was so full of sorrow that I didn't want to live anymore. And if you asked me today whether I would like to live my life all over again, I'd be hard put to say that I would. To be completely honest about it, I don't think I would. I know, Brother Ben, you think such talk is blasphemy. But that's the way I feel."

"It surely is blasphemy," declared Brother Ben, reproach in his voice. "God is the creator of life, and it is His, not man's, to decide whether it is worthwhile or not. Obviously He must have thought so, or He never would have created it. Also, does not the Bible itself tell us explicitly that God looked upon all that He had made and saw that it was not only good, but very good?"

"Of course. God sees things from His own point of view. . . ."

That did it. Brother Ben gasped as if the old man had struck him in the stomach with his fist – and as he drew air back in, his cheeks bulged out like a balloon and he looked as if he were about to explode.

"Blasphemy! Blasphemy!" he exclaimed.

Daniel Josiah went right on calmly. "I don't presume you claim to see things from God's point of view?"

"I, I certainly do not," Brother Ben sputtered.

"Well, that's all I was saying."

Brother Ben was squirming now in his seat more than ever. That oak seat was hard, and the longer he sat on it the more uncomfortable he looked, as if there was a growing fear in him that that old goat was harder and more diabolical than he had anticipated. Let him squirm, said Daniel Josiah to himself; I'll try to be civil with him but I didn't ask him to come.

"I repeat, it is God's place, not man's, to determine the worth of things," Brother Ben said firmly. "For his part, the good Christian, no matter how hard his life, has faith in God and the goodness of life. He is full of peace and joy whether the Lord giveth or taketh away."

"I have never claimed to be a good Christian," said Daniel Josiah.

"How can you make a statement like that?" retorted Brother Ben. "Perhaps you were a better Christian than you think. Perhaps a worse one. Only God knows for sure. But," and here he adopted a more conciliatory tone, "I must admit that I am curious about some aspects of your life. For my benefit, since I've known you only very late in your life, would you kindly tell me something about your past."

Daniel Josiah pursed his lips, as if he wished the question had not been asked. "I'll oblige you," he said finally, "though some things are most painful to relate."

That was all the encouragement Brother Ben needed. "You were born of good Presbyterian parents, were you not?" he asked quickly.

"Aye, I was. And they were probably good Christians too, if that doesn't seem a contradiction. Yet, good people as they were, I didn't think much of some of their views."

"Like what?"

"Well, for example, what they thought about God electing some men to salvation and others to damnation."

"That's in the Bible, Brother Daniel. . . . Unless, of course, you don't accept the Bible as the word of God who doesn't tell lies. The Bible explicitly states that God chooses for salvation whom He will. However, let's not get stuck on this point for we could argue about it until Doomsday. When you were a boy back in Hog Ridge, Tennessee, you were examined by the elders of your church, were you not?"

"I was."

"Did you pledge that so long as you were a member of the Presbyterian church you would not drink alcohol or gamble or commit fornication?"

"I did."

"Did you ever commit fornication?"

Daniel Josiah pursed his lips again. "No."

"Are you telling me the truth?"

"So help me! However, to tell the whole truth, I have to confess that I did have the desire." And then quickly he added, "But the way they watched over the young ladies around Hog Ridge I never had much of an opportunity." He chuckled.

Brother Ben was not amused. "Do you not know that Christ said that the man who lusteth in his heart is as guilty as the man who actually commits the act?"

"Then I guess I did commit fornication."

Brother Ben's eyes gloated with self-satisfaction. "Did you ever drink liquor?"

"Aye, I did. In fact, I've taken quite a few nips in my lifetime. And there were times in my life when I was so down and out with grief that I got stone drunk."

"In other words, you got stone drunk because you were unable to accept cheerfully what the Lord had sent you?"

Daniel Josiah wrinkled his brow. "I guess that's one way of looking at it."

"Now, how about gambling? Were you a gambling man?"

"I never gambled for a living, if that's what you mean. But I did like to play poker and faro. I found those games right exciting."

"Did you play for money?"

"Of course. That made it all the more exciting. Don't you think that most everything in life is more exciting when the stakes are higher?"

Brother Ben ignored the question. "Is it not true, Brother Daniel, that you won your first wife, Sarah Lou, in a faro game?"

"Well, in a manner of speaking, I did."

The minister pressed on. "From what I have heard, the years of your marriage to Sarah Lou were full of woe. Do you not see any connection between this fact and the fact that you won her in a game of chance?"

Daniel Josiah snorted. "I sure don't! In the first place, I only won her in a faro game in a manner of speaking. Jess Tomlinson and I both had our eyes on her, and since we were friends we made a deal that whoever won the game could court her. But Sarah Lou would have married me even if I had lost. If you want to know the truth, I had a lot more vim and pluck in me than Jess Tomlinson had, and Sarah Lou liked a man with vim and pluck."

"Ah, ha! What you're really saying is that the game of chance had nothing at all to do with your marriage to Sarah Lou, that she would have married you no matter what – that you were really elected to each other!" Brother Ben's eyes were wide and glowing with excitement. "So you really believe in God's election after all, don't you, Brother Daniel?"

"I believe some folks get along better with each other than they do with others. I had vim and pluck if you'll pardon my saying so again, and so did Sarah Lou, and we were both willing to take a chance if it meant a better life for ourselves. My woes had nothing to do with Sarah Lou, but with something else."

"Like what?"

"I'll tell you in due time. But first let me tell you what happened. When I first met Sarah Lou I was only an apprentice in a blacksmith shop at Hog Ridge, making six dollars a month. This wasn't enough for a married man to support a family, at least in decent style, so when Sarah Lou consented to marry me we decided together that I should open a shop of my own. But there were already two shops in Hog Ridge and so if I wanted a shop of my own we would have to go elsewhere. We had heard that in the new land of Texas there was a great need for black-smiths, and other opportunities, too, for any one willing to work hard, which I was. . . ."

"So that's how you came to Texas?"

"Yes. But we had to wait three years until we could save enough money to make the trip. In the meantime, our first son, Samuel, was born. This raised some doubts in Sarah Lou's mind about our making the trip. But she was a plucky one and when I put it up to her whether to move to Texas or not, she said, 'Let's go: If we stay here it'll always be the same. We can do better than this if we work hard and if we don't let fears take hold of us.' I suppose you'd say she was a gambling woman, too, wouldn't you, Brother Ben? But do you see anything wrong in folks wanting to better their lives? Wasn't that the reason your own grandpappy moved from Scotland to America, to better his life?"

Brother Ben grimaced. "No, it's not wrong to want a better life, if it really is better. My grandpa came to this country not in order to live an easier life or to make more money but because he had a calling to preach the Gospel to the settlers and the savages. But I'm not sure that you and Sarah Lou wanted to come to Texas for a really better life – a better one spiritually, I mean."

"Well, we weren't coming to Texas to preach the Gospel to settlers and savages, that's for sure. We wanted more opportunity for ourselves. That's the only way I can explain it. Perhaps that's selfish, perhaps it isn't. I don't know. In hindsight, if I had known all that was going to happen to us in Texas, maybe I would have been satisfied to stay in Hog Ridge. But, then, on the other hand, I'm damn glad we don't live by hindsight."

As he talked, the old man's eyes grew distant and there was a sharp pain in his chest as he relived that hard decision that he and Sarah Lou had to make, not knowing whether it would lead to opportunity or disaster.

"Pray tell me what happened when you arrived in Texas?" Brother Ben asked.

"Well, to get there we had to go by the steamboat up the Trinity River to the town of Liberty. But no sooner we got on the boat we found out that there was cholera prevailing all up and down the river. Seems like every boat that stopped at the towns was taking off people that died with cholera. Sarah Lou and I were both taken with fright, particularly in fear for little Samuel. But we decided together that we just couldn't go back. We just couldn't, without admitting defeat for all our plans. Still, when we got to Liberty the cholera was going there full blast and what we were frightened of happened. Little Samuel took sick and in two days he was dead. He was the apple of our eyes. He was so lively and bright. And when he died it seemed to us that all our hopes and pleasures were gone forever. . . ."

"I don't mean to interrupt," said Brother Ben, "but you say that you had a chance to turn back when you found out about the cholera. Yet you didn't. In hindsight, do you think that it was right to have risked little Samuel's life simply because to have turned back would have interfered with your plans? Do you not possibly see God's judgment upon you in little Samuel's death?"

"No, I don't," Daniel Josiah retorted. "Little Samuel died from cholera, not God's judgment. In hindsight, as I told you, I might have been satisfied to live in Hog Ridge if I had known all that was going to happen to us in Texas; little Samuel's death, in fact, was just the beginning of our woes. But I also said that I was damn glad that we don't have to live by hindsight. Does that answer your question?"

"Not fully. But pray tell me what else happened in Texas?"

"Well, it wasn't all bad. Fact is, there were good times as well as bad for us. Not that the good outweighed the bad. Still they were good while they lasted. . . .When we finally got to Texas my wealth consisted of exactly five dollars in money, a set of blacksmith tools, a loving and spirited wife, a good trade, lots of strength and energy, and a determination to do all that I could to make an honest living. I spent my five dollars in Liberty to buy two barrels of flour at two and a half per barrel. I killed deer and we lived fine. But I had no iron or steel to work on. However, the country around us was in desperate need of a blacksmith. So the folks got together and lent me the money to buy iron and steel on condition that I repay them by New Year's. I paid up promptly a few days before the debt was due. To make a long story short I did my work so well, never slighting a job no matter how small, that soon folks were coming from thirty and forty miles around to get their work done by me. I became quite prosperous. I had several apprentices to help me. My family was growing right along with my business, two daughters and a son having been born to take little Samuel's place. I began to take advantage of other opportunities, using my blacksmith experience to build a saw mill and a grist mill which were sorely needed by the community. But then, just when we were so prosperous I thought we would never have to worry again, my troubles started over. First, I crushed two of my fingers at the grist mill. Then one of my dear daughters, Myra, died from some sort of sickness. It took her swiftly and terribly. Finally, my wife got the sore eyes, so bad she went blind. I could not take anything more, so although I had several very prosperous businesses there in Liberty County and was known for a hundred miles around, I decided to pick up stakes and move farther west, where the climate was drier and there wasn't so much sickness."

"Brother Daniel," Brother Ben interrupted, with all the eagerness of a hound about to pounce on a rabbit, "your story is indeed a sad one, and it is not right for another man to judge. But did you not say that your troubles began again right when you were getting so prosperous that you thought you would never have to worry again?"

"I did."

"Do you not see any connection between thinking thoughts like that and the beginning again of our woes?"

"Only that happy times are few and far between for all men born of woman."

Brother Ben cringed. "Oh ye of little faith!"

"I have told you before," said Daniel Josiah, "that I did not consider myself a good Christian."

"Aside from that," cried Brother Ben, "do you not know from the Bible that the Lord exalteth the humble but layeth low those that put their trust in worldly possessions?"

"I know the Bible says that. But I still say that what caused most of my troubles in Liberty County was not God's judgment upon me. If it was God's judgment, then it was God's judgment upon the whole country thereabouts. That part of Texas we had come to was just sickly country back then. Why, I don't know, it just was. I saw that when we first arrived there. Big, fine houses along the main roads – altogether empty! Behind house after house you would find the graveyards, with whole families freshly buried in them. I told Sarah Lou at the time that we had come to a sickly country, and so it turned out to be. It was so dreadfully sickly that in the winter and spring of that year about fifty of our neighbors died."

Now it was Daniel Josiah who was breathing hard and squirming in his seat, like a worm on a fishhook.

But he went on. "So it was because it was sickly country, and not because of God's judgment upon me personally, that little Myra died and my wife went blind and all the rest. That was why we decided to move to drier country even though we were most prosperous in Liberty County and had very fine neighbors who begged us to stay and not to move. But what was the good of money and fine neighbors when the country was so sickly? As a matter of fact, just before we could get away, and just after I had sold my blacksmith shop and my saw mill and my grist mill, and I had my wagon and mule teams all ready for the trip, my loving wife and youngest daughter Caroline became dreadfully ill. After being sick only about ten days, Sarah Lou died. My hopes and my vigor for life were again dashed, and I felt as though the rest of my life would be spent in terrible sorrow."

"Your story is indeed a sad story," said Brother Ben. "But though you are by nature blessed with a good mind and though you have read many books in your lifetime, still I do not know if you have eyes to see the connection between one thing and another. But pray tell me whether your troubles ceased after you moved farther west?"

Daniel Josiah shook his head, and a most pained expression came into his eyes. "No, to tell the truth, they did not."

"Then pray tell me what happened there?"

"If you mean that God's judgment was pursuing me westward because I had troubles there too, I think you're wrong," retorted Daniel Josiah. "There were times, of course, when I thought just that, and sometimes I got so discouraged that I even took to drinking more than I should. I'll admit that and I'll also admit that maybe that wasn't the manful thing to do. Still at times that's the way I felt and that's what I did. But in what you're implying I think you're driving up the wrong trail."

"Pray continue," said Brother Ben. "Perhaps by the time you tell your whole story you yourself will see the connection."

"Well, after we left the eastern part of Texas things began to look up for awhile. The weather was pleasant and my daughter Caroline improved every day that we moved farther west. Then one night in December when we lacked only one day's travel of being at the journey's end and we were camped on Coyote Creek in Gonzales County, just about the worse blue norther you can imagine came upon us; the temperature must have plunged by forty or fifty degrees in the span of two hours. Little Caroline got worse and several days after we got to my uncle Pete's house near the town of Seguin she died. That left me only one child, Jonathan, out of what was once a family of a wife and four children. I was so discouraged that I didn't want to live much myself any more. . . . But here was little Jonathan to take care of and besides my time had not yet come, so I set to work again, though with a heavy heart. . . . I set up a blacksmith shop, even bigger than the one I had back in Liberty County, and before long I had another saw mill and another grist mill going along the Guadalupe River. About three years after moving west I married my second wife, Jo Ann Thompson, and with her to encourage me and to stand with me by my side, I decided that I would commence a new chapter in my life – one full of promise and hope."

Daniel Josiah paused at this moment to catch his breath. Brother Ben saw his opportunity and asked, "During all this time, when you were in Liberty County and after you had settled along the Guadalupe, were you a regular churchgoer?

"Yes, I was."

"How was that? Did you see nothing contrary between going to church and drinking alcohol and playing games of chance, which you said you did right along?"

"Well, as I told you, I was raised by good Presbyterian parents and was taught to read the Bible every chance I could. During my younger days I even went frequently to the mourner's bench. Both my parents and the preacher had told me that if I believed in Christ and trusted Him for my salvation, God would bless me and grant me peace and joy unspeakable. And, indeed, for many years I tried with all my heart to seek religion in just that way. But I never felt the peace and joy that they said I would. Finally, I gave up going to the mourner's bench, though I never gave up going to church – and hoping. When I married my second wife Jo Ann, and as we were starting to build a new life and a new family together, she prevailed upon me to give up alcohol and poker and faro, saying it was not right for a good Presbyterian to drink liquor or play games of chance. Thinking that maybe she was right and that maybe this had been the reason for all of my troubles in the past, I did as she said. For five years I never touched a drop of liquor or a playing card."

"Did your woes cease during the period that you abstained?" Brother Ben inquired.

"No, by damn! First, the Guadalupe went on a rise after a cloudburst and carried away both my sawmill and my gristmill. I had in the meantime built up a good herd of cattle in addition to my other possessions and I thought to sell these to rebuild my mills. But before I could do that some outlaw cattle rustlers came one full moon and made off with the whole herd, including all of my horses but one. It was several days before I could get enough neighbors to help me trail them. But before we could catch up with them we ran out of provisions and our horses tuckered out. . . ."

"Though all men are born to trouble out of Adam's sin," said Brother Ben, "you had indeed more troubles than most men."

"Indeed," said Daniel Josiah, "but when I was finally able to pull myself back together I went back to work. I made partners with two Germans to rebuild the mills. They put up the money and I did the bossing and the blacksmithing and the mechanical work. In four years we were on the way to prosperity again."

"But again not for long, I presume," said Brother Ben.

"That's right. First, one of my small daughters died of diphtheria. Then my oldest son Jonathan, from my first wife, Sarah Lou – who'd grown into a kind and noble young man – disappeared one Saturday morning while fording a creek on horseback. Four days later, his body washed up to the edge of the creek, five miles down from where he disappeared. Oh, who can describe the grief a father suffers when he is called to name his dear son's body! I thought I had known the blackest of nights already, but naming the body of a son – right when he is on the cusp of manhood, his whole life ahead of him – well, I can tell you, there is nothing blacker than that."

"That is certainly one of the worst of all misfortunes. I presume you went to church directly thereafter to ask God to forgive you your sins."

Daniel Josiah's eyes narrowed. "I know what you're getting at. Yes, I admit it, I was taking a drink now and then. I'd told Jo Ann that for the life of me I could see nothing wrong in taking a drink of whiskey now and then, or playing a game of chance for fun. I still feel that way. And I will tell you right here – after my son was drowned, I began to drink heavily and sometimes, as I said, even to become stone drunk. I know that was wrong."

"Still you did not see any of your misfortunes as signs from God?" Brother Ben asked.

"What can I say? The fact is that I was at church with my wife and I had about decided in all honesty to return to the mourner's bench when someone came running into the church shouting that our mill was on fire. We did what we could but it burned to the ground. Then, while we were at a camp meeting one night, our big two-story home which we had built during the good times caught fire. Brother Tom Smith was preaching to beat the Devil when the alarm of fire was made. By the time we got back to the house everything was in ashes. . . ."

"I do not mean to interrupt again," said Brother Ben, "but did you not see any connection between the two fires and the fact that you were at church both times when fire broke out?"

"My wife Jo Ann did point this out to me. But, Lord, what is a man to think? Does God afflict you when you are doing wrong and then afflict you again when you are repentant? What kind of God is that? After our home burned, that final straw, as it were, Jo Ann said to me, 'I don't think the Good Lord wants us to have what we had. I don't know what He wants for us, but I do not think we should try to put our life back together as it was.'"

"Did you not think over what your wife said?" declared Brother Ben. "Did you not consider possibly that she might have seen something that you did not see or did not want to see?"

"I considered what she said," Daniel Josiah replied, "but after thinking everything over carefully, and for a long time, I told her that I could not believe that it was God's will that so many of my beloved family members had died, or that my properties had burned down. After careful checking I determined that both the mill and house had caught fire from natural causes, and I thought that it was not only wrong – but, actually blasphemy, of a sort – to say that 'the Lord willed it.' The same was true about the flood that came in 1875 and washed away both our mills again. Anybody could see that both times the mills had been built too close to the water and did not account for the floods that happen every few years on the Guadalupe. Having seen the mistake, I determined not to give up just when I had seen my mistake, so, although I was now sixty-five and not as strong as I once was, I went to work again and built new mills and a new home a hundred yards from the river on higher ground. This cost me a lot of money and much time. But in a few years we were becoming prosperous again because people could trust the lumber and flour we made and they came from a hundred miles around to buy it. "

"I do not think at this point," said Brother Ben, "that I need for you to tell me that the good times did not last for long."

"You know the rest of the story, Brother Ben, because it was about that time that you were called to help minister to our community."

"Yes, I do," said Brother Ben, "but tell me, how many in all of your family did you bury?"

"Two wives, seven of my ten children, five grandchildren and three great-grandchildren . . . and I grieved over every one of them."

"It is indeed sad, even for a good Christian, to bury a member of his family," said Brother Ben. "But when we see that everything is in the hands of God, that He never calls any of His children except for good reason and out of His almighty wisdom, we can still feel, in the midst of our sadness, that peace which surpasseth understanding and that joy unspeakable which is the gift of God to His elect."

"All what you say is above my head," said Daniel Josiah, "though all my life I have tried with all of my powers to understand the Lord and His way with men. When I was close to seventy-five years old, I decided to make one last great effort. There was a camp meeting at the old Plum Branch school and I went to it every day and night with the determination that if there was any religion within me that I was going to seek it with all my heart. I wanted above everything else to be happy as some good Christians I knew seemed to be. Every night during the revival I went to the mourner's bench. But for some reason I just did not ever get any light. Finally, the preachers got around me and prevailed upon me to take the pledge again, to abstain from all alcohol and card games, to read the Bible some every day, and to hold prayer meetings in my home at least one night a week. I promised to do so. And I did it for nearly five years, during all of which time I was reading and searching for the Truth, asking questions and trying to get all the light I could on the subject of religion. But I was never able to get rid of my doubts. I never really felt that peace and joy unspeakable which you and the others promise to the faithful Christian."

"Perhaps you read too much and you asked too many questions," said Brother Ben.

"Perhaps," replied Daniel Josiah. "But when I saw no real evidence that I was saved according to what the preachers said, I decided that I would withdraw from the church. Of course, Parson MacDonald begged me not to do so, telling me that the Devil would get me for sure if I did. But I told him that I had decided that I had no real religion, according to the way he and others of the church saw religion, and that if the Devil did indeed take me, at least he would be getting an honest man and not a hypocrite. And so I did, indeed, withdraw from the church."

"Did that make you any happier?"

"No, it didn't. But at least I wasn't a hypocrite, pretending to believe something that I didn't. . . . Until this day I've continued to read and ask questions and to search for the light. But I have never found that peace and that joy unspeakable that you and some others talk about."

"This is the saddest part of your whole story," said Brother Ben, lowering his head.

"I think you are right," said Daniel Josiah, his own head bowed, his eyes clouded over by a profound darkness. Absent-mindedly he reached into his pocket, pulled out a blue handkerchief and wiped his forehead.

For a minute or so there was silence. Then Brother Ben spoke up again. "Brother Daniel, as you look back over your life now, would you say that it merited peace and joy unspeakable? I am not passing judgment; I'm only asking a question."

"That's too big a question for me to answer," replied Daniel Josiah. "Maybe my life didn't merit joy unspeakable. I'm willing to concede that. But after so many years of troubles and griefs, I do think that I might be entitled to a little peace. I am a very tired old man."

"I hope, from the bottom of my heart, that you do have peace," said Brother Ben. "But do not say that you are entitled to it. God owes no man anything. He created the world and it is His to do with as He pleases. Since all men are sinners, He elects some to salvation and others to damnation according to His own wisdom. But no one has any claim upon Him, neither those who are saved nor those who are damned."

"Well, then," said Daniel Josiah, "I hope it pleases God to give me peace."

"That's better," said Brother Ben. "Now one last question. You said in the beginning that if you could put the happenings of your life on two sides of a scale, the troubles and griefs would far outweigh the happy moments, and that if you were given the choice of living your life over again, knowing what was ahead of you, that you would not choose to live it over again. Do you still say that?"

Daniel Josiah dropped his eyes. He did not say anything for a few moments.

"I still stick to that," he said finally. "However, if you remember, I also said that it was a damn good thing that while we are living we don't know what lies ahead of us."

Daniel Josiah sighed.

And Brother Ben did too.

* * *

A mourning dove sitting in the crotch of an oak tree broke the heavy stillness of the cemetery with a long, plaintive call. The boy looked away from Daniel Josiah Williams' gravestone toward his mother. "How long do you think my great-great-grandfather is going to be resting in peace, Momma?"

"Forever I hope."

"Is resting in peace like taking a nap?"

"In a way," the mother replied, walking over to the crouched boy and bending down and ruffling his hair.

"But, Momma," said the boy, "you told me that when somebody dies, they go up to Heaven and God makes them happy. How can somebody be happy if they have to take a nap forever? I don't even like to take a nap 'til 3 o'clock."

The woman smiled. "Well, maybe he'll just take a nap until he's rested."

"Then what's he going to do?"

"Oh, I imagine God will find something for him to do," the mother replied. "Now, don't ask any more questions. Just say a prayer for Grandpa and for your great-great-granddaddy and for everybody else in the cemetery. Then we've got to rush and pick up your father. He's been working hard all day, and he'll be hungry."

"What should I say in my prayer?"

"Whatever you want, sweetheart. You could ask God to make sure that everybody who's buried in this cemetery is at peace – and that they'll all stay at peace, even after they get up from their naps."

"And God will do that?"

"God answers all our prayers, if we say them with an open heart."

"Do I have an open heart?"

"Of course you do. You're a very good boy."

"But I hit Frank in the mouth last week and it started bleeding down his chin. Remember? So does that mean God won't . . ."

"Jimmy, just say a prayer and don't ask any more questions."

"But, Momma, do you think that . . ."

"Hush, I said."

Hush.

ACKNOWLEDGMENTS

This book would not exist without Michele Stanush, my daughter, who saw the connection between seemingly disparate stories and urged that they be published together. She spent many hours checking details and when she came upon stylistic clunks, she helped me unclunk them. Many thanks, too, to Bryce Milligan and Robert Bonazzi for aspiring to an Old School tradition of publishing: taking risks with books that might not fit into a prevailing "market trend."

Six of these 13 stories appeared in earlier versions in literary magazines: "Bishop O'Hara," in *Four Quarters*, La Salle College, Philadelphia, Pa.; "A Pair of Shoes," *Kansas Quarterly*, Kansas State University, Manhattan, Kansas; "The Butterfly," *Jesture*, Thomas More College, Crestview Hills, Kentucky; "Some People Can," *Nimrod*, University of Tulsa, Oklahoma; "Live and Let Live," *Snowy Egret*, Williamsburg, Kentucky; "Morning Glories," *Phoebe*, George Mason University, Fairfax, Virginia.

AFTERWORD

I believe that "life" is what the great majority of us value most, whether it is the life in ourselves, or that expressed in a myriad other ways outside of ourselves – in other human beings, in nature, in works of art, in the incredible diversity of our world, even in the question whether there is life beyond this world.

When I graduated from college, I deliberately chose journalism for a career because of the potential it seemed to have for experiencing life in the widest range of possibilities. I was not disappointed. At the *San Antonio Light*, where I began as a cub reporter, I first covered the produce market and the stockyards, then wrote obituaries and church news, graduated to hotels and schools, and eventually covered the police department, city hall, the courthouse, and the state legislature. At *LIFE* magazine, where I next worked, I started in the Hollywood-Los Angeles bureau, where we covered everything from movie stars to alfalfa farms; I then went to New York where I wrote party, nature, science and religion stories; and finally, as chief of correspondents for the Washington D.C. bureau, I covered the government and national and international issues.

But even with such extensive experience, there was something missing. As a reporter, I was telling about life, not as a participant, but as an observer, a witness from the outside.

The reality is that all human beings live life not only on the surface but in the depth of their being, where decisions are made. At this complex level, we can hardly understand what goes on inside of ourselves, much less what goes on inside others. I was in my 40s when I first read the short stories and saw the plays of Anton Chekhov, and was so moved by his compassion and his intuitive insights into the lives of his characters that I was moved myself to want to write fiction.

Applied to storytelling, the word "fiction" is somewhat misleading. It derives from the Latin word *fictio*, meaning "to feign, to deceive," and in the dictionary it is defined as something "invented or imagined." Yet, paradoxically, if the test of good journalism is its factuality, the test of good fiction is its truthfulness about human life and all its many dimensions. Thus both journalism and fiction serve the cause of truth, but in different ways. And if newspapers or magazine work provide access to a wide variety of people in a wide variety of circumstances, then journalism is invaluable for any would-be fiction writer. The stories in *Sometimes It's New York* were, to a great extent, inspired by my journalistic experiences.

Some literary critics believe that the stories of a particular writer should be connected by the style of the writer, and be recognized by it. But in this collection there are no obvious or imposed connections beyond New York as the locale of six of the stories. Each story has its own style, its own rhythm and mood, for just as I believe in the uniqueness of every human being, I believe that every story should reflect that uniqueness in its style and resonance. What connects these stories is that all human beings, however different in other ways, are engaged in the same human struggle – not just to exist, but to live.

– Claude Stanush
San Antonio, Texas
2006

ABOUT THE COVER

My wife, Barbara, took the cover photograph of the brick and brownstone building that is located at 111 Waverly Place in the center of Greenwich Village, New York. I lived in the garden apartment of this building for some years as a bachelor, and many parties were held there for New York-Texans starving for a fix of tamales, enchiladas and chili.

I met Barbara shortly after she moved into an apartment on the second floor. One of the first things she did after we married and she moved downstairs was to clean the enchilada sauce off of the large western painting behind the old sawbuck ranch table. I couldn't explain how it got there.

Both of us loved living in this building, so reminiscent of New York's storied and literary past – of Henry James, Herman Melville, Edith Wharton, Edna St. Vincent Millay. Waverly Place, named for Sir Walter Scott's novel, "Waverley," is an extension of Washington Square North, and its townhouses are similar to those that were the background for Henry James' novel (and later the movie), *Washington Square*.

When Barbara's mother visited our basement apartment for the first time, she had a feeling of déjà vu. Back in the 1920s, it had been a speakeasy – to which the man who was courting her and would become her future husband had taken her as an adventure.

ABOUT THE AUTHOR

Claude Stanush has won both state and national awards for his writing. Starting out as a newspaperman, he then worked for 13 years on the staff of *LIFE* magazine. Accolades for his *LIFE* stories include awards from the World Council of Churches (for his work on the series "The World's Great Religions") and the American Association for the Advancement of Science (for his essay "The Geography of the Universe"). One of his *LIFE* stories inspired the film "The Lusty Men" (RKO Pictures), which *Premiere* magazine named an "unsung classic" of American cinema. As a freelance writer, he has written short stories, essays, film scripts, and recently, in collaboration with his daughter Michele, a novel. Awards for his fiction include a creative writing award from the National Endowment for the Arts as well as one of Texas' highest literary honors – the J. Frank Dobie Award and Fellowship (given by the Texas Institute of Letters and the University of Texas). He was a co-screenwriter on a feature film, "The Newton Boys" (Twentieth Century Fox); and a co-creater of the documentary film, "The Newton Boys: Portrait of an Outlaw Gang" (with David Middleton), which won the gold medal in its category at the Texas Film Festival and the International Film Festival in the Virgin Islands. Mr. Stanush also has a book of newspaper essays and an earlier collection of short stories. One of his short stories, published in the University of Nebraska's literary magazine *Prairie Schooner*, was voted "best story of the year" by the editors.

WINGS PRESS

Colophon

This first edition of *Sometimes It's New York,*
by Claude Stanush, has been printed on 70
pound non-acidic paper containing 50 percent recycled fiber. Story titles and initial
caps have been set using Caslon Openface
type, the text in Adobe Caslon, and book
titles in Parisian ICG type. Wings Press
books are designed by Bryce Milligan.